DUST
AND
DAZZLE

Book Two of THE DUST TRILOGY

HEATHER HAYES

Published by AH Digital FX Studios, INC 11/01/2023
AH Digital FX Studios, INC
10551 E. Ririe Hwy.
Idaho Falls, ID 83401
www.ahfx.net

ISBN: 978-1-945597-10-7

Library of Congress Control Number: 2023949589

Cover by Adam Hayes
Book Layout, Design & Editing by Adam Hayes

Paperback printed in San Bernadino, United States of America

For Mrs. Blosch's Class

Thanks for letting me practice
being an English teacher on you!

Chapter 1

THE STERILE TABLE and its paper covering crackle under my itchy legs. The guy I'm told is Dr. Hamble looks at me with a wary eye. "Tell me again how you fell into the cement truck?"

I look sideways at my friend Conrad who is sliding off the table next to me into a vat of vinegar water. He grimaces at both of us. I'm not sure if it's from the question or from the itchiness of his skin. Who am I kidding? His legs are covered mid-thigh in mostly-dried concrete. His skin is hating life right now, and my skin feels exactly the same way. I decide not to answer the doctor's question.

My advocate in this new country, Ernestine, and her adult son, Rocky, slowly waddle into the room with a vat of vinegar water for me too. "Are you going to cut off the legs of my pants, too?" I think about the single change of clothes I smuggled out with me when I went under the border wall.

The doctor looks at me suspiciously and nods. "Yes. I'm sorry, but these aren't going to be any good."

I hope my eyes aren't as frantic as I feel. "But—I don't have—I need these."

Ernestine shoots me a look of warning before saying, "I know it's hard to lose your luggage, but I'm sure we can find you something else for the next few days. The monorail will find your luggage eventually."

What in the world is a monorail? I look between the doctor's frowning face and the look of warning in Ernestine's eyes. Didn't she say that this doctor was a friend, a safe person? Why aren't we telling him what really happened?

I submit to Ernestine's non-verbal message and grimace at the doctor. "Okay. Go ahead and cut them."

The doctor looks at me curiously again. "Would you feel more comfortable if I moved you into your own room before I do this?" He gestures toward Conrad and Rocky and then makes the scissors *chomp, chomp* in his hand.

My aching skin answers his question for me. "No! My legs feel like they are burning off. Just cut them."

Dr. Hamble quickly cuts off the legs of my pants mid-thigh. I slide my legs into the water before anyone can delay me. A sigh escapes my lips. I start rubbing my legs as vigorously as I can, hoping to stop the itch and burn. It helps, but I can't squat like this forever. I sit down, wincing when a little bit of water splashes out onto the shiny wooden floor. I look apologetically at the doctor. "Sorry."

"Don't be sorry." He drops a towel on the floor as he hands me a soft-bristled scrub brush. "Do you want to scrub it off yourself, or do you want my help?" Ernestine's son, Rocky, looks at me crammed in my little tub and rocks from one foot to the other uncomfortably.

"I can do it myself. Thanks." After a hard look from his mom, Rocky leaves the room.

Dr. Hamble frowns as he looks at my red, irritated legs in the water. "Okay. Make sure all of the concrete residue comes off. I may have to do the scrubbing if you can't handle the pain." He walks over to Conrad and lifts his right leg out of the little tub. My friend winces as the air hits his fiery-red leg. His legs look much worse than mine. He stayed in the wet cement longer than I did when we escaped through the tunnel a couple of hours ago. The doctor lowers Conrad's leg back down into the water. "You won't like this, but it has to be done." He takes another soft-bristled brush and starts scrubbing away at Conrad's skin.

I realize that I'm not scrubbing hard enough on my own legs as I watch the doctor vigorously scour my best friend's hairy legs. Conrad's fingernails dig into the sides of the tub. He is showing more toughness than I knew he possessed as he suppresses groans and bites his lip.

When the doctor is done with Conrad's legs, he looks at Ernestine. "I don't care if these two are the clumsiest lovers in the world. Even if they were fooling around on the backend of a concrete truck, they have different depths of concrete burn on their legs. Something isn't right about your story. What's really going on here? Are they complex refugees?"

Ernestine bites her cheek as she looks at me. She sighs as she turns to the doctor and shrugs. "You got me. Is it obvious that they're refugees? It's not their fault that they couldn't tell a safe place to hide from an unsafe one."

The doctor sighs, "Yes, they look like caged animals. I can't imagine living on the run for two years or living in the Complex of Undesirables for any length of time, for that matter." He shakes his head. "I wish you had just told me the truth from the beginning." He taps his fingers together as he looks at Ernestine. "I hope my son's edict has nothing to do with this...." Ernestine grimaces and looks at her feet.

"Hmm." Dr. Hamble opens a cabinet and pulls out a pair of simple, light-green shirts and pants. He turns to Conrad and me. "I always keep some extra scrubs on hand. You can change into these once we treat your burns with aloe vera. You will need to soak in a tub of vinegar water two to three times every day and apply aloe at least five times a day for the next week. I'll need to check in on you again at that point."

Conrad lifts his weary head as much as he can from the edge of his tub. "Thank you for helping us. I don't have anything to pay you now, but—"

Dr. Hamble waves him off. "Don't worry about it. My daughter was in the complex too. I'm sorry to hear that you didn't have any family support when you got out. I just want all of you to get back on your feet. No charge. Do you have any internal problems that I can help you with?"

My head is swimming with all this unfamiliar information. Why would he ask me that? "I have—a headache."

The doctor starts examining my head. "Is it just a headache, or do you have deeper problems?"

Why doesn't he believe me? "It's just a headache."

He stops looking at my scalp. "Okay, I'll get both of you some pain pills to get you through the next week. We'll see how you're doing then." He still looks like he doesn't believe my headache diagnosis.

Conrad nods. "Thank you, Dr. Hamble."

The doctor looks from Conrad to me. "That's an awfully nice shirt, young man. Where did you get it?"

Conrad looks at me uncertainly. "I, uh, someone gave it

to me." That is a good answer. He doesn't have to say that the someone was his mom and his rich, hateful dad.

"Hmm." He doesn't look convinced. "Ernestine will help you find a place to stay. I'd offer you a place myself, but my wife and I adopted three children with heart problems when the complex law was disbanded, and they are taking most of our space and attention right now."

Ernestine nods her head. "I wouldn't dream of adding to your burdens right now, Ross. I have several housing options in mind."

Doctor Hamble throws away our cement-covered pant legs in the garbage. "I'm sure my daughter and her husband have some clothes that will fit the two of you. She's expecting, so she doesn't fit into most of her old clothes anyway. Next week I'll have you visit me in my actual office though, okay?"

I look around at the ornate home office I'm sitting in and notice the wall of books behind me for the first time. I've never seen so many books in one place besides the Tifton Library. I may have barely escaped from my awful country, I may be in terrible pain, I may be a refugee, but I am in a country that values books and education! That makes me smile.

The doctor gives Conrad and me our own bottles of aloe vera. "When you climb out of the water, gently pat your legs dry and then apply this liberally to all the irritated flesh."

As the doctor turns to leave, I call out, "Thanks, again, Dr. Hamble." He smiles at me and shuts the door.

6

Ernestine looks at the two of us and shakes her head. "That was close."

I can't hold back my curiosity. "Why did we lie to him? I thought he was your friend."

"Oh, he is. He and his wife, Florence, are my best friends in the world, but their oldest son, Brock Hamble, is about to become President of The United Cities, and I don't want to mess that up. People from your country will probably come looking for you, and Hambles harboring fugitives from a neighboring country won't help Brock on the ballot."

Conrad looks at me apprehensively. "I wouldn't be surprised if my dad comes looking for us before the Tifton Patrolchief does."

I roll my eyes and nod. "He certainly has more money and resources, but I don't know of anyone who has crossed the border wall in my lifetime. Surely, we are fine—right?" Conrad's eyes flash with apprehension.

Ernestine picks at a spot on her arm as she thinks. "Whether anyone comes looking for you or not, we are going to play it safe until after the election. That means keeping your story a secret from the Hambles."

I nod my head obediently. "Where will we all sleep?" I think about my mom, sister, boyfriend, and all of his friends who snuck out of the country with us.

Ernestine scratches her chin anxiously. "Well, that's the trick. I would normally have some of you stay here, well, in the

Hambles' basement safehouse, but they adopted three very sick little children that no one else wanted, or knew how to care for, when the complex emptied out, and with the election just around the corner, it just won't work."

Conrad looks at Ernestine curiously. "Is the complex where all the flawed people in your country used to live?"

She nods with a sneer. "Yes, but Brock put an end to that two years ago."

This sounds so familiar. "Oh—my dad told me about that senator—before he died."

Ernestine raises her eyebrows. "I'll tell you all about it later. It's a long, complex story." She taps her fingers together in concentration. "I will probably have the boys stay with us at our house. Having five more people will fill us to the brim, so—where should I send the girls?" Ernestine twists her lips as she thinks. "My second choice would be Elira, the Hamble's daughter, since she has a nice house and a big heart, but she's a Hamble too, so I better not. She's always being scrutinized by the media. I think that leaves Elira's friend's house. I can trust her not to spill the beans, but can I trust you guys not to let Elira know who you really are if she shows up for a visit?"

Conrad looks at me and then at Ernestine. "Yeah. I'm sure Dandra won't say anything, but I'd rather not be separated from her."

Poor Conrad. I feel the same way, but beggars can't be choosers, right? Since we know nothing and have nothing in this country, we are at the mercy of these strangers. I nod at Ernestine. "Yes, of course I'll keep our past a secret."

Ernestine narrows her eyes at me. "What about your mom and sister?"

I lift my shoulders. "Uh, I'll tell them how important it is to keep quiet. It'll be fine."

"Okay. Once you are lathered in aloe vera and changed, I'm taking you and the other girls to Shasta's house. Actually, I should probably call first." She chuckles at her own impulsiveness.

"Ernestine, thank you. Thank you so much," I say from the bottom of my heart.

I am so lucky that my boyfriend Baldwin became two-way radio friends with Ernestine before we made our escape. She was waiting for us on this side of the border wall when the nine of us literally squeezed and clawed our way through. Unfortunately, when I went back for Conrad, the escape tunnel was being pumped full of cement.

I cringe as I look at my red, cement-burned legs. If I had known a few hours ago that escaping through a tunnel filled with wet concrete would be so painful, would I still have done it?

I remember Patrolman Darius's crazed eyes glaring at me as I trudged through the cold, wet tunnel that my dad and I had dug for so many years. I had stayed one tiny step ahead of him even though Conrad's dad, Zane Chesterton, had paid him to guard me. They could control most things in the city of Tifton, and even the whole country of Layland for that matter, but they could not control me. Even though I feel like a fox that sacrificed its legs to break into a hen house, I would do it all again.

Chapter 2

I FEEL LIKE I WAS IN the doctor's house for just a short visit, but a blanket of blackness has claimed the streets since I entered. It has to be about 10:30 pm. Was I really escaping with my life just a few hours ago? There are plenty of streetlights out here in this new and unknown country. The streetlights combined with the lights on the Hambles' house give me an excellent view of the doctor's mansion. I can't help but stare at it. It's so big and clean and beautiful. I used to think Conrad's house was the prettiest house in the world, but Doctor Hamble's is—dazzling. Conrad and I shuffle on the slick sidewalk with stiff legs to Ernestine's van, which is—empty. My heart jumps into my throat. I can see my breath in the air as I cry, "Where did my family and friends go, Ernestine?" Rocky waves at us from the driver's seat. He's the only person in sight.

Ernestine puts a calming hand on my shoulder. "They are at my house. I had Rocky take them there while you guys met with the doc. I was afraid they would cause a scene with the Hambles or anyone else who walked by, really."

I feel my eyebrows knitting themselves together. "What do you mean? They were just sitting in the van."

Ernestine snorts. "It was the right move, missy. First, it's freezing cold out here. Second, they kept looking around wide-eyed like they'd never seen buildings and streets before." She raises her eyebrows at me as we all climb into the van. "Don't worry, my husband Frank has been keeping them company."

I check to make sure my own jaw isn't gaping open because these streets really are shockingly clean. There is no litter in sight at all. I feel like I'm on an alien planet. Conrad leads us to the car and gingerly places his legs in the backseat, so they won't bump into me or anything else. We are such a mess. I feel bad about putting Conrad through this, and I feel bad for leaving my family and boyfriend with strangers. I'm sure I'll be feeling bad about a whole lot more before this week is through.

The drive to Ernestine's house takes only a couple of minutes since she lives on the opposite end of the same street as the Hambles, the less-affluent end of the street, for sure. Ernestine helps me out of the van while Rocky helps Conrad. I feel like a little old woman who might slip on the ice. Seriously, this icy sidewalk is nerve-wracking.

I look at my friend as we approach the smaller, plainer, older house. "Are you ready for this, Conrad?"

"Mmmhmm," is all he says. He is hiding his pain well as he slips, but I can tell Conrad is in agony because his smile doesn't reach his eyes.

The door opens as we get to it, and my boyfriend Baldwin bursts through and takes my arm from Ernestine. "How are you feeling? Are your legs still burning?"

I turn the corners of my mouth up for him. "Yeah, but I know how to give them some relief now." I hide my discomfort as I remember Dr. Hamble saying that pain and itchiness will be my new normal for the next few months. "I have pain pills." I shake the bottle at my boyfriend reassuringly.

He kisses my forehead. "You just tell me what you need, and I'll get it for you—or at least I'll try to get it for you." He looks at the unfamiliar house we're walking into with apprehension. Honestly, he owns nothing in this country or the country we left. He is poor, but he is the smartest guy I know.

He doesn't say anything or spare a glance for Conrad, but my friend follows Baldwin and me into the house anyway.

Ernestine leads us into a cramped living room where my mom and sister are sitting with Baldwin's friends, the anti-gamers we escaped with, and a man who looks like a lumber jack. The lumber jack stands up and offers me his seat. "Please sit here; I've heard about your cement burns. That must be very uncomfortable." I lower myself into his worn armchair. He smiles at me. "You must be Dandra. I'm Frank Moore, Ernestine's husband and Rocky's dad."

I shake his hand as I get situated in the surprisingly comfortable old armchair. "Thank you. I'm Dandra Metty, and this is my good friend, Conrad Chesterton."

Frank shakes Conrad's hand. "It's nice to meet you. I hear you also have cement burns. I got a cement burn on my right hand when I used to work in construction. It took over six months to heal all the way. It was terrible. I'm sure someone will let you use their seat, so you don't have to sit on the floor." He looks at the anti-gamers on the couch expectantly, but they don't budge.

Finally, Marcella stands up, shakily, but Gordon pulls her back down on the couch and plants himself on the floor in front of her. Conrad looks warily at the empty spot on the couch between Adamar, who's still distraught that his girlfriend didn't make it out of the country with us, and a frightened Marcella before he slowly slinks down into the open seat. He's careful to

14

keep his legs pointed straight ahead, so he doesn't bump into anyone.

He looks so uncomfortable, and not just because of his cement-burned legs. My anti-gamer friends don't like him. Well, it's more that they don't like his father.

Baldwin sits on the floor in front of me and leans against my legs, which of course makes me screech.

He looks mortified. "I'm so sorry, Dandra! I forgot." He scoots over so he doesn't touch my legs at all.

I bite my lip to keep myself from wailing as Ernestine comes in with a basket of fruit. "I'm sure you're all hungry after that horrendous escape tonight. Please take as much as you need. Rocky, will you bring in the cheese and crackers for me? I need to make an important phone call to Shasta."

"Yeah, sure," he says as he leaves the awkwardly silent room.

We nervously watch as Ernestine hands the basket to my mom who takes a banana and passes it to my little sister Everley, who takes an apple and walks it across the room to Marcella. When Ernestine returns from making her phone call, her thin, lean body squats down on the floor next to her husband Frank and sighs. "Well, I'm thrilled that I figured out where you were coming through under the border wall with so little information. It was pure luck that Rocky heard you calling for me on the radio this morning." We all nod in appreciation for everything they have done for us. "I think we should call this night a success. You all made it through, and there are no helicopters shining search lights from Layland's side of the wall."

Adamar's voice cracks, "Not all of us made it through." He covers his face with his hand so that we can't see his emotions spilling over. We all mumble our condolences that his girlfriend didn't come with us.

I feel so bad for him. I swallow a bite of banana before saying, "Adamar, Charlisa made her choice. She wasn't ready to leave her mom. It was a huge decision to make in such a short amount of time."

"I know," he says through his hand. Rocky comes back with the cheese and crackers and decides not to start the tray with Adamar since he won't look up.

Ernestine leans forward to examine each of us carefully. "Do any of you have any broadcasting devices that will lead the authorities here?"

Baldwin and Ed look at each other furtively as Baldwin says, "No. We don't have anything that can broadcast anything without being set up." He glares at Conrad. "He is the only one who might have a GameCom on him."

Conrad glares at Baldwin and lifts up his empty wrists. "We left them covered in cement by the escape hole. They probably don't work anymore, but if they do, they can't lead anyone to us here."

Baldwin cocks his head to the side. "I'm not so sure about

that. Those things listen to everything around them. They may have picked up Ernestine's voice."

I try to break the tension. "Zane Chesterton may have a recording of her voice, but he doesn't know who the voice belongs to. We'll be fine, at least for now."

Ernestine looks at us all curiously but then focuses in on me. "These GameComs sound disturbing, but are they really worth leaving your country for? You ruined your legs running through that cement." She watches me as I peek at my red, swollen calves under my borrowed pants.

My mom clears her throat. "We were in a bad situation, Ernestine. Our country has given up on education and those of us who were fighting to keep it were despised and destitute, and a powerful man started..." Mom looks at Conrad who is looking at his hands, "targeting us. He killed my husband, he was having all of us watched, and some of us were being escorted around by his thugs." She gestures to my sister, me, and lastly to Conrad, who had it worse than the rest of us from his own father.

Ed scowls at Conrad. "It doesn't help that the powerful man is his dad."

I scoot forward in my seat before saying to the room at large, "Conrad told Patrolman Mark the truth about who really ran over my father even when it incriminated his own dad. We owe him a lot." I pull the legs of my pants up as high as I can. The sting of fabric touching them is killing me. I look at my mom's tired face and say, "I can't believe our tunnel under

17

the border wall is full of cement now. Years of work gone in a couple of hours. We almost didn't make it out."

Ernestine's eyes linger on Conrad's downturned face. "Well, I hope you find the United Cities better than Layland. Unfortunately, we have our own set of problems."

Gordon speaks up through a mouthful of cheese and crackers, "It doesn't look like you have problems. The streets are so clean."

"Our problem isn't cleanliness or slothfulness, it's bigotry."

I feel my eyebrows come together. "I thought you said the complex law is gone, and all the flawed people in your country have been free for two years."

"Well, technically, yes. No one has to live in the Complex of Undesirables or the Complex for the Elderly anymore, but not everyone in the United Cities likes mingling with flawed and elderly people."

I hate hearing that. My curiosity gets the best of me. "Will we stand out since we just appeared out of nowhere?"

Ernestine purses her lips together as she thinks. "I don't think so. There is a lot of moving and shuffling these days between cities. People of all philosophies are trying to decide where they feel most comfortable. Most of the moving and shuffling is still an act of bigotry, but fortunately for you, nine people can show up in a new city without work or a school placement and not be questioned too much about it right now."

I feel my hopes rising. "I can go to school with lots of people who want to be there?"

Ernestine looks at me like I have two heads. "Uh, yeah. You're too young to drop out. Do any of you want to drop out?"

Gordon clears his throat. "We were encouraged to end our education at age 16 in our country. None of us wanted to do that, but we just assumed we'd need to get jobs to survive over here."

Frank looks at his wife before turning to Gordon. "Most of you still will, but you can do both."

I feel happy for the first time tonight. "This is why my dad started the tunnel so many years ago! When can we start school?"

Ernestine shrugs. "The schools are about to start Christmas break, so after that."

I clap my hands excitedly. "Perfect."

Ernestine gives me a sad smile. "I don't know if perfect is the word I would use. Some people will assume you are from the complex, and they may not be kind."

Mom clears her throat as her eyes wander apprehensively around the cramped, little living room. "But before we think about that, where are we going to sleep?"

Chapter 3

I HATE SEEING THE ABANDONMENT in
Conrad's eyes as I pack up my mom, Everley, and Marcella into
Ernestine's van. How did everything fall into place like this? I
worry about separating from the guys. I'm especially worried
about Conrad, who isn't friends with the rest of the boys we
escaped with. In fact, Baldwin can't stand him.

I give Baldwin a quick peck on the lips as I pause by the
van door. "Can you believe we did it? Everyone we wanted out
is out!"

He smiles at me and pushes a piece of hair behind my ear.

21

"Everyone except Charlisa. But you're right. We're out, and we're safe. That's a lot to be thankful for."

I can see over Baldwin's shoulder a look of abandonment in Conrad's eyes. It kills me a little. I take Baldwin's hand and say softly, "Adamar and Conrad are missing the people they left behind the most tonight."

Baldwin softens as he looks at Adamar, who is barely keeping it together. "I think you're right."

My eyes wander to my mom who is holding Everley like her life depends on it. I softly admit, "I wish we could all stay at the same house, but this is temporary."

Baldwin steals one more kiss. "I know. We'll be together soon."

I squeeze his hand. "I'll miss you. At least we'll get to go to school together." Conrad is behind my boyfriend looking at the ground. I lean in and whisper, "Baldwin, Be nice to Conrad, please."

Baldwin guffaws. "I'm the nicest guy I know."

"He isn't his dad, remember that."

"I'll try." He gives me a quick hug and then assists me into the van and shuts the door.

Conrad hobbles with stiff legs up to the door of the van. I lower the window and reach out to give him a quick one-armed hug. "Just take care of your cement burns. Don't worry about anything else, okay? I'll try to find jobs for all of us, so we can move closer together soon."

Conrad's eyes don't leave my face. "Remember when I tried to get you to work with me at the gaming district?"

I smirk as I think about the place that is taking over so many people's lives in Layland. "Yeah, I chose the dusty old library instead, and I would make the same choice again," I say as I smile at the memory.

Conrad sighs, "I still want to work with you."

That library was mysterious and a little bit creepy, but it led me to Baldwin and where I am now. I look at my friend's gloomy face and say, "I'll try to find a job we'll both like, and I'll see you soon."

Conrad's hand grips tighter to the window frame. "I wish you could stay here. I will give up my bed and sleep on the floor."

I look at my mom's worried face and the back of Ernestine's head and lower my voice. "I don't think that is an option right now." Conrad's face droops. "I'll find a better option soon. I promise."

Conrad's face doesn't look convinced as he mutters, "Okay."

My heart breaks a little as I drive away from half of the people who have been my world the last few months. I hope we're doing the right thing trusting Ernestine and splitting up like this.

My mom pulls me close and guides my head to her shoulder. She whispers, "I hope this country is going to be better. Your dad was so sure that it would be."

23

I wipe a tear off my cheek. "I hope so, too."

Everley and Marcella are silent as we drive for 10 minutes to a house that is about the same size and age as the house that we left behind in Layland. The one thing that is noticeably different is that there is no litter blowing across the road or stuck in the hedges. The buildings in this part of town are simple and clean. A few of them look like they could use a fresh coat of paint, but those few are the exception, not the rule.

Ernestine climbs out of the van and opens my door as she stretches her back. "Don't be alarmed at how tall Shasta is. She has a condition that makes her extremely tall and thin. She gets enough judgement from the narrow-minded people of Herrington without you guys making it worse. She has the kindest heart I have ever seen and has taken in many former complex residents that were rejected by their families. In fact, she has four little girls living here who were rejected by their families but are too young to live on their own, so you'll have to get used to them." Ernestine scratches her chin before going on, "Shasta has helped six other women find the schooling or jobs they were looking for and places of their own. She's a very protective person, and she'll take good care of you."

I worry about what to say when I meet this Shasta person. I hope I like the answer to the question I ask Ernestine. "Does she know our real story, or did you tell her the same story you told Dr. Hamble?"

Ernestine smiles at me reassuringly. "I told her your real

story because I know how hard it will be to keep that kind of secret from someone you're living with, and I know your secret is safe with her."

That news is a relief. "Oh, good. Thank you."

When I hear the door open, I turn to see a blonde woman walking toward me. Wow. She is extremely tall, at least 6'2" and unnaturally thin. I don't have time to stare at her though. My legs are starting to burn again. I think it's time for a new layer of aloe. I hope Shasta has a tub I can soak in tonight.

My mom waits for Everley and me to gather the three small bags that came through the tunnel with us and slowly walks us up the sidewalk to our new host. Mom's voice shakes slightly as she says, "Hello. You must be Shasta. My name is Laurel Metty. These are my daughters Dandra and Everley." Mom wraps her arm around Marcella and pulls her closer. "This is our friend Marcella. Thank you so much for taking us in."

Shasta's eyes focus on us. "No problem. I hear you had a breath-taking escape out of your country. I'd love to hear all about it. Won't you come in?" Her face is significantly less expressive than her voice sounds.

Mom smiles hesitantly. "Yes. Thank you."

Ernestine shuts the sliding door of her van and opens the driver's door and says, "I will check in on you tomorrow. Shasta will take good care of you." She climbs into the van and yawns as she rolls down the window. It has been a long night for all of us.

I nod at Ernestine and wave. "Thank you, Ernestine. I don't know what we would have done without you."

Ernestine yawns once more before saying, "I like to help people find freedom. It's my thing." She waves one last time and drives away.

I try to be brave as I force my painful legs to put one foot in front of the other and follow Shasta into the house.

My mom has a very maternal air about her as we tour the house. She's making a special effort with Marcella, which is exactly what she needs. I'm sure my friend is feeling kind of like Conrad at the other house tonight.

This mid-sized house uses its space impressively well. We are all staying on the smaller second floor because Shasta and the four girls living here have already claimed the three main-floor bedrooms. We don't peek into the little girls' rooms because they are asleep. Shasta says that the two girls in the first room are five and six and the girls in the second room are eight and nine. Everley bounces on her feet, excited to meet them in the morning. Shasta's room is small and simple. She seems like a woman of simple taste. I think she'll have a calming influence on us anxious refugees. The staircase to the second floor is narrow and steep. My mom and Everley are going to share a room right at the top of the stairs. Marcella and I are going to share the other room next to that one. The two bedrooms and a full-size lavatory are the only rooms on the second floor. The hall is wide enough for a desk, a bookshelf, and a few chairs. The roof is gabled on this floor, so Shasta would hit her head constantly if she slept up here. The clean, flowery scent of the lavatory lures me in as soon as I see it. My legs are dying for a bath.

Shasta takes a couple steps down the stairs so she's looking me in the eye. "Are any of you hungry?"

I am so wound up I don't know if I can eat, but maybe everyone else wants something. I look at them but get only yawns. "Uh, I think we need rest more than food."

Shasta nods. "You aren't the first refugees who have told me that. Get some sleep. We can have a big breakfast and get to know each other tomorrow. There should be plenty of blankets and pillows in both rooms."

I smile as I take in my new surroundings. "Okay. Thank you so much," I say through a yawn as my mom gets everyone situated in the bedrooms. Shasta smiles and walks down the stairs, careful not to hit her head on the ceiling as she goes.

My mom hugs me once we're alone and insists that I go soak my legs in the tub. That sounds heavenly, so I walk into the lavatory and start running water for a bath.

My legs are so red and irritated, I worry about putting on

pants again. There are a few soap options in this tub, but I don't use them. My skin simply can't handle it. I forgot to ask Shasta for vinegar. Oh well, my skin feels so much better in the water than in the open air.

A soft knock on the door wakes me up out of my daze. Mom's muffled voice calls, "Dandra, honey, I think you should come to bed."

"Can't I have another 20 minutes?"

"Well, you could, but your sister needs to use the lavatory."

"Oh. I'll get out. Sorry."

I gently pat my legs dry and force them into the thin green pants that Doctor Hamble gave me. I bite my lip as the fabric drags across my skin. Where did I put those pain killers and aloe?

My mom holds her face together as I hug her good night, but I can tell that she wants to cry. Patrolman Mark lied for us tonight, but we didn't take him with us or even thank him. Mom is going to miss him. Everley can barely fit a "good night" between her yawns. She's been through a lot today, poor kid.

I collapse on my bed and think about what I've done. I'm glad to be away from Patrolman Darius, but I feel sort of empty and sad at the same time.

I don't know what I expected, but this is not it. I am in a house like the one I left, I'm with my family, and I have a new roommate. This isn't too bad, but it would be better if I knew the way back to Baldwin and Conrad on these clean, unfamiliar roads.

I'm almost asleep when a loud sound wakes me up. "AHHH!" Marcella shrieks from her bed.

I remember Baldwin telling me that Marcella has nightmares, a lot. She was not only homeless in Layland, but she also used to earn money through creepy men. She has a lot in her past that would keep anyone from sleeping soundly at night. I scoot onto the edge of Marcella's twin-sized bed and shake her shoulder. "Wake up, Marcella! You're having a nightmare. Everything is okay."

My friend doesn't open her eyes. "Don't touch me! Get away from me!" she shrieks and flails. One of her hands inadvertently smacks me in the face.

"Ow!" I screech.

Hearing that wakes my friend up. She looks mortified. "Sorry, Dandra! Did I hurt you?"

I gently touch the stinging spot on my check. "Nah. I'm fine." My friend looks embarrassed, so I try to make her outburst seem like no big deal. "Don't worry about it." I doubt she'll share, but I ask anyway," Do you want to tell me what your nightmare was about?"

Marcella hesitates a long time before answering me. "You don't want to know. I'm sorry. I'll try not to do it again." She pulls the covers up to her chin and turns her head away from me.

My heart goes out to her. I say reassuringly, "It's fine, and you are safe here. If there is anything I can do to help you, just let me know."

She mumbles through the blankets, "Okay. Thank you."

I hear her breathing slow down and eventually turn into a soft snore. What a crazy day this has been.

Chapter 4

THE BED AND MY BODY START SHAKING like crazy. Is it an earthquake? No, it's just Everley. "Dandra, wake up!" Why do 10-year olds have so much energy first thing in the morning?

My voice sounds like a dying frog as I answer, "But, I just barely fell asleep."

"Shasta made pancakes, eggs, and—bacon, and I really want to eat them with the other girls down there, but I want someone I know to come downstairs with me!"

I refuse to open my eyes as I answer. "Okay, fine. Where is Mom?"

"She's taking a shower."

"Where is Marcella?"

A high-pitched, unfamiliar voice answers, "She's already downstairs."

I immediately sit up and open my eyes. "Who are you?" I ask the unfamiliar red-head peeking through the door.

"I'm Nelle," she says as her freckly face turns as red as her hair.

Everley smiles at her new friend. "Nelle is nine, so she's only a year younger than me. She says she'll share her painting kit with me."

I pull the covers up to my throat. "That sounds fun. Can you guys give me a few minutes to get dressed? Where is my bag? I can't remember what I stuffed in it yesterday."

Everley picks my scruffy school backpack up off the floor and dumps it on my bed. "Here it is. We only packed one change of clothes per person, remember?"

"Oh, yeah. Thanks. I'll be down in a minute."

"Okay, be quick," my sister says as she and her new friend leave. I notice that her friend has a club foot as she hobbles out of the room. I understand why she has a bedroom on the main floor now.

Mom holds a bite of pancake in her mouth and closes her eyes briefly before she swallows. "Shasta, these pancakes and eggs are amazing. Thank you."

"No problem." Shasta extends a plate of bacon towards her. "You haven't had any bacon yet. Take some."

Mom shakes her head. "Oh, no. I couldn't. It's too expensive. Let the children have it."

Shasta opens the fridge and points to several packages of bacon sitting there. "I have tons more. Please take some."

Mom hesitantly takes two small slices off the plate and then hands it to Marcella. "I hate to be a burden to you. Do you know of any jobs available around here?"

Shasta waves off her comment. "You are not a burden. This is what I do."

My mom shakes her head in disbelief. "I've never seen or even imagined a society that is so willing to help other people out without compensation."

Shasta smiles at her. "Other people helped me out of a bad situation, so I want to spend my life helping others in any way I can." Shasta gives the pancake batter in front of her a good, swift whip. "There is no rush, but there are always jobs posted on the community boards at city hall if you want to go check them out."

My mom's eyes light up. I hope she doesn't mind getting

a job that won't use her education. We can't afford to be picky in this new country. I clear my throat from the doorway of the kitchen. "What kind of jobs are posted there?"

Shasta takes a drink of orange juice and shrugs. "Anything from janitorial to professors at the University."

My mom looks at her curiously. "Do they ever need bank help?"

Shasta scrunches her eyebrows together as she thinks. "Occasionally they do. I know that the last time I was at city hall, there weren't any bank jobs, but there were two clothing stores needing help and three different tutor jobs posted."

Mom's eyes light up as I sit down beside her. "You need tutors here? I am a tutor. Does it pay well?"

Shasta nods. "Yes, we have a teacher and tutor shortage in Herrington right now because those of us who used to go to school in the Complex of Undesirables need a school placement out here now. I bet it pays well, and more importantly, it probably doesn't require any government documents."

Mom smiles as she crunches on a piece of bacon. "I'm so happy to hear that! I mean, I'm not glad that there is a shortage, but I'm glad that there is a job I can do."

I start to worry about all nine of us needing government documents to get jobs and to cash future paychecks. "Will the rest of us need government documents to get jobs, Shasta?"

"Actually, now is a great time to get away with not having documents. Because so many former complex residents are getting low-level jobs in the cities, businesses are allowed to hire without paperwork and even to pay in cash," Shasta says with a smile.

Three little girls burst through the door to the kitchen and join Everley and Nelle at the table. Everley looks like she is in little girl heaven.

I smile at her. "Who are your friends, sis?"

Everley points to a chubby girl with blonde curls. "This is Peggy. She's eight and she shares a room with Nelle. She jabs her head toward the smallest two girls. "I can't remember their names though."

The second smallest girl has a recently repaired cleft lip. Her brown hair is thin and barely makes two little pig tails on the top of her head. She holds up her hand and an additional finger and looks me in the eye. "I'm Deedee, and I'm six."

She is adorable. I smile at her and say, "It's nice to meet you, Deedee. What is your friend's name?"

Deedee turns to the little girl sitting next to her. She is sucking on a piece of her long black hair. "This is Mina. She's five. She doesn't talk, so I talk for her."

I look at Mina to confirm this statement, but she won't look at me. I look at Deedee instead. "Does Mina want some pancakes?"

"Yes, she does, but no eggs. Mina hates eggs."

I fill up a plate for Mina as Shasta fills up a plate for Deedee. "Does Mina like orange juice?"

"Yes. We both like orange juice."

I nod. "Okay. Does anyone else want orange juice?" Peggy, Nelle, and Everley raise their hands like they're in school, so I grin and get juice for all of them.

Everley takes the juice from me and smiles. "Thanks, Dandra."

I look around the well-stocked kitchen in awe as I put a few pieces of bacon on my plate. "Who pays you and pays for all of this food, Shasta?"

"The Hamble Foundation."

I add a pancake and a scoop of eggs to my plate. "Do you mean Doctor Hamble? Or his son, Brock?"

Shasta gives Everley and Nelle fresh pancakes off the hotplate. "I mean Doctor Hamble and his wife mostly. They are the most generous humanitarian contributors in the city. Their sons and daughter donate some, too."

Knock Knock. I feel a jolt of dread run up my spine even though no one who wishes us harm knows we're here.

The door creaks from the other room as it opens. I brace myself, ready to run if need be. A sweet-sounding feminine voice calls from the front door, "Shasta, are you here? I brought two bags of clothes. My dad called me this morning to tell me to bring them here."

A pretty girl with a big purple birthmark over one of her eyes walks through the kitchen door. I try to decide what stands out the most, the purple birthmark over her eye or her protruding stomach. She's a thin woman who looks like she's six months pregnant. Her kind face and sweet smile make her the cutest mother-to-be I've ever seen.

I'm pretty sure I know who this is. This has to be Elira Hamble, Dr. Hambles' daughter who used to live in the complex. I need to be careful about what I say to her. She can't know that we are wanted escapees from Layland. I whisper some quick instructions to my mom and Marcella while Elira talks to Shasta.

Elira smiles at the room at large. "Something smells good in here! Can I grab a plate?"

Shasta takes a few more pancakes off the hot pan. "Sure. Help yourself."

Elira sits down next to Marcella at the table like she's known us forever. "I love a good pancake. Especially right now. I'm always craving breakfast food." She rubs her pregnant belly affectionately. She suddenly looks right at me and extends her hand. "Sorry. I didn't introduce myself. I am Elira Yesterly. I hear you were in the complex but didn't stay once the law was revoked."

I nod bashfully. "Aren't you a Hamble, though? The doctor I saw yesterday mentioned you."

"Yes. I'm Dr. Hamble's daughter. I don't live with my parents anymore. I was married six months ago," she says through a bite of pancake.

I spin my glass of juice around and around nervously. "He's a good doctor."

Elira swallows a bite of pancake and smiles. "Yes, he is." She looks questioningly at my mom and then back at me. "My dad said that you didn't have any family support when you left. Where have you been sleeping?"

I have to think quickly. My mom's scared look might give us away. "I uh, guess you could say that we found any old space and made it our own."

She looks at my mom curiously. "You guys look a lot alike. Are you related?"

Mom clears her throat. "Uh, I am her aunt, Laurel, and this little girl is her cousin, Eva. We just met up with Dani and her other refugee friends yesterday. We've been looking for them for a long time."

Everley frowns at being called little. She opens her mouth to ask why Mom is lying when I shake my head at her. I smile at Elira then turn to look at Marcella. "This is my friend Marcy. We have several other friends staying—" Mom elbows me before I say too much. "...in this city, so we're excited to live here, too."

Elira watches me carefully as she eats her pancake. "Were you in the green dorm or the blue dorm when the complex law was disbanded?"

I have no idea what the difference between the two dorms is, so I just choose one. "Marcy and I were in the blue dorm."

Elira does some quick math in her head. "I was just old enough that I wouldn't have shared a dorm with you in the complex. Why didn't you just stay at the complex if you didn't have anywhere to go? They would have let you stay and paid you to work."

I look at Shasta for some help. She smiles at Elira and says, "They were only 14 when the complex law was repealed. They had to be 16 in order to stay to work for pay. I would have lived in the wild, too, if my only other option was staying, unpaid, in the complex with Mentor Roberta."

Elira nods her head. "Good point." She grabs a piece of bacon, looks at my mom and asks, "So, what happens now? You have found your long-lost niece."

My mom looks at Shasta for more help. Luckily she is ready to answer for us. "They are going to stay with me until they have found work and school placements in Herrington. Once they have that, they will do like my other guests have done and find their own house or apartment to stay in."

Elira looks at all of our wary faces before responding. "Well, that is as good a plan as any. Do you want me to help look for jobs? I bet my brothers have something for you. Brock always needs campaign help and Greggory's department usually has openings at the National News Station."

Shasta shakes her head forcefully. "I don't think these ladies want to work in the public spotlight, but thanks anyway. Some of them have lived for two years on the run, in constant turmoil, so I think we'll just find some quiet jobs and quiet school placements around here."

Elira looks at her friend curiously as she stands up and puts one hand on her protruding stomach, gently stretching her aching back. "Okay, I just wanted to help. Can I at least do the dishes?"

Shasta is nodding right as my mom says, "No, I'll do it."

Elira smiles at my mom. "If I wash, will you dry?" My mom nods bashfully. Elira turns to Marcella and me. "You girls should go look at the bags of clothes I dropped off in the living room. There are some super cute hand-me-downs in there."

I nod at our guest and take Marcella's arm and drag her up from the table. I will feel more comfortable in another room where I don't have to keep secrets. I smile at Elira and say, "We love new clothes! Thank you and thank you for breakfast, Shasta." We take our dishes to the sink and then go to the living room to see what kind of clothes Elira brought us.

My mom looks at Elira's belly as she starts washing dishes. "Are you sure you want to be on your feet right now? I remember my back hurting once I was six months pregnant."

"Oh, I'm only four months along, but I'm having twins."

My mom puts a hand to her mouth. "Then I definitely don't want you hurting your back washing my breakfast dishes."

Elira smiles. "Nonsense," I overhear her tell my mom as I leave, "Your niece and her friend have impressively good manners for being raised in the complex, and to be honest, I remember having no idea that the morning meal was called breakfast…."

Chapter 5

I CAN PRACTICALLY HEAR MY LEGS sighing with relief as I swish them around in the tub filled with vinegar water. I am almost asleep when my mom's knock at the door startles me awake. "Dandra, Ernestine is here to bring us some news. Can you come downstairs?"

I should rush downstairs, but my legs dread being in clothes again. "I need like, 15 more minutes, and then I'll be down, Mom."

"If you say so, but she brought Baldwin and Conrad with her."

I don't need telling twice. "I'll be right down!"

I hurry as fast as my blistering legs will let me. I throw on a lightweight, lavender dress from one of the hand-me-down bags. It's probably meant for warmer weather than December, but it feels so much better on my legs than restricting pants do, and it's very pretty. I don't want my wet hair to become a blonde fluff ball in an hour, so I braid it as quickly and tastefully as I can, quickly rub some aloe on my legs, and run-hobble down the stairs into the living room. I feel like a toy soldier or a doll with unbending legs. I slow down only after I see two sets of eyes looking at me in anticipation. Baldwin runs to me and helps me down the last two stairs. Conrad is right behind him hobbling worse than I am.

Ernestine gets the first word. "I didn't mean for this visit to be a get-together, but these two refused to be left behind once they knew I was coming to see you."

Baldwin leans toward me. "You look beautiful in that dress. I feel like I should have made more of an effort." He looks at his own worn-out shirt and pants self-consciously. He, of course, has only two scruffy outfits to his name, like the rest of us. His well-worn green sneakers finish his look.

I don't care what everyone is wearing. I'm just glad we're all alive and away from Patrolman Darius and Conrad's crazy dad, Zane Chesterton.

I give my boyfriend a quick peck on the lips and point to a big bag by the door. "Make sure you take that bag of clothes home with you to share with everyone. Doctor Hamble's daughter brought them this morning."

He nods appreciatively. "Yeah. I will."

Baldwin leads me to the couch and sits down uncomfortably close to my blistering legs. My gasp makes him retreat a few inches. "Sorry. I keep forgetting. It's hard when I just want to be near you."

I don't want him to feel bad, so I smile. "It's fine."

Conrad watches my every move and sits gingerly down in a chair next to Everley and Nelle, who are making bracelets out of beads on the floor. Nelle immediately puts a man-sized flowery bracelet on him. Everley tries to hide her snort.

He holds it up to his face. "Does it go well with my eyes?" He bats his eye lashes for effect. The girls break into uncontrollable giggles. When he looks at me and Baldwin, his playful face goes blank.

Ernestine looks at my mom and sighs. "I just talked to a man named Jim in Layland on my two-way radio, and he says that you guys are big news over there."

Conrad's eyes fill with fear as he looks at me. Baldwin reaches over and takes my hand. He looks at Ernestine. "It's not a big surprise, really. This is the first time someone has illegally left the country in over two decades."

Ernestine nods. "According to Jim, there is a lot of turmoil going on. A man named Zane Chesterton wants permission to cross the border wall to search for his son." She looks at Conrad. "Are you the son he is looking for?"

Conrad nods his head. "Yes. Unfortunately."

She frowns at his lack of love. "He is your father. Do you have any regrets about leaving?"

Conrad shakes his head. "My dad is a liar and a— murderer. He put me on house-arrest when I refused to keep lying for him. I'm never going back." He looks right at me and the message in his eyes is clear. I promised to help him if he told the authorities the truth about who really ran over my dad, and he expects me to keep that promise.

Ernestine scratches her chin. "The only reason Zane isn't over here right now is because some of the peace officers or patrolmen or whatever you call your men in uniform over there are investigating him for murder. They are fighting hard to put him away, and he is fighting to put them away for defending the Metty family. He claims that you are a bigger threat to the country than he is because you did, in fact, dig a tunnel under the border wall."

I shift uncomfortably in my seat. "Did Jim say how likely it is that Zane will get permission to cross the border?"

"He thinks Zane will pay the right people the right price and will have himself or one of his cronies across the border within a week."

Baldwin's body tenses beside me. "We need to think about this logically. There are nine lives at stake here. If Zane gets permission to cross the border, which is very possible, we might have no choice but to give Conrad back to save the rest of us."

Anger rolls through my body as I turn to face my boyfriend. "No. I promised Conrad I would help him if he told the patrolmen the truth."

Baldwin doesn't back down. "I understand that, and we'll try our best to protect him, but if worse comes to worst, shouldn't we think about the eight of us who are not related to Zane Chesterton?"

I feel blood rushing to my cheeks as I drop Baldwin's hand. "I thought you of all people would hate to give the rich, power-hungry man what he wants and punish the only person in his family who told the truth."

He takes my hand again, softly this time. "Dandra, I want to keep us all free. I just think we need a plan B and maybe a plan C if Zane finds us."

I shake my head. "I won't let his dad take him back to Mrs. Graight and house arrest."

He squeezes my hand. "I think the main reason Zane hired Mrs. Graight was to keep him away from you." I open my mouth to object, but Baldwin lifts a finger to silence me. Conrad looks at me sheepishly as my boyfriend continues. "Okay, maybe we'll just cross that bridge when we get there. We're sure the GameComs won't lead them to us, right?"

Conrad nods. "I'm sure they won't lead anyone anywhere.

They are still sitting by our exit hole in the church yard, and they are probably ruined from the cement."

Ernestine looks at us with worry. "If authorities from Layland come over here looking for you, I can guarantee that they will search my house. I have a reputation for getting people out of places that aren't good for them, and you said that they may have a recording of my voice."

Conrad sits up straighter. "If that happens, where will we hide?"

Ernestine scratches her chin. "I can hide two people in closets easily enough, but I don't know about five."

Baldwin taps his fingers together as he thinks. "Okay, well, we need to find some jobs and get a place of our own, then."

Shasta pipes in. "There is a reasonably-priced apartment building two blocks from here that my former complex refugee house-guests seem pleased with. I can check to see when they expect to have vacancies."

Ernestine nods. "If we can get one for the girls and one for the boys, that would be great. You all could split the cost of the rent and utilities which would make it quite affordable."

"That's what I thought, too," Shasta says quietly. "Even if they only have one apartment available, we could get the boys moved before the search parties arrive."

Baldwin nods his head. "That means we need to get jobs as soon as possible. Who wants to go job hunting?"

Chapter 6

ERNESTINE TAKES BALDWIN BACK to her house to get the other anti-gamers. Conrad insists on going with Shasta, my mom, and me. Baldwin and Ernestine don't love that, but Conrad says he will only work a job if I work there too. If that's the case, he may as well search for jobs with me. Marcella is feeling anxious today, so she says she'll stay at Shasta's house to watch the little girls.

I pull on my coat and assure Marcella, "We'll bring you back a stack of job applications to look through. Don't worry. No one knows where we are." Marcella nods and scoots closer to Everley, the bravest of the two staying home. The cold December air requires us to dig through Shasta's closets for coats that are mostly too big and too small for us.

Shasta has a van kind of like Ernestine's, but it's much newer. She climbs into the driver's seat and smiles nervously. "I've only been driving for a year and a half, so I hope my driving doesn't scare you too much." My mom gives me a wary look as she climbs into the passenger seat. Conrad and I climb gingerly into the back.

My mom tries to sound optimistic. "Where should we start?"

Shasta pulls slowly onto the road. "I think we should start by looking at the community boards at the city building, and then visit as many of the businesses that are hiring as possible. On the way home, we'll stop at Larkside Apartments to see if they have any openings."

My mom has worry in her voice when she asks, "How much does an apartment cost per week?"

Shasta slams on the breaks when a car pulls out in front of her, which also means that we skid on the ice. We brace ourselves as quickly as possible, but my raw legs don't fare well. Shasta doesn't notice our anxiety as she answers, "It depends on how many bedrooms it has. The three-bedroom apartments cost more than the two-bedroom apartments. I try not to put more than two people in a bedroom, but it can be done if that's the only way to make it affordable."

50

Mom braces herself as another car pulls out in front of us. "So, if the boys get a three-bedroom apartment, how many coins a week will it cost them?"

"Uh, I don't know about coins, but it will cost $1500 a month for the rent plus utilities."

Conrad uses his fingers as he adds in his head. "So if all five of us contribute $300 a month, that should cover our housing, right?"

Shasta's voice is cautious. "Yeah, but you'll need money for a phone, food, clothing, transportation, and other supplies too."

Conrad's eyes are far away as he thinks. "So I need a job that makes at least $500 a month. I can do that."

Shasta speeds up when the car behind us honks its horn. "Yeah, that should do it, but you have to find something that will let you work after school."

Conrad leans toward Shasta. "Well, yeah. But maybe I can put in full days until school starts to save up."

My mom nods as she pats Conrad's knee. "That's a good idea, Conrad." She looks sorry when she sees him wince from the pressure on his inflamed skin. Shasta slams on the breaks two more times—which causes more sliding on the ice before we reach city hall. Conrad and I try to hide the pain we feel in our legs, but it's almost impossible. Our legs will have an imprint of the seats in front of us before we get home. My poor knees are absolutely throbbing.

Mom sighs with relief when we get out of the van. Maybe

she should offer to drive. We follow a random man dressed in casual clothes from the parking lot into the city building. He looks like he just bit into a lemon. He probably wasn't impressed with Shasta's parking job. He does not hold the door open for us. Goosebumps erupt on my arms as I walk into the fancy building right as a man in a suit finishes pinning a new help-wanted advertisement on the community board.

The man in the suit gives us a passing glance as he goes into some kind of clerk's office. I hope he can't tell that we aren't from here. My eyes search the advertisements hungrily, hoping to find the perfect job opportunity for Conrad and me.

The sour-faced man we followed in here is searching the community boards beside me. He glares at me as I take a step towards him. He makes sure to take another step to keep the same amount of space between us.

Conrad talks aloud to himself as he reads the notice board. "Night janitor, no. Snow removal, no. Child care, no. Tutoring, no. Bakery, no. Department store shelf stocking, no. Department store gift-wrapping, hmm, sounds temporary." Conrad looks defeated until he reads the last job posting. "Arcade game technician, perfect! Let's apply here together, Dandra!"

I stand there shocked for a minute. "Are you kidding me?"

Conrad's eyebrows furrow together. "What?"

My voice shakes as I say, "I just spent the most horrific day of my life trying to get away from gamers, and now you want me to work in a gaming place? No way."

My friend finally realizes his error. "Sorry. I just thought it might be something I'm good at."

I cringe. "If you want to work with me, forget it."

Conrad rolls his eyes. "Fine, but there isn't anything here that really sounds like my thing."

My mom gives our shoulders a squeeze. "It's not about finding 'your thing' right now; it's about getting a roof over your head and food on your table."

The man who keeps avoiding me overhears what my mom says and exclaims, "You all should go back to where you came from! The complex fed you and put a roof over your head. Now you're out here taking jobs away from respectable people like me!" He sort of growls at us, or Shasta in particular, and storms out of the building without looking back.

My jaw drops as I look at my mom and Shasta. "What was that about?"

Shasta shrugs and says, "Not everyone is happy that the Complex Law was disbanded. My condition is very obvious, so I'm not always treated very kindly. Maybe I should just wait in the van."

I shake my head as the man who went into the clerk's office comes back out and pauses as he passes us on his way to the front door. When he opens his mouth to speak to us, I feel myself cowering away from him, afraid of another angry rant. He looks right at Conrad and me and asks, "Are you two looking for jobs during your Christmas break?"

Conrad grins at the man. "Yes, we are!"

The man smiles back at him. "I am the manager at Casswell's Department Store, and I need four full-time gift wrappers as soon as possible. Would you two be willing to start tomorrow?"

The grin slides off Conrad's face. "But—isn't this job over once Christmas is over? We need jobs that will continue once school starts up again."

The man's eyebrows come together as he thinks. "Well, the full-time gift wrap will stop after Christmas is over, but I'd be happy to keep you on as evening shelf stockers after that."

Conrad doesn't look enthusiastic. "Uh, can we talk it over?"

The man shrugs. "Sure, but if you agree to start tomorrow, I'll up your pay from minimum wage, and you can keep any tips you get. I'm desperate."

I smile at the man in the suit, glad to have found a kind person who is hiring. I give Conrad a nudge and whisper. "He needs help, and we could start tomorrow, working together. What do you say?"

He wrinkles his nose for a second then smiles at me. He turns to the man. "Okay, we'll take it."

The man's face breaks into a grin. "You are lifesavers. I will see you tomorrow at Casswell's at 9:00 am sharp. I'm Mr. Bronson by the way." He shakes our hands and whistles as he holds the door for someone, or multiple someones. Baldwin, Adamar, Ed, Gordon, and Ernestine pour in the door. Mr. Bronson gives us a last wave and leaves. Baldwin wraps his snowy, cold arms around me and gives me a kiss that would make people think that we were separated for way longer than an hour. Conrad takes a couple of steps back and looks away.

Ernestine directs all of the boys to the community board. "I'll take you around to any of these jobs that appeal to you." She joins my mom and Shasta. "Sorry we're late. Adamar took some convincing to come with us."

Shasta shrugs at Ernestine. "Dandra and Conrad already have jobs. The man who let you in the door hired them on the spot. That was way easier than I expected," she says as she smiles at my mom.

Mom nods as she writes down the names of the three students looking for a tutor. "I wish everyone was as friendly as Mr. Bronson." Shasta nods in agreement. Mom continues by asking, "Are these tutoring prices for real? If I remember the money transfer rate between our countries correctly, I've never been paid that much per session. "

Shasta leans over the loud anti-gamers and looks closely at the board. I wonder if something is wrong with her eyes. She nods. "Yes, I've seen similar amounts for tutoring on these boards before."

Mom looks longingly at the tutoring advertisements.

"With school out for over two weeks, do you think anyone will want a tutor right now?" Ernestine shakes her head.

Shasta shrugs. "Well, probably not until school starts again. Maybe you should wrap gifts until Christmas is over, too."

Mom looks at Conrad and me and nods. "Yeah, that's a good idea."

I watch Conrad's shoulders slump at the same time as mine. It's true that this is probably the best option for Mom, but does she have to work side-by-side with me? I sigh. Oh, well. It's just for a few weeks. I jot down the bakery, the child-care center, and reluctantly, the arcade's addresses for Marcella.

I bump Baldwin with my hip. "Do you see anything that interests you?"

He speed reads the community board and shrugs. "Not really. I'll let everyone else have first pick, and I'll work at whatever's left."

I just love how generous he is. "You'd rather work in radios or something mechanical, right?"

"Yeah."

A thought pops into my head. "A lady who stopped by with some clothes this morning said her brother might be hiring at The National News Station—but that kind of job might be too conspicuous for us."

"Really?" he asks. I nod. He seems deep in thought for a minute. "I'm pretty sure Rocky works there, but it's probably not the best way to stay hidden," he says with a sound of longing in his voice.

I share the rest of Elira's offers for jobs. "She said her other brother needs campaign help, but that's a job in the public eye, too."

Baldwin looks at the community boards one more time. "Huh, I'm sure I'll find something that will pay the bills."

Mom squeezes my shoulder. "We should get going. Are you ready?"

"Sure." I say and then turn to give my boyfriend a parting hug.

He leans into me, including my legs. "Maybe I can work with you."

I bite my lip as pain shoots up my legs. "Yeah, maybe, but my mom wants to work there until school starts, too."

Baldwin finally realizes what he's done and takes a step back. He covers his mouth with his hand. "I'm so sorry. I never realized how easy it is to bump into your legs." He really does look sorry.

I shrug. "It's fine. I'll see you soon." He takes my hand and refuses to let go of it until the last minute. *Sigh.* He's so sweet sometimes. Conrad waits patiently for me then follows me to the door. I love the smile and optimism radiating from Mom's eyes as we leave the building. She likes to be in charge of her own destiny.

Once Shasta has her seatbelt clicked in place, she turns

57

to me. "I'll take you to those places you wrote down to get applications for Marcella. I'll also show you where Casswell's is. It's only a few blocks from here."

I realize that Shasta can't be my personal chauffeur every day. Gas is ridiculously expensive in Layland, so we never drove if we could help it. I'm used to walking everywhere I go. "How far is Casswell's from your house? Can I walk there?"

"You could walk there. It'll take you about 15 minutes. It'll be five minutes closer once you move to your apartment."

I nod and say, "That's not bad. It used to take me 13 minutes to walk to my last job."

Conrad clears his throat. "What about me? How long will it take to walk there from Ernestine's house?"

"Oh, well, it would probably be smarter to drive or take a bus, but you could walk there in about 30 minutes, longer with your legs in blisters."

I can see the wheels turning in my friend's head. I don't think he likes coordinating with or even talking to the anti-gamers. I stop him from getting crazy ideas in his head. "You are not going to walk. I'm sure Ernestine or Rocky can drop you off. I don't want you to walk that far on icy sidewalks."

Conrad's focus comes back from wherever it was. "We'll figure something out, I'm sure."

Casswell's is a huge department store. It's at least triple the size of our department stores in Tifton. The building is four stories tall with giant windows on all floors displaying ornate, rotating Christmas trees and self-moving toys as big as I am. Maybe I won't have to work alongside my mom after all.

We stop at the childcare center to get an application for Marcella, but it gets crossed off my list of possibilities for her immediately. The woman with black, slicked back hair who meets us at the door stops us from walking in further after she takes one look at Shasta. She says, "I'm sorry, but we don't have any openings, for children or employees."

I frown at her and say, "We just came from city hall. You have two job openings according to the notice board."

The woman turns her nose up at me and says, "We have certain standards that management feel need to be upheld in these times of—societal decline." She sneers at Shasta's unnaturally tall form and continues, "We wouldn't want the rising generation to learn from anyone but those of the highest caliber, now, would we?"

My jaw drops, and I'm about to respond angrily when Shasta puts a hand on my arm and says, "We understand. Thank you for your time." We leave without a backward glance. Once we're back in the van, Shasta says, "There are a lot of prejudiced people in this city, but there are also plenty of other jobs that are open to anyone, despite their flaws. Don't be discouraged."

My mom nods at Shasta as she buckles her seatbelt. "That was uncomfortable, but we aren't discouraged."

Shasta says, "I can stay in the van if you think that will help your chances."

Mom and I both answer together, "No!"

Mom smiles at our similar outrage and says, "We want you with us."

I try not to notice, but Shasta definitely wipes a tear off her cheek as we drive away.

Once we have several acceptable job applications for Marcella, we stop at the apartment complex that Shasta thinks we should consider. It's not new, but it's not old either. There is a skiff of snow on everything which makes the white building seem even whiter. We follow Shasta into the building like chicks following their mother hen.

The smell of flowers and fruity candy overwhelms me in the office area. "Hello, Mrs. Abbot. How are you today?" Shasta says to a plump woman with poofy blonde hair.

Mrs. Abbot isn't as hostile as the childcare woman was, but she doesn't smile when she says, "Just fine, Miss Shasta. How 'bout yourself?"

Shasta smiles in her calm way. "I couldn't be better. I actually have some houseguests looking for two apartments. Do you have any vacancies?"

Mrs. Abbot looks us over as if expecting flaws and says, "No. I don't have anything right now."

Conrad's face drops.

Mrs. Abbot's eyes linger on him before she starts admiring her pretty pink fingernails. "But, I have a three-bedroom apartment that will be available the day before Christmas.

The residents decided to buy their own house as a Christmas present."

Shasta lights up. "Could you put us down for that one?"

Mrs. Abbot looks us all over curiously. "Are these more of your complex refugees, Shasta?"

Shasta frowns and asks, "Do they look like complex refugees?"

Mrs. Abbot grunts. "Everyone you bring me looks like a complex refugee. Luckily, I desire money more than respectability. How many people will be living there?"

Shasta takes a piece of candy out of the bowl on Mrs. Abbot's desk. "Five."

The woman purses her lips for a second. "You know my rules. No pets, no smoking, first and last month rent due before you move in. The rent on a three-bedroom is $1500 a month which includes power."

Conrad gulps. I bet he's wondering if the boys can come up with $3000 before Christmas.

Shasta smiles sweetly. "We are happy to follow your rules. Please write us down."

"All right. What's the name?" She looks at my mom expectantly.

Conrad steps forward. "Conrad. Conrad Ch—"

"Churchill," I finish for him. "Actually, you should probably use your first name instead of your middle name, so you're legally correct, right?"

Conrad looks confused for a minute. "Oh yeah, I go by Conrad, but my first name is actually—John."

Mrs. Abbot looks from my mom to my friend suspiciously. "Your first name is John, but you go by Conrad instead?"

Conrad finds confidence in his lie and says with a smile, "Yeah. If you had as many Johns in your family as I do, you'd do the same thing."

"I'll take your word for it," Mrs. Abbot says as she finishes typing things into her computer. "You need to be at least 18 to rent an apartment. Is that going to be a problem?"

Conrad doesn't miss a beat. "No, that's fine. There are two of us who are over 18 who will be moving in." He's so confident that I almost believe him.

"Do you want to sign the contract now, or when you move in?"

He looks unsure. "Uh, now, I guess."

I wonder how weird Conrad feels signing the name "John C. Churchill" on the contract. He should write that name down, so he doesn't forget it when he moves in.

I let out a sigh of relief when Mrs. Abbot takes Conrad's signed contract without any questions. That was way easier than I thought it would be.

Mrs. Abbot refills her candy bowl. "Oh, I almost forgot. I'll need to make a copy of your ID."

Conrad pats all of his pockets like he is searching for

something. "I forgot to bring my wallet. Is it okay if I bring it in later?"

Mrs. Abbot's face is less than excited. "I suppose that will be fine." She digs around in her candy bowl for the perfect piece without looking up. "I look forward to getting to know you better when you move in." Her eyes suddenly stare at Conrad.

Conrad grins at her. "Thank you. I'm sure we'll become the best of friends." He raises his eyebrows up and down in a way that he probably thinks will lure her in.

Mrs. Abbot raises her eyebrows and tries to hide a grin.

Mom leans forward to interrupt their special moment. "My girls and I are also interested in an apartment when you have one available. How much is a two-bedroom?"

Mrs. Abbot is all business again. "It's $1000 a month."

"Do you have one that I could see by chance?" my mom asks hesitantly.

Mrs. Abbot starts to shake her head, but then sees Conrad smiling at her and lights up. "I don't have an open apartment right now, but I guess you could look at mine. It's just next door."

Mrs. Abbot takes out a key ring and waddles around the desk to an inconspicuous door in the wall. She unlocks it and lets us into her very clean and very feminine apartment. My mom does a good job oohing and ahhing at all the right things. Conrad looks less than impressed with all the lace and pink décor but manages to smile every time Mrs. Abbot looks at him. I imagine what it will be like to have Mom and Everley in the master bedroom and Marcella and me in the other bedroom. It will be nice to have two lavatories for the four of us. I feel kind of bad for needing the tub upstairs in Shasta's house so much right now.

I thank Mrs. Abbot for letting us look at her apartment, but she only grunts at me. She could talk all day to Conrad though. When I ask if it's absolutely necessary to have the first and last month's rent to move in, she kind of snaps at me. "Yes, it is necessary. I am not running a charity house here! I barely have enough to keep this place running. Don't be surprised if I raise the rent next year!"

Conrad comes to my rescue and assures Mrs. Abbot that we will have the first and last month's rent before Christmas. She has one last smile for him as we walk out the door.

The van is a welcome sight. My stomach starts growling like a lion. I'm surprised that no one else's stomach is growling too. It's past our usual dinner time. I realize that my friend is deep in thought about more serious things than his stomach. I elbow him in the side as we approach the van. "What did you think, Conrad? I'm glad Mrs. Abbot's prejudice stops at you."

He smiles feebly and shrugs as he gently climbs into the van, carefully avoiding contact with his blistering legs. "It's not what I'm used to, but it will be fine."

Chapter 7

I HOPE MY MOM isn't this nervous when we get to Casswell's. She won't quit adjusting her clothes and touching her hair. I remember her acting like this when she started working at the bank back in Tifton. "Mom, this is just a temporary job. You don't need to fret about it."

"I know. I just don't like the way some of the people we talked to treated Shasta yesterday."

I nod. "I know what you mean."

She goes on, "I also hope it isn't obvious that we aren't from here."

My legs start itching like crazy, as if they know that I'm trying to keep their blisters a secret. "If Ernestine is right, then no one is fitting in very well right now. The more I think about things, the more I feel that hiding in plain sight might be the best way to go unnoticed."

Mom rebuttons the top button on her shirt that she just unbuttoned. "I hope you're right."

Conrad is waiting for us at the front door of Casswell's when we get there. I don't get the chance to ask him who dropped him off before Mr. Bronson rushes over to us and takes us into the back of the store. His friendliness is refreshing after the treatment we received yesterday. He bounces on his feet as he says, "Welcome, my new gift wrappers! What were your names again?"

Conrad doesn't miss a beat. "I'm John Churchill. Is there any paperwork I need to sign?"

Mr. Bronson smiles as he pulls out a few sheets of paper. "Yes, but not much. Ever since the disbandment of the Complex Law, we aren't required to have as much documentation on beginning level jobs. Just fill out your name, address, and phone number right there, check the box for payment preferences, check or cash, and sign right here." His thick finger points to the final line on my paperwork until I have signed it.

Conrad fills out the information like he's lived in this country his whole life. I had to fill out a cheat sheet with my fake name and Shasta's address and phone number. I only have to peek at it once. Mom barely keeps her composure as she fills out her paperwork. She's fiddling with her top button again.

Mr. Bronson doesn't seem to notice my mom sweating as she fills out her paperwork. "What is your name, ma'am?"

Mom blushes as she looks up from her paperwork. "Oh, I'm Laura Moore. This is my daughter, Dani Moore. We just moved here, so I hope it's okay that I came along. I could use a temporary job until school starts again."

Mr. Bronson smiles as he takes the signed paperwork out of my mom's shaking hands. "I'm glad to have an extra person. We're only one person short now." He winks at Mom as he files her paperwork. When the file drawer clicks shut, Mr. Bronson gets down to business. "We have five gift wrap stations manned by six employees during the holidays. Two stations are on the second floor and three stations are on the main floor. On the main floor we have two people wrapping at the same station near the front door and one near each side door. Do you care which station you work at?"

My mom and I both shake our heads as Conrad says, "I'd like to work with Dani near the front door."

Mr. Bronson winks at me. "All right. I can make that happen. I'll send Shelly and Lupe to the second floor when they come in. Please ask to see the receipts of the items you're asked to gift wrap before you wrap them. If they have spent $50 or more, the gift wrap is free. If they spent less than that, the gift wrap is $4 per gift. If they don't have a receipt, don't wrap it.

Here are your cash boxes. If you run out of small bills, flag me or another manager down to get you more. Do you have any questions?"

I open the cash box and look at all the paper bills in there. Layland only uses paper money for $100 bills and up. It seems like these paper bills would be easier to counterfeit than coins. I hope I can figure this out. Conrad looks in the box only briefly. "I'm sure we can figure it out."

I look around at all the wrapping paper options in the room. "Am I supposed to use a certain kind of wrap for certain presents?"

Mr. Bronson shakes his head. "No, let the customer decide. If they don't care, use the plain red and put a gold bow on top. We bought twice as much of that as the other options."

Mom clears her throat. "Where do you want me?"

Mr. Bronson smiles and winks at her. "I'll put you on the right-side door. Hopefully your matronly presence will keep the cashiers from sneaking out for unappointed smoke breaks."

Mom's cheeks start to redden. "Oh, well, I'll try my best."

Once we're all in our places, Mr. Bronson insists that we smile. "It's Christmastime. Everyone wants to be greeted with a smile."

I can tell that my cheeks won't be able to stay turned up all day. They are already getting sore ten minutes in. Conrad is doing well at the smiling though. I haven't seen him this happy in months. He doesn't even lose his smile when he gets a papercut on the second gift he wraps. "Thank you for shopping at Casswell's, ma'am, and have a Merry Christmas," he says with a grin.

The middle-aged woman wearing too much makeup gives my friend a coy smile. "Thank you, young man. Here's a little tip for your trouble." She slips a $10 bill in his shirt pocket and pats it. It kind of gives me the creeps.

Conrad doesn't seem affected by the woman at all. He pulls the $10 out of his shirt pocket and stuffs it into his pants pocket instead. "I think I'm going to get a new shirt with my tips today."

I don't think my friend knows that broke people have to act differently than rich people. I give him a sideways glance as I organize the cash box. "But, I thought you guys needed $3000 to get into your apartment."

Conrad shrugs. "Surely I can use a little bit of my hard-earned money on myself. I don't have very many clothes even with the hand-me-downs."

I lean in close to his ear and whisper. "I know what you mean, but would you rather have a new outfit or be safely moved into your own apartment when your dad and Patrolman Darius come looking for you?

The customer-ready smile slides off his face. "I—guess if you put it that way." He pats the $10 bill in his pocket. "I'm at least going to buy you a nice Christmas gift." His smile reappears as a young stylish woman sets an armful of clothes on our table.

As sweet as that sounds, I have to teach my spoiled friend how to live a low-cash life. I whisper so the customer can't hear me, "No, you're not. We're all going to give up Christmas gifts this year so we can get into our own apartments. Starting a new life in a new country is its own gift, right?"

Conrad looks at me like I'm the most ridiculous person he's ever met. "If you say so." He handles the fancy suit he's wrapping for his customer so lovingly that I worry he won't ever change his ways.

I am amazed at how much money flows through Casswell's. Beautiful people flock through the doors and leave with arms full of beautiful things. Conrad isn't as shocked as I am because he's always had nice things. I don't think I could even afford the cheapest thing in this store. I am just a little bit jealous when a girl my age has me wrap a beautiful plum-colored velvety coat with fur around the hood. It is freezing cold outside, and my coat is thin and has a few holes from our escape. I tell myself that it's okay though. I want to save my money for the greater good.

Marcella should have come with us today, but she said that she didn't want a job that would require her to talk to people. She said she was going to try the bakery first since she already has experience doing that, and she likes the added perk of taking home any mess ups. While filling out the application for the bakery, she said, "If you mess up wrapping someone's gift, do you get to take it home and eat it? Of course not. That's why the bakery is a better choice." That is a good point, and it's embarrassing how many times I am asked to rewrap an ugly wrapping job by the customers this morning. As the morning wears on, I can tell that each gift I wrap looks better than the last one, thankfully.

I am surprised by how many people tip us for wrapping their gifts. If I actually had $50 to spend on gifts, I would be happy to get the free gift wrap, but I wouldn't spare a single cent to tip the person who wrapped it. I have a whole pocket of crackly bills right now from tips. When we get our lunch break, I want to count how much I have.

Mr. Bronson comes to relieve us once we finish wrapping for a rush of people. He takes a quick look through our cash box and smiles. "The lunch rush appears to be over. Go ahead and take your lunch break. The employee lounge is through the room I took you to this morning."

Conrad looks at him questioningly. "Are you going to cover for us?"

Our boss gives us a flashing smile. "Yep. There aren't too many people here right now. I'll probably just read the paper."

I laugh because I know that won't last long. He sits down with a contented sigh on one of the chairs that I've only sat on once all morning. I stretch my arms and say, "Thank you, Mr. Bronson. I'm starving." I notice the headline on the paper as

71

we walk away. "Layland's Border Wall Breached: Peace Officers Asking for Leads."

Mr. Bronson puts on his reading glasses and takes a sip of coffee. "No problem."

I try to slow down my heart as Conrad and I walk through the storage room to the employee break room together. Mr. Bronson doesn't know that we are the people they are looking for. I need to stay calm and quit feeling like a convicted criminal. Blend in, Dandra. Hide in plain sight.

There are a bunch of tables and chairs and high-tech food and beverage machines in the break room. I take a seat and count my tips. I have $24 in tips. Maybe I should buy something from the high-tech machines for lunch. As I'm thinking about it, my mom comes in and sits next to me. She pulls a couple of sandwiches out of her coat pocket, or Shasta's coat pocket, actually. "Shasta said I could make these for our lunch. Are you hungry?"

My excitement drops. "Yeah. I am hungry. Thank you." My sandwich takes less than five minutes to eat. And it doesn't fill me.

Conrad finishes counting his tips. He has $40. I don't know why he was lucky enough to get all the big tippers. He buys a strange-looking beverage, a bag of potato chips, and a chocolate bar from the high-tech food and beverage machines. My stomach growls as I watch him take a long drink. When he comes back to our table, my mom clears her throat. "Conrad, do you think Ernestine will let you pack a lunch from home tomorrow, so you can save for your apartment?"

Conrad looks like he didn't even think of that. "Oh, uh, probably."

Mom smiles at him in a motherly way. "That would be a good idea since you are on a timeline to get out of Ernestine's house. Your dad will look there first when he gets permission to cross over the border." My heart starts pounding as I think about the newspaper headline. I hope Mr. Bronson isn't suspicious of us.

Conrad swallows loudly. "Yeah. I'll do that." He looks at me. "Do you want a chip?"

I take one as I hesitantly look at my mom's frowning face. "Thank you."

Conrad turns his smile up another notch when we get back to work. Is that why he gets more tips than I do? Are my smiles less impressive? I try smiling different ways for the rest of the day. Surely one of them will get me good tips. When our shift is over, my mom meets us at our table right as Mr. Bronson comes over to our station and takes most of the money out of our cash box. "Would either of you like to stay an extra shift tonight? I'm still a person short, so I could use the help."

Mom shakes her head. "My daughter Ev—Evelyn is probably missing us. We better get home to her."

Conrad pipes in, "I can stay for another shift, Mr. Bronson. Can I stay at this table?"

"Yeah. That would be great. Thank you, John."

I look at my friend with concern. "But, what about your ride?"

He waves me off. "Can you let Ernestine know what I'm doing? Don't worry about me. I need to pull my own weight."

A teenage boy and his mom place some nice-looking clothes on the table to be wrapped just then. The mom asks, "Can we get these wrapped please? This is the only way I can keep him from trying to wear them before Christmas."

The teenager rolls his eyes. "Mom, I'm not a baby."

Conrad flashes another killer smile. "Hey, I've had my eye on this shirt, nice choice, my friend."

The teenage boy smirks. "Thanks."

I try to get Conrad's attention as we leave. "Okay. I'll call Ernestine for you. See you tomorrow. Bye." Conrad doesn't stop talking to the customers, but he throws me a wink as we walk away.

Mom grins at my friend as we exit the main doors. "Conrad is doing well at his first job, don't you think?"

I let out a long breath as we walk away from the big building. "Yeah, I'm as surprised as you are. I just hope he doesn't spend as much as he makes."

Chapter 8

I FEEL SO SPOILED when I come home to Shasta's house with hot ham and potatoes waiting for us on the table. I haven't eaten this much meat since—long before my dad died. I try to show my gratitude by washing the dishes and sweeping the kitchen floor. Everley is glued to my side telling me about all the games and projects she did with Nelle and Peggy today. I can only get her to let me have a minute alone when I show her my red legs.

"Your legs look gross. If you need help with your green goo stuff, I'll do it."

"Thanks, sis."

The bath does make my legs feel good, but something else happens that makes me feel even better. Baldwin calls me and asks me what my favorite kind of cookie is. We rarely had the ingredients to make cookies in Layland. The last time Everley and I made them was at Conrad's house. I shudder as I remember that day; it was full of emotional upheaval because Conrad was still lying for his dad. I have to think hard about how to answer. I finally say, "I like all cookies, really, but especially ones with chocolate and nuts."

He answers cryptically, "Okay, that's all I need to know. Have a good night and I'll talk to you tomorrow! I miss you!"

"I miss you too, bye!" I'm not sure what he is planning, but I grin imagining what he is up to. I soon get lost in the story that Everley asks me to read her. Shasta has several enormous bookshelves throughout her house full of books for all ages and interests. I absolutely love to just look at all the beautiful covers. It makes me feel like I'm back at the Tifton Public Library again—but without all the dust.

I'm to the climax of the story when the hero is about to die when I hear a scratch at the window. I pause for a second, but Everley begs me to go on, so hesitantly, I do. A few seconds later, I hear a tap at the window behind me. It's dark outside, but I peek through the curtains anyway. I don't see anything. I put the book down and start to question my sanity. Does my brain think that any time I read I'm in a mysterious library full of mysterious noises? I get two more lines of the book out of my mouth before I hear the distinct sound of a pebble hitting the window. That's it. I stand up and march to the door to investigate. I grab the doorknob and hope I'm not about to get kidnapped. I open the door and ask, "Who's out there?"

I don't see anyone at first as my eyes adjust to the darkness, but I'm pretty sure I can see Ernestine's van parked at the top of the driveway and Rocky in the driver's seat. What in the world could he want? I take a cautious step out onto the icy step when someone jumps out from the side of the house and grabs my arm. My automatic response is to pull my arm away and try to run. Unfortunately, the icy sidewalk takes me down, and the firm hand on my arm makes that person go down too. I land partially on my assailant which helps cushion my fall, but the pressure of their body against my legs makes me scream in pain.

I flail and struggle to get up when a familiar voice says from underneath me, "Hey! Stop flopping around like an octopus, Dandra! I brought you your favorite cookies. I just made them. They are hot and everything." My boyfriend's voice sounds excited and uncertain at the same time.

I roll over onto the cold sidewalk and sigh with relief, "Baldwin, you scared me." I don't know how I'm going to stand up with these painful legs, so I just lay there and catch my breath. When I notice Balwin's warm breath on my ear, I turn my head and kiss him. He kisses me back, and despite the pain in my legs, I would be glad to just stay here on the ice kissing him until the sun comes up, but my little sister decides to cough very loudly in the doorway.

"You two are gross! Knock it off!" she says with irritation.

Baldwin gingerly helps me up and smiles at my sister. "I brought cookies! Do you want one?"

She gives him an unimpressed look and says, "No thanks." She closes the door and turns on the porch light. She continues to frown at us from the living room window.

Baldwin smiles at her and waves anyway. "Tough crowd."

I unstick my pants from the flesh of my legs and push my hair out of my face before answering him. "You scared us to death! Why didn't you just knock on the door?"

Baldwin looks at me like his reason was obvious. "I wanted to surprise you! Hold on to my arm and see how I've set up the van. It's a fancy candlelit dessert on wheels."

It's easy to forgive him as I feel his warmth spreading into me, and I see the little candlelit table through the window of the van. When he opens the sliding van door, the aroma of fresh-baked cookies washes over me. The little table has a deep red tablecloth and milk in two fancy long stemmed glasses. Each place at the table has three warm, gooey chocolate chip cookies with a pecan pressed into the center of each.

Baldwin points to the cookies before he helps me into the

back of the van. "Ernestine only had a few pecans in her pantry, so I made these cookies as chocolatey and nutty as I could."

I realize how much Baldwin must have gone through and the favors he must have asked to make this little date for us in our new country happen. It is the sweetest thing he could have done. I lean across our little table and kiss him again. This time it's Rocky who coughs out loud. I forgot he was here. It was nice of him to be Baldwin's driver and accomplice, but now he's also a third wheel....

Baldwin looks at me like I've just made his dreams come true. "I thought we should celebrate your first day at your new job. How was it?"

I take a bite of one of my gooey chocolate chip cookies and sigh with pleasure. "It went well, I think. My boss is very nice, and I got to keep my tips. The nice customers outnumbered the mean ones. My legs and feet are tired from standing all day though."

Baldwin reaches across the table and wipes the melted chocolate out of the corner of my mouth. "If I had any money, I would shop there every day just so I could see you."

I feel myself melting into a puddle. This is so different from how I felt all day at the store. I thought I was the ugly duckling next to Conrad who had more customers and more tips than I did. I smile at Baldwin. "Thank you for this. I don't know how you pulled it off, but thank you! This makes me think that anything is possible in this new life of ours."

Baldwin reaches across the table and pushes my hair behind my ear. "Seeing you read to Everley tonight reminds me why I like you so much. You are all the things I admire in a person, and in this country, I'm pretty sure our pasts can't stop us. If we work hard enough, we can do anything!"

I feel a tear in the corner of my eye as I soak in the truth of what he is saying. "You're right! No one can tell us what we can or can't do here!" I think of all the books in Shasta's house and the school I'm about to start, and I am the happiest I've felt in a long time.

Conrad lifts his glass of milk and says, "To us and our unstoppable future!"

I laugh as I raise my glass. "To us!"

Chapter 9

MY LITTLE DATE WITH BALDWIN gives me the energy I need to get up in the morning and go to work. I find that knowing Baldwin cares about me and believes in me keeps me optimistic about my future in this country. It takes me about a week to get used to my work, eat, bath, aloe, sleep routine. Even though some of the customers are rude, I just keep my chin up and work as hard as I can so my boyfriend can move closer to me, and we can all get apartments of our own as soon as possible.

I'm surprised when Ernestine is parked outside of

Casswell's as we're leaving for the day. She rolls down the window to her van and says, "Jump in, you three. Dr. Hamble wants to check up on the cement burns."

We jump in and my mom says, "Can you drop me off at Shasta's first? Everley is always waiting for us by the window after work. I don't want her to worry about us."

Ernestine nods. "Yes, I will. Dr. Hamble hasn't seen you yet, Laurel, and I don't want him to. Especially with how much your escape has been in the news."

When we get to Shasta's house, my mom jumps out, waves, and promises to save me some dinner before Ernestine whisks us off to a part of town that I haven't been to before. It appears to be some sort of medical district. When we get to Dr. Hamble's office, there are only two other cars in the parking lot. I climb out of the van cautiously with Conrad right behind me. "Are you sure they're open, Ernestine?"

Ernestine walks to the front door without stopping. "They are closed, but Dr. Hamble said he'd stay late since you both had to work. Let's not keep him waiting."

Conrad and I shuffle as fast as we can with our pathetic legs. A receptionist is gathering her things as we walk in. She calls back where we can't see, "They're here, Dr. Hamble. If you don't need anything else, I'm going to lock the door on my way out."

Dr. Hamble's voice answers, "I can take it from here. Thank you for locking up, Liz." A door to the side of the reception desk opens, and Dr. Hamble's smiling face greets us. "You two are looking much cleaner and happier than the last time I saw you! Come on back and let's have a look at your burns."

The room he takes us to has one examination table and several chairs. Conrad nudges me toward the examination table, so I jump up on the crackly paper while he takes a seat to the side. Ernestine says she needs to use the bathroom, which I believe is what they call a lavatory here. Dr. Hamble seems surprised to see me in pants. "A skirt or dress would probably lessen the pressure on your burns you know."

I give him half a smile. "I know. I just don't want people to look at my legs funny at work."

He nods. "This is a prejudiced city." He gently pulls up the legs of my black work pants. Hmm. How often are you soaking in vinegar water and applying aloe vera?"

I know he wanted me to do those things three times a day, but I can't do anything while I'm at work. I try to explain myself to him. "I work most of the day, so I soak and put on aloe vera morning and night."

Dr. Hamble nods and gently examines my red flesh. "Try to soak as soon as you get home from work, and then again right before bed. It will speed up the healing process considerably." He sprays a mist over my skin that feels cool and almost numbing. He puts on plastic gloves before he touches my knees.

My knees get bumped into the most and look the worst. "How is your pain level? Do you need more pain pills?"

I cringe as his glove tries to stick to my knee. "I took my last pill this morning. It would be nice to have more to help me get through Christmas."

Dr. Hamble nods and starts applying aloe vera to my legs. "I will give you some of this numbing spray, another bottle of aloe vera, and enough pain pills to get you through Christmas. Hopefully you won't need them after that. If you feel like you do, come see me again." He gently rolls my pant legs back down and helps me off the examination table. He looks at Conrad and says, "It's your turn, young man."

Conrad looks at me with apprehension as we trade places. He gingerly climbs on the table after Dr. Hamble changes the paper covering and starts pulling up his pant legs. Dr. Hamble's face darkens as he looks at Conrad's legs. My hand jumps to cover my mouth once I see how much worse Conrad's legs are than mine. My flesh is red and irritated, but I see tiny improvements each day as my skin heals itself. Conrad's legs look just as bad, actually worse, than they did a week ago. There are bits of black and patches of white on his red flesh. Dr. Hamble frowns and sprays the numbing mist on his legs. "How often are you soaking in vinegar water and applying aloe vera?"

My friend looks sheepish as he says, "I try to remember to do it every day."

Dr. Hamble points to the black spots on his flesh. "Do you

see this? This is your skin dying instead of healing." He points to the white spots and says, "Do you see this? This is infection. You have to make your skin a priority. It is more important than anything right now, even work." Conrad rolls his eyes. Dr. Hamble sees him do this and his voice gets more severe. "These cement burns are eating your flesh away. It could eat clear down to your bone if you don't take care of it. Do you want to lose your legs?" Conrad looks worried for the first time as he shakes his head. Dr. Hamble continues. "Promise me that you will soak in vinegar water and apply aloe at least morning and night."

Conrad looks down at his blackened flesh and realizes what is at stake if he doesn't obey the doctor's orders. "I promise. Morning and night."

Doctor Hamble doesn't apply aloe to Conrad like he did to me. "I have a therapy tub down the hall. I'm going to make sure you get a good soak, scrub, and lather before I send you home. You'll need to start a round of antibiotics as well to stop the infection. I'll be right back."

I frown at my friend once we're alone. "Why haven't you been taking care of your burns? You could lose your legs!"

Conrad looks at me sheepishly. "I work a double almost every day, so I'm too tired when I get home late at night, and there are so many of us getting ready for work in the morning that I feel bad locking everyone out of the lavatory."

"If you won't stand up for yourself and your legs, I will."

I shake my head in frustration. "I'm going to have a talk with Ernestine."

I make sure to relay all of the information we received about Conrad's skin to Ernestine before she drops me off. I have eaten dinner and put Conrad's troubles out of my head and am almost asleep when Marcella barges into our room. She's home five hours later than usual. She looks annoyed as she exclaims, "Argh. What a long day."

I squint as the light of our room blinds me. "Bad day at the bakery?"

"Yeah. I made 50 loaves of bread, 20 dozen rolls, and 20 dozen donuts with a broken mixer. It took twice as long as usual, and I had to talk to a customer about why her order wasn't ready on time."

I try to hide my giggle that Marcella is mad that she had to talk to a customer.

Marcella goes on to say, "The customer told me that I was a disgrace to humankind and should go back to the Complex of Undesirables where I came from." My friend scowls. "I still don't understand what that means, but I could tell it was not a compliment."

More prejudice. I shake my head in disgust. "That's terrible. I had a rough day too. Conrad and I got told off by our doctor. We need to take better care of our burns." The smell of pastry fills the air as Marcella plops on her bed. I bat my eyelashes at her. "Do you have any mess ups by chance?"

Marcella smiles and throws me a small white bag. "Here's a messed-up donut."

I grin as I open the greasy bag that smells like heaven. "Thanks!" I take a bite of the soft maple frosted pastry. It's like taking a bite out of a sweet, gooey cloud. Marcella laughs at the look on my face. I should probably be more discreet in my enjoyment. As I lick my fingers, I ask, "So, are any of the other anti-gamers working at your bakery?"

Marcella nods as she pulls some hand-me-down purple pajamas out of her bag. "Yep. Gordon just got a job as a janitor at the bakery. I didn't get to see him for very long before I left, but it was nice to see a familiar face."

I lick the last of the donut glaze off my fingers. "That's good. I wonder if Baldwin has found a job yet. I'm guessing he has since I haven't talked to him in five days."

"Yeah, he did. Didn't you know? He got a job at the National News Station."

I jolt upward at the news. "What? He was supposed to find a job that was out of the public eye!"

Marcella shrugs as she climbs into her bed. "He isn't a news anchor. He is behind the camera, so he shouldn't be seen."

It takes all my restraint not to slap my knee. "But if he has to be the cameraman for interviews with government officials, someone might recognize him!"

Marcella yawns, "Don't kill the messenger."

I don't know what to think as I climb back into bed. I know Baldwin likes radios and broadcasting, but he is putting us all in danger. I growl as I pull the covers up to my chin, "He should have told me this himself."

"Conrad, you look beat. I don't think you should do anymore double shifts," I say as I stick a gold bow on a wrapped train set. "Doctor Hamble made it pretty clear last night that you have to make your legs a priority or you will lose them."

My friend rolls his eyes as he takes a giant teddy bear from a sweet little grandma to wrap. "Oh, stop. I'm fine. It's the walk more than anything that wears me out."

I pause as I hand the wrapped train set to a young father. "The walk? You're supposed to get a ride." The young father has to tug the gift out of my hands. I feel silly, so I let go and give him a big smile and say, "Thanks for shopping at Casswell's, have a nice day!"

The father frowns and says, "Oh I will, after you wrap the doll."

My eyes drop to the doll on the table that I clearly forgot, which makes me feel incredibly stupid. I grab some shiny gold paper and say, "Of course, I will have this done in a jiffy!"

Conrad smirks at me briefly, but then turns back to the teddy bear wrapping. "There aren't enough rides for everyone going every direction in the morning, so I volunteer to walk."

I accidentally rip the wrapping paper I'm tucking around the doll. "That's crazy! You have the longest distance to walk."

Conrad hands the wrapped teddy bear to the grandma with a smile. He tucks the five dollar tip she hands him into his pants pocket as he says, "No, I don't. The National News Station is the farthest away."

Hearing about that place gets me even more riled up. "Why didn't you tell me Baldwin is working there? I told him it was too risky."

I force a smile as the man I wrapped the doll for gives me five cents for a tip and says, "You ripped the wrapping paper! Hasn't two years out of the complex taught you anything?"

Conrad smiles big enough at him to cover for my frown. "Merry Christmas, sir, and thank you for shopping at Casswell's." I just glower as I watch the man leave.

We have a small break in customers for a minute, so Conrad turns around to face me. "Dandra, I had nothing to do with Baldwin getting that job. That's between you and him. I have nothing to say to him. I don't think it's a big deal, to be honest. Rocky already drives there to work anyway."

I slam the lid of the cashbox down hard. "If anyone recognizes him, we're all going back."

Conrad carefully pulls the cashbox away from me. "I don't think anyone knows who to look for, so quit worrying about it."

That's easy for him to say. I honestly thought that we would all be staying together and making decisions as a group when we broke into this country. That is not happening, and I think it will get us into trouble. We should at least make sure everyone has a ride to work, right? I sigh in defeat as I say, "I worry about your legs, and I worry about someone recognizing Baldwin. Will you please ask Ernestine to drive you to work?"

"Nah. We'll be in our own apartment in a week anyway. I can walk here in 10 minutes from Larkside apartments."

"How long does it take you now?"

"Well, 30-40 minutes, depending on the traffic and the ice."

I look out the window at the snow coming down. "It's freezing cold out there. It's crazy to walk that much every day."

"I don't mind it, Dandra. It's not like I'm missed while I'm gone."

I let that sink in for a minute. "Is that why you keep working double shifts?" I ask quietly.

Conrad looks at his shoes. "You and Everley are the only friends I have here. Your anti-gamers don't even acknowledge my existence." He slides the cashbox back to where it was.

I can't imagine how lonely my friend must feel. I look at him sympathetically. "I'm so sorry. I didn't realize it was that bad."

He looks down at the table and starts picking up little scraps of wrapping paper. "I don't want you to worry about me. I'm fine."

I think of all the fame and money Conrad left behind in Layland, well, before his dad went psycho anyway. I look at him curiously. "Do you wish you hadn't left?"

Conrad pauses for a second. His eyes look thoughtful. "I miss my brother and my mom, but—no. I don't miss anything else."

I rethink how great our plans are now that I know Conrad has no friends at home, and he's in danger of losing his legs. I look at my friend apologetically. "I thought this apartment thing would make life better for you, but I'm not so sure now. Is there anything else we can do?"

Conrad shrugs. "No. The apartment will be better. Baldwin said he would share a room with Adamar and Ed would share a room with Gordon, so I will have my own room. Right now there are three of us in each room."

I'm thrilled with my boyfriend's generosity to my friend. "That's nice of him to let you have your own room for the same price as everyone else."

Conrad looks at me like I'm missing something. "Uh, it

won't be the same price as everyone else, but that's okay. I'll pay more for my own space."

Mr. Bronson interrupts us as he plops his newspaper and coffee on our table. "The lunch rush is over; go ahead and take your lunch breaks. I'll be sitting here reading about the Layland break-ins." He starts pulling on his reading glasses when I recognize my own picture on the front page. I have to think fast. I grab his coffee cup and splash some of the brown liquid on the pictures of Conrad, my mom, and myself.

I make a show of how horrified I am. "I'm so sorry, Mr. Bronson! I was trying to hand it to you. I'll just mop that up." I grab several tissues from the box on our table and roughly wipe the brown, wet spots on the paper so it blurs our faces until they aren't recognizable.

Mr. Bronson frowns when I hand him his splotchy newspaper. "I think your blood sugar is low. Go feed yourself some lunch, Dani."

I don't argue with him. "You might be right. I better go eat."

Mr. Bronson pulls some coins out of his pocket and tosses them at me. "Have a Fizzopolis on me, kid. That's what I drink when I feel droopy. It's B10 in the beverage machine."

"Thank you, Mr. Bronson," I say as I grab Conrad and march him to the break room.

Chapter 10

"WHAT ARE WE GOING TO DO, MOM?" I ask as I unwrap the sandwich Mom packed for me.

My mom frowns. "I'm glad you reacted so quickly, but we could easily be recognized by customers or other employees."

"I think we need to change our looks," Conrad says as he takes a bite of apple. "Not just us three—all of us who crossed the border."

I remember my picture staring up at me from the newspaper. "How do we do that?"

Conrad smirks like it's obvious. "Hair cuts, hair dye, glasses, fake blemishes or tattoos."

Mom touches her lips anxiously, "I'm afraid to look anyone in the face now. I will ask Shasta what she can do to help us tonight."

Luckily for us, Shasta has lots of ideas on how to disguise ourselves. She says, "There are lots of ways to change your appearances, but those of you who have established jobs can't go too dramatic, or your co-workers will wonder what is going on. I would have one of you cut your hair, one of you dye your hair, and one of you start wearing glasses and a hat."

Shasta helps me dial Ernestine's number so I can talk to Conrad and Baldwin. Conrad isn't home yet because he worked another double shift, but Baldwin is home and sounds concerned about me.

His voice is delicious to my ears when he says, "I hate that we haven't been able to see each other yet this week. I miss you."

I feel myself melt as I say, "I know! I miss you, too."

Baldwin insists, "I will be over as soon as I shower. I'm so glad you spilled the coffee on your picture."

I smile as I rub aloe vera on my legs. "I know, but at

least we're getting you closer to your apartment, which is closer to me."

Baldwin answers with longing in his voice. "Yeah, that will be nice. So, how much are you going to contribute to our apartment?"

I didn't expect this change in tone. I stumble on my words for a second. "Uh, as much as I can, I guess. I kind of thought you boys would pay for your apartment and we girls would pay for ours."

"Well, yeah. That's what will eventually happen, but we are in a time crunch. Haven't you heard that the United Cities is inviting emissaries from Layland to come over to look for us? It's the first time this has happened in 25 years!"

I feel my face tighten. "No, I didn't know."

"Well, you should watch the news more. Things could get bad really fast for us."

I don't love Baldwin's criticism of my common knowledge, and I have criticism to hand right back to him. "Speaking of news, why are you working at the news station? You are going to get noticed by people who know who we are."

Baldwin makes a noise in his throat of disbelief. "I don't think so. I don't leave the station, and my boss really likes me. I don't think he'll turn me in."

"Is your boss a Hamble by chance?" I ask through gritted teeth.

"Yes. His name is Gregory Hamble."

"Ernestine said to stay away from the Hambles until the election is over!"

"I know, but he thinks my name is Winston Blake, and he really likes my work ethic and my curiosity."

"This is a recipe for disaster."

"I've already changed my appearance, Dandra. I have blonde hair, glasses, and a fake tattoo on my neck. Ernestine even agrees that my disguise should keep me safe."

I feel my jaw drop. "What? Why am I the last to know?"

Baldwin exhales into the phone. "I didn't think you'd like me changing my looks or—working there, so I—didn't tell you."

My voice raises an octave. "I don't want you working there! Are you absolutely sure that they've never seen you looking like you usually do?"

"Yes. Rocky had the stuff I needed before I started this job."

I sigh, still annoyed. "Fine."

"Will you forgive me for not telling you?"

I feel my eyebrows knitting themselves together as I think about how to answer that question. "I hope you aren't ugly now."

Baldwin chuckles. "Uh, well, Rocky says I look better, but Josie says I look worse."

I sit up as I hear this. "Who is Josie?"

Baldwin sounds unsure for the first time tonight. "Um, Rocky's friend."

I am not thrilled with everything Baldwin is doing behind my back, and I'm especially not thrilled to hear that there is a girl who has seen Baldwin from before and after his makeover when I have not. I can't keep the frustration out of my voice. "We were eating cookies and toasting to our future only a week ago, and now—I—just—I feel like I don't know you anymore, Baldwin, or should I call you Winston?"

Baldwin laughs uncomfortably. "Win will do just fine. That's what everyone else is calling me now."

I force my anger down before I respond to his flippant response. "Well, I'm glad to finally know that, Win." I pause before asking, "Is Conrad home yet?"

I can hear Baldwin shuffling around before he responds. "Um, yeah. He just walked in the door."

"Is he limping?"

"Well, yeah, kind of."

"You guys are a bunch of jerks for making him walk to work for 35 minutes both ways with blistering, infected burns all the way up his legs and making him pay the most for the apartment."

Baldwin goes on the offensive. "It's your fault, not mine, that he has the burns, and he should pay more if he gets his own room. It's just common sense."

"Hand him the phone, please," I say angrily.

Baldwin's voice turns apologetic. "Dandra, don't be mad at me about this."

"Hand him the phone," I repeat.

Baldwin's voice begs, "Can I still come over tonight?"

I can't handle him tonight. I need to sleep on this. "No. I'm not in the mood to talk to you any more tonight."

Baldwin sounds upset. "Really? I never get to see you. We would be getting along better if we saw each other more. At least let us meet up tomorrow and try this again. I'll bring cookies and milk again! What do you say?"

I hope I'll be cooled off by then. "Whatever, tomorrow."

"Good," Baldwin says with a sigh of relief. He sounds like he is truly sorry for upsetting me. "I hope your legs are feeling better, and I miss you so much."

I roll my eyes. "Yeah, but not enough to tell me that you've changed your looks. Give the phone to Conrad, please. Bye, Baldwin."

My boyfriend's voice gets hesitant and quiet. "I'll see you tomorrow, Dandra. Bye."

I am fuming as I wait for Conrad to pick up the phone. I can hear Baldwin mumbling something in a grouchy tone as he hands off the phone to Conrad.

"H-hello?" my friend says haltingly.

"Hey, Conrad. How long has Baldwin's hair been blonde?"

Conrad pauses before answering, "I don't know. This is the first time I've seen him in four days."

I guess that is a good excuse. I feel my anger cooling off a bit. "Huh. If you had known before now, would you have told me?"

Conrad pauses again. "Probably..."

I nod feeling reasonably satisfied. "Good. I feel so out of the loop, and I hate it."

"I'm sorry. I'll try to keep you updated about your boyfriend more," Conrad says with a touch of malice in his voice.

I feel bad for giving him that impression. "No. That's his job, not yours." I take a deep breath and refocus my attention on what we need to do moving forward. "Anyway, the reason I wanted to talk to you is because Shasta thinks we should make small changes to our appearances since our coworkers will notice if we do something drastic. What would you like to do?"

My friend pauses before answering. "Um, I think I need my eyes checked anyway, so I could wear glasses, and I bought a hat to wear today," he says.

Of course he bought a hat, he is always spending money. At least a hat will help us out. "Perfect. Mom wants to dye the gray out of her hair, so I guess that means I get to cut mine."

I can hear the smile in Conrad's voice. "Nice. I can't wait to see it tomorrow."

"You might hate it."

"I don't think I could ever hate anything about you."

I am at a loss for words. "Well, you—thanks, Conrad. Go soak your legs."

His voice is eager to please. "I will, and I'll take my pills and put on aloe, Doctor Dandra. See you tomorrow."

I can't help but smile. "Thanks for being a good patient. See you tomorrow."

Chapter 11

I CRY A FEW TEARS when I look in the mirror. I've always had medium-length or long blonde hair. It doesn't reach the bottom of my ear lobes now. *Knock, knock.* I wipe my tears before opening the door. My little sister and her new friend Nelle greet me as I open the door to the lavatory. "Hi, girls. Come in."

"Why are you crying?" Nelle asks.

"I've never had hair this short before. I don't really like it."

Everley's hair is cut into a bob just under her ears, but she looks cute. She smiles into the mirror. "I like my haircut."

"That's because you are the cute sister," I sob.

Everley shakes her head and says, "I've always thought that you are the cute sister. You and Mom always look beautiful."

"Blonde doesn't mean beautiful, sis. Mom's hair dye made her blonde hair too bright in my opinion, and my hair just— looks bad."

"You're just not used to it yet. It will grow on you," my sister says encouragingly.

Nelle opens a drawer and pulls out some products. "I have an idea. There was a girl who used to live here, and she showed me how she spiked her hair. Do you want to try it?"

I look at my frowning face in the mirror and shrug my shoulders. "Sure. Why not?"

Nelle giggles as she fills her hands with goop, transfers the goop to my hair, and spikes it out. I realize I kind of like it. Everley looks at me and says, "You kind of look like a blonde, girl Conrad now, well, how he used to look in Layland."

"Thanks—I guess," I say as I shake my head in the mirror. The blonde spikes don't move much.

My sister looks at me curiously. "Is Baldwin coming over tonight?"

I frown as I turn my head side-to-side in the mirror, watching my new spikes as I move. "No."

Everley raises her eyebrows. "Is that really why you're crying?"

My sister is smarter than she looks. "I don't know. Maybe a little bit."

"If he makes you cry, you should dump him," Everley says with a serious expression.

I laugh at her simple response. "I wish people were that easy to figure out, sis, but they aren't. Baldwin has some amazing talents and is driven to do amazing things that will help lots of people, but he has his faults too."

Everley nods in agreement. "He cares more about..."

I stop my sister before she can say another word. "I don't want to go into his faults right now. I've cried enough today. Let's think of something fun we can do before we go to bed." Everley looks like she'd like to finish her sentence, but she thinks better of it and closes her mouth.

"I know what we can do!" Nelle says eagerly. "We can play spies!"

Everley's face lights up, and she jumps up and down. "Yes! This is my favorite game! Let's go in Nelle's room and play spies! Come with us, Dandra!"

My curiosity is stronger than my exhaustion, so I follow my sister and her friend down the stairs on tiptoe, as best as I can with my sore legs. When we get to Nelle's room, we find Peggy fast asleep in the top bunk of the bunk bed already.

Nelle quickly pulls a box from under the bottom bunk and digs out some binoculars. I am not sure if this game is going to be appropriate when she opens the curtains to her window a bit and finds a comfy position to camp out with the binoculars pressed to her eyes. "Look, Everley! The peace officer headquarters' blinds are still up!" She hands the binoculars to my sister.

Everley turns to me with authority in her voice. "Peace officers in this country are like patrolmen in Layland." She puts the binoculars to her eyes and shrugs. "I don't care as much about the peace officers. I like to spy on the guy who dresses his cats up in weird costumes!"

I am shocked to hear that this house is near enough to the peace officer headquarters to see in the windows. "Let me see," I say as I take the binoculars from my sister. This bedroom window faces the backyard, and we can see into the backyard neighbor's kitchen window. On his table, he has his big orange cat dressed up like a pirate, and his skinny black cat dressed up like a fairy. He teases them with treats to get them to stand on their hind legs. This is pretty hilarious, but the two-story building at the end of the street catches my eye more. The solemn gray exterior makes me think that this must be the peace officer headquarters that Nelle is talking about. I adjust the binoculars to zoom in more. It's 8:00 pm, but the lights are still on, and the blinds are open. I figure the janitors are probably cleaning the windows as I press the binoculars into my eyes.

The men I see in the windows don't look like janitors. They have official regalia on their jackets. As a matter of fact, the man with his back to me is wearing regalia that I recognize. That black jacket with that symbol on the back is what patrolmen from Layland wear—I press the binoculars into my eyes so hard that it starts to hurt. The man in the patrolman jacket throws his hands in the air as he speaks to one of the peace officers from this city. The peace officer is holding the GameComs that Conrad and I left by our escape tunnel and looking sheepish. I gulp nervously. Those arms flailing around in the air—they also seem familiar. My heart starts beating faster as the patrolman turns around and I see Patrolman Darius, my former bodyguard, staring out the window in my direction.

Chapter 12

"DID BALDWIN TELL YOU WHY I called him back last night?" I ask Conrad as I hand a wrapped shirt to a teenage girl.

"Yes," Conrad says as he adjusts his fake glasses.

I lower my voice. "What should we do if he walks into the store?"

Conrad rolls his eyes. "He won't walk into the store. He's not in the United Cities to go Christmas shopping."

I lean close to his ear. "But you never know. There is still a help wanted sign in the window. He might think that the sign will draw us in."

My friend shrugs. "If he does waltz through that door, which he won't, just act normal. Acting normal is the best way to blend in."

I open the cash box and start organizing the bills inside. "I'll try." I shouldn't be talking this much with customers close by, but I can't help it. I whisper, "I can't believe Patrolman Darius is here. It's like my worst nightmare has come true." I put the last dollar bill in the right spot and shut the lid of the cash box. "At least you get to stay with us tonight. Where are Baldwin and the others going to stay again, the Longs' house? That's what Baldwin told me when I called him back with the bad news last night."

Conrad scratches his forehead under the brim of his hat. "Uh, sure. It's Josie's house. I don't know her last name," my friend says as he throws away a piece of scrap wrapping paper.

I stop what I'm doing and stare at him. "What? Josie's house! Whose stupid idea was that?"

Conrad looks at me hesitantly. "Well, Rocky's, I think. She is the only one outside of Ernestine and Shasta who knows who we really are."

I growl, "He was supposed to come over tonight, but now he's spending the night at Josie's house! This is the worst day ever." I am so busy wrapping a fluffy blanket that is almost as big as I am that I fail to notice that Conrad has gone unusually quiet.

He suddenly whispers to me, "Your worst day ever is about to get worse."

I look up from my wrapping job to see a familiar uniform standing ten feet in front of me. Patrolman Darius has his back turned toward me, but I duck behind the enormous fluffy blanket anyway. My heart starts beating its way into my throat. What do I do? He will take me back to Layland if he sees me!

Conrad doesn't miss a beat. He just adjusts his hat and glasses and keeps smiling and sweet talking all the little moms and grandmas who have flocked to our table with their gifts, but he uses a fake accent. Only I notice that his hands are trembling. I reluctantly hand the enormous gift that is acting like a shield for me to its owner and whisper to Conrad out of the corner of my mouth, "What should we do?"

Conrad graciously accepts a $10 tip and puts it in his pocket before he slides a big box of dishes in front of me to shield me again. He whispers so only I can hear, "You need to act natural. Pretend like he isn't here. Keep wrapping gifts and acting like you belong here. Whatever you do, don't duck behind the gifts or the table like a weirdo again."

I stand up tall and hold it together as I watch Patrolman Darius out of the corner of my eye. He wanders around the left side of the store for a bit. I'm not the only one stealing glances at him. Many of the customers pause to look at the unfamiliar, metal GameCom on his arm. Their eyes then travel to the unfamiliar insignia on his jacket. I cringe as I see him meander over to the right side of the store where my mom is working. She hasn't noticed him yet, or at least she's pretending like she hasn't noticed him, but he's getting awfully close to her...

Right as he's about to approach her table, Mr. Bronson comes out of his office and gets rather close to my mom as he tells her to go on her break. I see my mom's eyes pop when she sees Darius's familiar uniform behind Mr. Bronson's back. She smiles and leaves quickly for the break room. That was close.

Conrad suddenly wraps a red fluffy scarf around my neck, high enough to cover my mouth. "Surprise! I decided to give you your Christmas gift early! Go look in the lavatory mirror at yourself! I'm sure you'll love it! Go!" He gives me a not-very-gentle shove toward the public lavatories. I am too scared to argue, so I just go.

I know my rushed breathing is suspicious, so I purposely slow it down as I lock myself in a stall. I take as much time as possible to relieve myself and wash my hands. I try to appreciate the scarf wrapped around my neck, but I know that the fear in my eyes is stronger than my disguise. I wonder if Patrolman Darius is gone yet. I wonder if he talked to Mr. Bronson. I wonder a lot of things as I stare at my terrified face in the mirror. I can't stay in here forever and should peek out the door to see what is going on. As soon as I open the lavatory door, a strong hand grabs my wrist and pulls me out.

I let out a small shriek before I realize that it is Conrad who has a hold of me. He pulls me close and whispers, "Mr. Bronson told us to go on break. I told him you had to pee, and that I'd wait for you here. Don't look at our table; just keep walking." I swallow all of my questions down and walk a step behind Conrad. I feel myself walking a little bit stiff, like a soldier. What does a casual walk feel like again? Conrad suddenly slows down, bumps into my arm and starts laughing. "That's a good one, Freckles!"

I fake a laugh and try to loosen up my stride as we walk into the break room. My mom is holding her sandwich but not eating it as terror distorts her pretty features. We sit down next to her and finally let the weight of our situation fall into our laps. My mom looks at me and says, "Did he recognize you?"

I look at Conrad and say, "I don't know; what happened after I left?"

My friend sets his shaking hands on the table and takes a deep breath. "I don't think he recognized either of you because your faces were always partially hidden from him. I looked him squarely in the face though."

My heart drops into my feet. "What did he do?"

Conrad swallows and says, "He was distractedly talking to Mr. Bronson. He said that he was looking for illegal refugees from Layland. He said he would need to see pictures of all new employees from here on out. His eyes didn't stay on me long."

I hope that being a current employee saves us from this

111

new command. "Does that mean that we don't have to show our pictures?" I ask.

My friend answers, "I don't know. But I think we are okay. Mr. Bronson said that all Casswell employees are fine, upstanding citizens who always obey the law."

"Did he recognize you when you looked him in the face?"

Conrad shrugs. "His eyes lingered on mine just a second longer than was comfortable, but he was so busy chatting up Mr. Bronson that I don't think he recognized me." Conrad takes off his fake glasses and shakily cleans them on his shirt.

None of us eat anything. We don't have the stomach for food. We don't have the stomach to work or leave the break room either. My mom finally pats our hands with her own. "Our break time is over. We better go back to our stations before Mr. Bronson gets suspicious." I nod, but I've never wanted to do anything less.

I am thrilled to see Patrolman Darius's back exiting through the door as I walk toward our station. He appears to be giving a report into his GameCom. I guess it's no secret anymore that there are microphones in those things. I wonder what Darius is telling Zane Chesterton… Mr. Bronson stands up irritably as we approach. His voice is harsher than I've ever heard as he says, "I have never had to deal with such an overbearing government official before. How dare he tell me what I can and can't do with my own business."

Conrad smiles at him and tries to sound understanding. "He seemed like a bossy guy. What does he want you to do?"

"He wants to see a picture of every employee I have. He started by saying that he needed to see a picture of all new employees from here on out, but when I said that I had enough to do during the holiday season without all that extra work, he said that because I was being uncooperative, I would have to send pictures of all my employees."

Conrad acts outraged. "That is preposterous! You can't let him tell you what to do. He should do his own job and let you do yours!"

Mr. Bronson nods enthusiastically. "That's right! He won't get a single thing out of me! If he wants to see who works here, he'll just have to come and see for himself! Hmph!" Our boss marches away like he's about to give someone a piece of his mind.

I'm relieved that we dodged that bullet, but how long will it be before Patrolman Darius comes back to get what he wants?

Chapter 13

THE WALK BACK TO SHASTA'S HOUSE is long and quiet. Conrad and I can't walk very fast with our sore legs anyway, but the weight of being actively hunted makes me feel like I'm dragging a ball and chain behind me. I'm also not sure where Conrad is going to sleep tonight in Shasta's snug little house, but Shasta will know what to do.

Shasta's usually unanimated face is flushed as we walk in the door. She's on the telephone. She covers the mouthpiece with her hand and whispers, "Bad news! I'm so sorry, but—bad news!"

Everley runs up to me and hugs me tightly around the waist. I gasp as she bumps into my legs. I turn to Shasta and mutter, "What happened? What did Patrolman Darius do?"

Shasta holds up one finger to silence me. "Thanks, Ernestine. I'll send word once I decide what to do. Bye." Shasta hangs up the phone and looks at us with worry tensing every line in her face. "Patrolman Darius has been busy today. He has a patrol of Herrington peace officers assigned to him to help him search the city. He and his patrol have already searched the entire south half of Herrington including Ernestine's house."

I feel my heart rate rising again. I say, "But I told Baldwin that Patrolman Darius was here last night. Didn't they get out in time?"

"Well, yes. They got their stuff out and made it to work before Ernestine's house was searched, but they can't go back. Rocky says that there is a peace officer parked across the street from their house, and it doesn't look like he will be moving anytime soon."

This news isn't great, but it could be worse. "Why are you so worried then?"

Shasta twists her hands together nervously. "Ernestine was taken into custody."

I gasp, "Why?"

Shasta shrugs. "She thinks it's for protesting the search. But maybe it's because her voice was recognized on the GameComs.

She wants me to bail her out. I don't know if I should, though, and—they will be here to search this house by tomorrow."

"Oh no." I look at my innocent little sister and wonder where we can go in this strange country to keep her safe until the house search is over. My mom hugs Everley like she is wondering the same thing. I add my arms to their hug until the ringing of the phone brings us back to reality.

"Hello? Oh, hi, Mrs. Abbot," Shasta says with enthusiasm. "It will be available tomorrow? That is great news. Yes, the first month's rent and last month's rent deposit won't be a problem. You can talk to Con—John if you want more reassurance. Okay, here he is." Shasta hands the phone to Conrad. We all eavesdrop on his conversation.

"Hello? Hi, Mrs. Abbot! Yes! I have been anxiously awaiting your call. My roommates and I have the deposit, and we will be over as early as you'll let us show up tomorrow morning. 8:00 is great! Thank you, and Merry Christmas to you too."

Conrad is as excited as a little boy in a candy store. "The three-bedroom apartment is ready for us a few days early! This is exactly the break we need! We can all move in until the searches are over!"

I can see a problem with this plan, so I have to ask, "That might work for a day or two, but they will search the apartment complex too, won't they?"

117

Conrad nods. "Well, yeah, I guess, but the important thing is getting you girls out of here before tomorrow."

Nelle pops her head out of the kitchen. "The soup is ready! I helped make it. Come and eat!"

I am mentally and physically exhausted as I plop down at the kitchen table to a bowl of hot vegetable soup. It smells good. I take a small spoonful. It tastes good too. The basil and tomato base reminds me of the Metty soup my dad used to make. The memory of eating soup with my dad gives me the energy I need to form a plan. Shasta makes sure the four little girls have seconds and a slice of bread and butter each before taking them to bed. Once it's just Conrad, Mom, Everley and me at the table, I ask, "Conrad, how much money do you and the other guys have saved for your apartment? Do you have the $3000 you need to get in?"

Conrad wolfs down his third bowl of soup like it's his last meal. "I think we're close. If we each have $600, then we're there." He leans over to his bag and pulls out a wad of bills. My jaw drops. I thought he was spending all of his money at Casswell's. Some of the bills are big, but there are quite a few ones in there too. This is obviously his paycheck and his tips mixed together. I help him separate the bills out by number. He has $524.

My friend slumps back into his chair looking defeated. "I guess you were right, Dandra. I shouldn't have bought you guys Christmas gifts." He leans over to his bag again and pulls out a fluffy scarf like the one he already gave me and hands it to my mom. "Merry Christmas, Mrs. Metty." She smiles but holds it hesitatingly. He hands another identical scarf to Everley, who of course squeals with joy.

My sister rubs the scarf on her cheek. "Thank you, Conrad! It's the most beautiful scarf ever, but Christmas isn't for another three days!"

Conrad grins. "I know, but I would rather give you your present early than not get the chance to give it to you at all." He looks at me with pleading eyes. He makes it too hard to scold him. Everley yawns and excuses herself to go to bed after she thanks Conrad again and gives him a hug.

I add up what the scarves probably cost in my head and realize that Conrad still wouldn't have had $600 if he hadn't bought the three scarves. But then Conrad pulls a white velvety coat with fur around the hood out of his bag and slowly hands it to me. "Merry Christmas, Dandra."

My jaw drops. It is like the one I wrapped for a customer on our first day of work. This white coat is even more beautiful than that plum-colored one though, and I would normally absolutely love it—but this is why he doesn't have the $600 he needs tomorrow. I stammer as I say, "Conrad, you shouldn't have."

Conrad looks at me sheepishly. "I know. You told me not to, but you need a warm coat, and this one will make you look less—fugitive-like." Conrad runs his fingers over the soft fabric.

119

"I can take it back if I have to, but if you lend me the $76 I'm short, I'll give you every tip I make until I've paid you back."

I should make him take it back, but this coat feels so—soft, and he had such a thoughtful reason for giving it to me. I've never wanted to keep something I can't afford so badly. I'm usually so rational and thrifty that I feel selfish wanting to keep it. I have $76 I can lend him, and I know he'll have enough to pay me back by tomorrow or the next day, so—I give in. I grin and say, "Okay, you've got a deal."

Conrad wraps his arms around me. "Thank you, Dandra, and Merry Christmas." I hold on to him longer than I usually would, but he hangs on a full second longer than I do. It feels good, but kind of weird. I start to wonder if he still has feelings for me. I haven't had someone spend time and money like this on me in a long time. My mom and Everley smile at us, which adds to the weirdness.

Mom clears her throat. "Do we have any way to get a hold of Baldwin and the others? We need to know if they have saved $600 each."

Conrad's bag of tricks has one more treasure for us. He pulls out a card with Ernestine's phone number and address with the same information for Shasta and Josie. "Baldwin gave us all a card like this last night in case we got separated."

My mom takes it and dials Josie's number hoping to find Baldwin. I run or shuffle-run upstairs to get the $76 I promised to lend Conrad. All of my money is shoved into a black sock that I found in the hand-me-down bag. I quickly count the money I have left. Not quite $400, $390 to be exact. I put the sock back in my bag of earthly possessions and pull out my bottle of aloe instead. I rub a new layer of aloe on my legs to get me through the night. I better make sure Conrad takes care of his legs too.

I overhear my mom saying to someone on the phone, "Oh, well that is too bad. We'll count what we have and see what we can do. I'll call you back soon. Bye."

I dread what I'm about to hear. "What did they say, Mom?"

Mom shakes her head in a defeated way. "They don't have $600 each. Gordon hasn't been paid anything at all yet, and the other three only have $400 each."

Conrad does the math in his head. "We need $3000, but with my $600 and their $1200, we only have $1800, which is $1200 short. We can't move in tomorrow. Where will we go during the searches?" he asks hopelessly.

I cringe as a thought comes to me. "Does Josie have room for five more?"

Conrad nods. "That is probably our best option. I'll call her and ask." He redials Josie's number from the card and waits patiently for someone to answer. "Hello? Josie? Hi! This is Conrad. Is there any way you could fit five more of us in your house tonight?" He pauses on the phone for an uncomfortably long time. "Oh, I see. Thank you anyway. We'll keep you updated on what we decide to do. Bye."

I look at my friend without optimism. "Bad news?"

"Yeah. Her parents are fuming mad to have four boys sleeping on the floor of their living room right now, and they refuse to give up their hall and laundry room floor for five more. So—there goes our only other option," my friend says like he has accepted that he's on his way back to Layland.

My mom is deep in thought. She excuses herself from the table and goes upstairs. When she comes back, she has a wad of cash of her own. "I have $450 dollars. How much do you have, Dandra?"

I can see where my mom's thoughts are going. "I have $390."

Conrad calculates where we are at on the back of the card Baldwin gave him. "That puts us to $2640. We're still $360 short."

I look at my mom. "Should we ask Shasta if she can help us?"

"Help you with what?" Shasta asks as she walks in the kitchen and starts putting the leftover food away.

Mom says, "We just added up all the money we have, and it looks like we are $360 short of getting the apartment tomorrow for the boys."

Shasta frowns. "I see."

My mom looks at her apologetically. "Is there any way you could loan us the $360 dollars we need to pay the deposit?"

Shasta sighs. "I wish I could, but my contract for this job is very clear that I can feed and house you, but I can not give any cash to any of my residents." My mom's face falls. Shasta goes on, "I've never housed people on the run from another country before, so I feel like this situation is different than usual. Do you want me to ask the Hambles to make an exception this one time?"

My mom shakes her head vehemently. "No. Asking for an exception will only give away that we are the refugees they are looking for. We promised Ernestine that we would keep the Hambles out of our troubles." She pauses for a second and then looks at Shasta and Conrad. "Do you think Ernestine can lend us the money?"

Conrad looks skeptical. "I think we've been eating them out of house and home. I'm not sure they have any extra money."

Shasta nods her head. "Even if they do, Ernestine is locked up and needs bail money to get out. She called me to ask for help instead of her husband. I don't think we should ask her."

We all slump heavily into our chairs. We are so close yet so far. If we had two or three more days of working, we would be fine, but Patrolman Darius will be here to snoop around tomorrow. Where will we go? A cave? Into the forest? A hole in the ground? I would go anywhere to stay away from Patrolman Darius.

Bam. The sound of the front door shutting wakes us out

of our stupor. Marcella walks in with a box of donut mess ups. "Why the long faces? Who needs a donut?"

My face lights up like a Christmas tree when I see her. How did I forget to count Marcella's money into our total? Everyone else at the table smiles and jumps up to give Marcella a hug. She looks bewildered as she sets the box on the table and tries to squirm out of our hugs. I'm sure this is a lot of attention for a shy person like her, but I don't let her get away from me so easily. "Marcella, we just found out that Ernestine's house has been searched and is being watched. They are coming here to search this house tomorrow. The boys' apartment is available if we can pay the $3000 deposit. We don't have quite enough though...Do you happen to have $360?"

Marcella's eyes go from anxious to disappointed. "I wish I did, but I just got paid today, and I only have $300."

I hope my heart can handle all these ups and downs. We are still so close, but not quite there. I wish I had something to sell, but I barely have any clothes to my name. I sit down at the table and set my arms down on the coat Conrad gave me. The price tags are still on it, and they scratch the side of my arm—which gives me an idea. I jump out of my chair and lift the coat up. "We will have exactly enough if we take this back."

My mom sighs with relief and starts laughing. Shasta smiles and pats my back. Conrad looks at me with regretful eyes. "I wish you could keep it."

I squeeze his hand and tell him, "It was a beautiful gift for the day, and it is the thought that counts, but being safe from Patrolman Darius is a better gift."

Conrad takes the coat from me and carefully folds it so it will fit in his bag. "This is a temporary sacrifice, Dandra. I will buy it back for you when I can."

I squeeze his hand. "Thanks, Conrad."

We are all so relieved to have a place to go tomorrow during the search that Shasta has to remind us to be ready in the morning. "Make sure you have everything you own packed and ready to go by 7:45 in the morning."

My mom looks at Shasta, "We don't have much."

Shasta smiles. "That's good because I don't want to lie about every little thing the search party might find. You guys should take some bedding just in case." Shasta looks around until her eyes land on Conrad. "I'll make you a bed on the couch for the night. Tomorrow is going to be a busy day." She looks at the rest of us. "We should all get some sleep."

We all yawn in agreement and head to our rooms.

I think of how much my legs need a vinegar water bath and realize that Conrad needs the same thing. There are two lavatories in this house, so he can use the downstairs lavatory once Shasta goes to bed. Nine of us in this house makes it pretty crowded. Nine of us in a much smaller apartment is going to be chaos. Not to mention it will be completely empty....Good thing it's only for a day.

Chapter 14

"DANDRA, WAKE UP!" my mom says as she shakes me awake. "Marcella, you need to wake up, too!" My friend groans and slumps out of her bed and heads to the lavatory.

I wipe the sleep out of my eyes as I watch my mom shoving my clothes into my worn-out backpack. "Is everyone else up?"

"Yes. Shasta is taking Conrad to Casswell's right now to return the coat. They are going to meet us at Larkside Apartments. You need to soak your legs and aloe them quickly."

My sleepy brain imagines us walking with all our stuff

down the street and can see a problem. "We can't just carry tons of bags and bedding down the street. The search patrol will see us for sure!"

Mom explains as she packs, "Rocky is going to drop off the anti-gamers and then come pick us up in the van. We need to hurry so we aren't late for work."

I yawn, "And so we aren't here when Patrolman Darius shows up."

Mom shudders. "Yes. That too."

I force myself out of bed and stretch. "Will Shasta come and get us when the search is over?"

"That is the plan but pack your bedding just in case."

My legs beg for more time in vinegar water, but twenty minutes is all I can spare. I rub aloe on them as quickly as I can and throw on the outfit my mom laid out for me. Everley calls my name up the stairs. "Dandra, are you ready? Mom says Rocky is here. I put two muffins in a bag for you."

I put on a brave face and gather up my bags, bedding roll, and a gallon of vinegar. Here goes nothing.

Rocky helps us load our things and doesn't wait for us to buckle our seatbelts before he zips off in the wrong direction. My mom and I look at each other completely confused. "Where are you going, Rocky?" I ask. "We're going to Larkside Apartment, remember?"

His face is tense as he keeps going in the wrong direction.

"I know, but there are peace officers marching down the streets the usual way. I just came from there."

"Are they at Larkside Apartments now?"

"Probably. They were either just leaving there or just going in. We need to find out before I drop you off."

I feel the blood draining out of my face as I imagine Baldwin walking into a trap. "Are Baldwin and our other friends already there?"

"Um, sort of..." A drip of sweat starts running down Rocky's forehead despite the cold morning. "When I dropped them off with their things, I couldn't see any peace officers, but once they were out of the van, all of the sudden, they were everywhere." I slump down into my seat.

My mom pats my knee and says calmly, "Let's hope that they had already searched the apartment building. It is possible."

I shake my head in fear. "Possible, but not probable."

As we approach the apartment building from the back end, we see Shasta sitting in her van at the back of the parking lot by a thick hedge of bushes, but we don't see Conrad with her. We pull up next to her and roll down the window. Shasta rolls her's down, too. My mom asks, "What happened? Where is Conrad?"

I screech as Conrad's head pops up from the backseat. I see his mouth forming the words, "Shh! I'm hiding until the peace officers leave!" His head disappears again.

Shasta climbs out of her van and looks around nervously.

"I'm going to check things out and talk to Mrs. Abbot. I'll be right back."

I am so worried about Baldwin and the others that I'm not sure what to do with myself. Everley ducks down in her seat and pulls me down to her level. "We should hide like Conrad. It's just like playing spies." I motion to my mom and Marcella to do the same. It's a quiet ten minutes that feels like ten hours.

Rocky suddenly whispers, "I think they are leaving. Shasta is heading this way." After a few minutes he turns around in his seat. "Go ahead and sit up. The peace officers have moved on down the street."

Shasta walks to our van and says, "Mrs. Abbot says that every apartment has been searched and the peace officers have left. I would still go in the back door just in case." We all breathe a sigh of relief. Shasta's eyebrows come together. "Where are Baldwin and the others? You need everyone so you can pay the deposit." She looks at Rocky expectantly.

Rocky looks uncertain. "I don't know. I dropped them off here. They went in the front door with their things before I realized that the peace officers were on their way here."

Shasta turns her head toward the apartment building. "I didn't see them inside. Mrs. Abbot didn't say anything about them. She just said that the peace officers were making her job difficult this morning, and she's ready to do paperwork and hand out keys."

I open the door to the van and look around hesitantly. I

watch the last peace officer walk out of sight, and yet there is no Baldwin to be seen. Where can those four boys be? A blonde guy with a tattoo on his neck suddenly appears in the doorway of the van. I shriek as Baldwin jumps inside next to me and kisses me in one fluid motion. "Let's go sign some paperwork!"

I'm so happy to see him that I kiss him back but then push him away from me. "Where have you been? We've been worried sick."

Adamar, Gordon, and Ed jump over the hedge and join us at the vehicles. I look at my boyfriend in disbelief. His new blonde hair and glasses look—okay, I guess. His fake neck tattoo is another matter though. It looks like a snake is slithering up his neck and about to bite my face. I don't love it. He takes my hand and gives it a squeeze. "I noticed two peace officers climbing out of a vehicle down the street as we walked into the apartment complex, so I told Mrs. Abbot that we would have to postpone our check-in until we'd had a word with them." He notices the muffins in my breakfast bag and snatches one out and takes a bite of it. Once he swallows, he says, "We left the building and jumped over the hedge. They never saw us. It got a bit cold after half an hour in the snow, so let's either get inside or crank up the heat in here!"

I screech as he puts his cold hands on either side of my neck to warm them up. I push his hands away and roll my eyes. "Where is your money? We need to make sure we have enough."

Everyone dumps their money in my lap. Everley helps me organize the bills by number, and we come up with exactly $3002. I sigh with relief. That's hurdle number one. I'm still not sure we're going to get away with not showing ID to Mrs. Abbot. That is hurdle number two.

Chapter 15

SHASTA AND I WALK in with the boys, but my mom, Everley, and Marcella wait in the van since this apartment technically is not for us girls. I try not to shake from the cold or my nerves as we walk in the door. Mrs. Abbot shakes her head as she sees us enter. "What a long morning it has been already. Those peace officers were super nosy, and I had to have a keysmith make three more keys for apartment 218 so there are enough keys for all five of you." Mrs. Abbot looks at me funny. "What are you doing here? I don't have your apartment ready yet."

Shasta comes to my aid. "We just want to help our friends move in since we have some extra time this morning."

"Oh," Mrs. Abbot says without enthusiasm.

Conrad pushes his way through the crowd to the desk. "Mrs. Abbot! Today is the day! Your favorite tenant has arrived!" my friend coos to the landlady. I've never been so thankful for Conrad's charm. Mrs. Abbot's bad mood quickly changes like he has put her under a spell. He talks to Mrs. Abbot like she is the most interesting woman in the world and somehow gets her to hand out the contracts without taking her eyes off his face. He helps her count out our deposit while telling her jokes. He even gets her to hand out keys to apartment 218 while she's enraptured with a story about a gaming competition he won.

A janitor interrupts our business dealings when he pushes through the crowd of bodies and hands Mrs. Abbot a yellow piece of paper. "Apartment 218 is clean, but I need Jack to show up before I can haul out the couch and bed they left behind." Mrs. Abbot doesn't look happy as she skims the information she has just been given. I'm not sure if it's because her employee is late or because the previous tenant of the apartment left things behind.

Conrad bats his eyelashes at Mrs. Abbot. "No worries. We are happy to do a favor for our favorite landlady. We'll haul those things out for you." He waves his hand in the air like it's nothing. "If they are nice enough things, maybe we'll even keep them!"

Mrs. Abbot's frown turns into a smile. "Thank you! It will be nice to have some extra muscle around here!" Her eyes linger on Conrad's physique for an uncomfortably long time.

Conrad doesn't seem to notice. "Any time, Mrs. Abbot. If you ever need an extra set of hands to haul off furniture, just give us a call."

We almost get away with not showing IDs, but Mrs. Abbot stops us as we're walking out the door. "Wait! I need a photocopy of everyone's ID!"

Baldwin gives Rocky a look and Rocky hands his ID to Mrs. Abbot. She takes it and makes a copy without even realizing that Rocky didn't sign a contract with her. Baldwin pats his jacket and pants pockets like he is searching for something. "I think I packed my ID deep in a box somewhere. Can I bring it by later?"

Conrad does the same pat-the-pockets routine and says, "I think I did the same thing. I guess that means I will have to come by later with it." He bats his eyelashes one more time. Gordon and Ed nod and mutter the same kind of story.

Mrs. Abbot giggles and says, "Okay. Since I have one on file, it will be fine if the rest of you who are over 18 stop by later after you've unpacked."

Conrad smiles at her and pats her hand. "You are the best,

Mrs. Abbot. I will see you later." Mrs. Abbot makes a sound that is a combination of a grunt and a giggle.

I roll my eyes as we leave.

Shasta and Rocky move their vans closer to apartment 218's door. I make sure to give Shasta a hug before she leaves. She has helped us so much already, and now she's going to have to lie to the peace officers for us and move us back once they're gone. I make sure to hug Rocky too. His eyes open wide as I squeeze him. I whisper, "I'm sorry about your mom, Rocky. She wouldn't be locked up right now if it wasn't for us. I will make it up to her some day."

Rocky lets go of me quickly and shrugs. "She would do as much for anyone. This isn't the first time this has happened, so we're kind of used to it. They'll let her out in a few days, I'm sure."

"Thanks just the same," I say. Baldwin, Gordon, Ed, and Adamar all shake Rocky's hand before he drives away. As Shasta follows him out of the parking lot, I feel very grateful to have come this far in our plan and yet—very exposed. "There go our protectors in this country, Mom," I say as the vans disappear.

"Come on, Dandra. Let's get these guys moved in," my mom says as she takes my hand. Mom, Everley, Marcella, and I follow the boys to an outdoor staircase and march our bags up the stairs.

I'm surprised to hear Baldwin compliment Conrad for his persuasion with Mrs. Abbot as we walk up the stairs. It sounds like it pains him to say it. "Conrad, you did well there. I'm not sure we would have keys right now without your help, so thank you."

Conrad looks at my boyfriend with equal pain on his face and says, "You're welcome."

Baldwin is the first one to the door and unlocks it with his new key. The apartment is simple and clean, and way smaller than Shasta's house. I walk through the entryway and scoot inward to the living room area to make room for everyone coming in behind me. The ugly green couch that the previous tenants left behind doesn't look promising, but when I sit on it, I see that it's actually quite comfortable and doesn't have any rips in it. The nine of us fill the place up even without any more furniture. My mom and Everley look nervous as they peek into the small kitchen, the three bedrooms, and the two bathrooms. Marcella, on the other hand, actually looks at home for the first time since we broke into this country. I think she misses living with the anti-gamers. She attaches herself to Gordon almost immediately.

Baldwin helps me up off the couch with a quick kiss and picks up my bag. "Is it okay if we put all four of you girls in the biggest bedroom for tonight? You'll have your own lavatory and the big bed they left behind." I peek around Baldwin to see what my mom thinks.

My mom nods with relief written all over her face. "Yeah, that's a good idea. I will start unpacking." I laugh to myself because we don't have much to unpack.

As we walk into the bedroom, I'm pleasantly surprised that it feels big enough to accommodate two on the bed and two on the floor. The bedding that my mom and Everley used at Shasta's house fits perfectly on the bed that was left behind. Marcella knows that my legs are in pain when they bend, so she makes beds for the two of us on the floor. We each have two bags of clothes that sit beside our beds and enough toiletries to fit in a single drawer in the lavatory, so I guess that means we're unpacked. Hopefully Shasta will send word that the search is over, and we can come back before we have to use our temporary beds. Baldwin watches us settle in for a minute but then leaves to make his bed in one of the other bedrooms.

My mom wrings her hands as she looks out the bedroom window at the back parking lot outside. She peeks into the lavatory and then sits on the edge of the bed. "Do you have to work today, Marcella?"

My friend stretches out on her two-blanket floor bed and says, "No. I worked a double yesterday. I have today off."

My mom nods. "Would you be willing to keep Everley company today while we're at work?" she asks anxiously.

Marcella nods. "Yep. Don't worry about her. We'll draw and read and eat some messed up rolls from the bakery."

"Thank you so much! I don't want her to spend too much time with these boys until I know them better." Marcella nods with understanding. My mom looks around the room one more time and exclaims, "Dandra, we better get to work. We're already late."

I stand up and put a reassuring hand on my mom's arm. "Okay. I'll grab Conrad. Thanks for babysitting, Marcella!"

"No problem."

Everley growls at me, "I'm not a baby."

I peek into the first bedroom on the other side of the living room, but Conrad isn't there. Baldwin and Adamar are setting up beds on the floor and stacking books in the corners. "I'm heading to work, Baldwin. I'll see you later."

He jumps to his feet. "I work a late shift tonight, so I won't see you until very late, or maybe you'll be back to Shasta's by then, but I'll be thinking of you," he says as he kisses my cheek.

The spot on my cheek sends tingles through the rest of me. "I'll wait up for you. See you later." He pulls me in and kisses me for real this time. My mom clears her throat behind me. I force myself to let go of him. "Uh, yeah. See you later."

We find Conrad in the other bedroom trying to lay out a single blanket on the floor in a corner for his bed with his stiff legs. It makes me mad to see him trying to push his breaking-down flesh to the limits while his roommates just sit there.

139

"Hey, Ed, help him out, will you? He has dead tissue and an infection on his legs."

"He does? I didn't know that." Ed says as he straightens out the corners of the blanket for him.

I fold my arms across my chest. "Yes, he does, and he needs to soak in a tub of vinegar water three times a day to stop the burns from eating his flesh to the bone."

Ed scratches his head nervously. "Yeah, well, good to know."

I notice that Ed and Gordon have two thick blankets to sleep with while Conrad only has one thin one. This biased group is probably not going to like having me under the same roof. I sigh, "Let's get to work, Conrad. We're late."

Conrad grabs his coat without any emotion on his face. "I'm ready. Let's go."

Conrad seems happier as the three of us walk to work. It is in sharp contrast with my mom who is agonizing about Everley staying all day in an apartment full of teenage boys.

Work goes by fast. Maybe it's because we are 15 minutes late, or maybe because it's crazy busy with only two days left until Christmas. Patrolman Darius does not show up. I hear customers complaining about the house and business searches, which makes me glad that I'm not the only one being inconvenienced, but sad that I'm causing problems for so many undeserving people. Conrad buys several chocolate bars and a bag of chips from the employee snack machine before we leave.

He also has a Casswell's bag full of who-knows-what on his arm. It makes me mad. "You owe me $75 plus everyone owes me $390. Stop spending money on junk!"

Conrad looks bashful. "You're right. I'm sorry." He digs in his pocket for a minute. "If it makes you feel any better, here's this." He hands me $40 in cash from his tips today. It does make me feel a bit better.

When we get back to the apartment, I'm surprised to see another two chairs in the living room. The worn-out red and gold overstuffed armchairs don't match the green couch at all, but they are better than sitting on the floor. "Where did these come from?" I ask Ed.

"Gordon said that the bakery was throwing them away and getting new ones, so we brought them here."

The faint smell of pastry coming off the chairs makes my stomach growl. "Did he bring any mess ups with him?"

Ed plops down on one of the chairs with a book. "No, but I'm sure Marcella will tomorrow after work."

I feel miffed that we basically have no food. I really want a donut. I whine, "We won't be here tomorrow. Shasta said her house was getting searched today."

Ed looks up from his book. "It didn't happen today. You guys will have to stay the night."

"How do you know?"

"Rocky went to the bakery for lunch and told Gordon."

I frown as I look at the empty kitchen. "What will we eat?"

Gordon overhears our conversation and pulls a box out of an otherwise-empty kitchen cabinet. "We have a box of crackers and four apples we can cut up. It will last us until tomorrow. Somebody should have some money by then."

I look at Conrad and feel bad for telling him off for getting some food. I should have bought a few things myself. My hand tightens around the $40 of tip money that Conrad paid me back today. I have $35 in my own tips. Should I go out and buy some food?

Conrad looks at me like he's reading my mind and shakes his head. "They are still searching houses and businesses out there. Just wait until tomorrow. We can pick up some food after work if we need to."

I force a smile and nod at my friend. Gordon chops two of the apples into slices with his pocketknife and offers them to me on a flattened box. I take three slices of apple and six crackers and wander to the room where my mom, Everley, and Marcella are waiting for me. My mom and sister's anxious faces break my heart as I walk in. I lift up my meager portions and say, "Dinner is served. Help yourself." Marcella and Everley jump up and head for the food. I hope Marcella really did have messed up rolls to share with my sister since breakfast this morning.

My mom hangs back and looks at me with concern. "Are you okay?"

I don't look at her while I eat the smallest of my apple

slices. "Yeah, but how are we going to make this work? We have food for today, but what if we have to hide tomorrow and the next day?"

Mom takes me into her arms. "It will be okay, sweetie. Just take it a day at a time. Tomorrow will take care of itself. We will probably be back at Shasta's where plenty of food and warm beds will be waiting for us."

"What happens if the peace officers set a watch on her house too?"

Mom shrugs. "Then the nine of us will really get to know each other."

The apple in my mouth loses its flavor. "Merry Christmas to us."

"It will be a Christmas to remember for sure, but it will help us appreciate next year's Christmas and the Christmas after that." She kisses me on the forehead.

I give her a quick hug. "You're right, of course."

Mom gets to her feet. "Finish your food and then have a long soak in the tub. It will help you feel better."

It is becoming a habit of mine, falling asleep in the tub. *Knock, knock.* I flail as the knocking wakes me up. The water I splash on the floor is not going to be easy to mop up with our limited supplies. Oops. I hear Everley's voice say urgently, "Get out, Dandra. I need to pee."

I force myself awake and out of the tub and dress myself quickly so my sister can use the toilet. When I stumble out of the lavatory into the big bedroom, I see that it's late. I've been asleep in the tub for a couple of hours. My mom is yawning, already tucked into bed with a book, but Marcella is nowhere to be seen.

I find her in the living room sitting on the couch next to Gordon. They look happy. They have turned a box into a table with a checkerboard drawn on it. They are playing checkers with pieces made from cardboard and markers. Ed and Adamar are fiddling with a scruffy-looking radio that is playing Christmas music quietly. They probably found it in the trash. My friends' smiles and laughter make me feel silly for complaining about our lack of food and supplies a few hours ago. A contented feeling settles over me as I watch my friends happy to just be together even if they have almost nothing. Well, most of my friends. Where are Conrad and Baldwin? Baldwin probably isn't home from work yet, but Conrad should be here. I peek into the two smaller bedrooms and don't find anyone, but I do see something hiding behind Conrad's backpack. It's the Casswell's bag I saw on his arm earlier. I sneak into his bedroom and am about to move his backpack when Conrad walks into the room, his black hair still wet from his bath.

I feel like I've been caught red-handed. "Oh, hi, Conrad. How are your legs doing?"

My friend doesn't answer right away. He looks at me

suspiciously and drops his dirty laundry in the corner of the closet. "What are you doing in my room, Dandra?"

I hope my cheeks aren't red. "I was looking for you—or Baldwin."

His eyes look skeptical. "It kind of looks like you were about to peek through my stuff."

I laugh humorlessly. "No! I would never do that."

He looks at me like I'm the worst liar in the world. "Right."

My shoulders cave in. "Okay, I could see the Casswell's bag behind your backpack, and I was tempted to have a peek."

There is a smile behind Conrad's eyes. "Were you hoping it was something for you?"

I feel like I have to defend my character. "No, I know that this apartment is our Christmas gift this year."

Conrad takes a step closer to me and puts a hand on my arm. "It's okay to want things, Dandra. It's okay to want things that don't benefit everyone else, too. It's okay to want things just for you."

Full-defensive mode erupts in me. "Why do you think I want something just for me from you? Am I that kind of person? Do you think I'm selfish? Or needy?"

Conrad takes another step closer and puts his arm around my shoulders. "No, you are definitely not selfish or needy, but even the least-selfish person in the world deserves to have something special just for herself."

"Hey! What is going on in here?" Baldwin's voice booms

out from the doorway. "Get away from my girlfriend!" he says as he flings Conrad's arm off my shoulders.

I take a step back and reach out to Baldwin. "I was just making sure Conrad had enough aloe for his legs. The doctor made me promise to look after him." Conrad raises his eyebrows, surprised at my response.

Baldwin growls. "You don't have to have your arms around each other to ask about aloe."

Conrad glares at my boyfriend. "Hey, nothing happened. She needed a little reassurance after this crazy day, and I was giving her that since we have been friends since, you know, forever."

"Well, I'm here now, so leave the reassuring to me."

Conrad's eyes have nothing but fire in them. "Fine, but this is my room, so go somewhere else to do it."

Baldwin sneers at Conrad. "Wouldn't want it any other way. Come on, Dandra."

Baldwin takes my hand and pulls me out of the room. I see a look of hurt mixed with—triumph on Conrad's face as we leave. I give him a feeble wave as we exit through the door.

Baldwin gives me a look of slight disappointment as we walk into the kitchen. "Have you eaten yet?"

I shrug. "Yeah. I had six crackers and three apple slices."

Baldwin picks up the cardboard box plate with the remaining four apple slices and a fistful of crackers and leads me into his room. He plops down on his blanket bed on the floor and pats the spot next to him. "Sorry for overreacting. I know you two have been friends for a long time. I think I'm just—it has been a long day. But enough of that. I want to hear about you. How was your day?"

I carefully sit down next to him and watch my boyfriend who doesn't look like himself wolf down some crackers. "My day started off rather nerve-wracking. I was so worried that you'd been caught, but it ended all right since I'm safe in this apartment with you."

He squeezes my hand and sighs. "I'm glad your day ended better than it started. Mine did too. I got to take the high-speed monorail for a story we're shooting."

"Tell me about your day. We haven't talked in forever."

He grins as he eats a couple of apple slices. "You're right. We never get to be alone like this." He offers me a cracker and then says, "Work was fine. We shot three different interviews. One on the monorail and two in the studio. Since Rocky's job is to listen to the peace officer radio frequency so we can put those stories on the news, he kept updating me about his mom, Shasta, and the peace officer house-searching patrol."

"Did they let Ernestine out yet?"

Baldwin shakes his head. "Unfortunately, no. They are sure that she knows something about our escape, so they haven't let her go."

"What about her house?"

"It is still being watched. So is Shasta's."

I'm not thrilled to hear this. "Why is Shasta's house being watched? Ed said her house has not been searched yet."

"Her house hasn't been searched yet, but because Ernestine called Shasta from the detainment center, the peace officers think that she is in league with Ernestine."

I smack my forehead with my hand in frustration and whisper, "They aren't wrong."

My boyfriend shrugs. "I know, so we can't go back to either house for a while."

I am surprised to hear this. I thought we'd be back to Shasta's house tomorrow after it was searched. I'm thankful for once that Baldwin works at the National News Station with Rocky. "Thank goodness for Rocky. We would be caught for sure and on our way back to Layland without him."

Balwin brushes off the crumbs from his dinner, takes my hand, and starts caressing it with his thumb. "You're right. Rocky is just as helpful to us as his mom."

I wish I had something to give Rocky to say thank you. "And he's taking you to and from work with no compensation."

Baldwin pauses for half a second. "Most of the time."

I am confused by his response. "What do you mean, most of the time?"

My boyfriend shrugs. "Josie took me home today to save Rocky some time and gas."

Yay. Josie. "What does Josie do at the National News Station?"

Baldwin sneaks a kiss before saying, "She is a broadcast technician."

I'm not thrilled with this news. "So, you two work side by side all the time."

He shakes his head. "Not all the time, but sometimes."

"Is she Rocky's girlfriend?" I ask hopefully.

Baldwin rolls his eyes. "No, but they are good friends." He looks like he's about to come in for another kiss.

I ask before he reaches my lips, "How close of friends are you with her?"

Baldwin pauses. "We're good friends, too." His kiss is colder than I expect it to be.

I have to be honest with him. "I don't like how close you two are. She knows what you're doing before I do."

My boyfriend rolls his eyes. "She is just a pal, a chum. You know how important it is to have friends at work." I give him a questioning look. He goes on, "Josie is the same kind of friend for me that Conrad is for you at work."

I think that makes me feel better. "Oh, okay. If your relationship is just like Conrad and I's relationship, then that is just—fine."

Chapter 16

MY JOINTS ACHE AS I WAKE UP on my floor
bed. Today is Christmas Eve. It will be the busiest day of
work yet because all the last-minute Christmas shoppers can't
procrastinate a single day more. My stomach growls, and my
legs burn, but I am happy to be safe with all the people I love.
I kind of hope that my Christmas present will be getting paid
back all the money I loaned to the guys for this apartment. Will
it happen? Who knows.

I get myself bathed, aloed, and dressed before my mom
has to remind me. I wish we had some food, so I could make

breakfast for everyone. Even a small container of oatmeal and two tablespoons of brown sugar would be better than nothing. My mom, Conrad, and I are the first ones to leave for work today, so I walk into the empty kitchen and take a peek into all the cupboards. I don't find anything, which isn't surprising. Conrad watches me from the couch as he puts aloe on his legs. "Did you check the fridge?"

I shake my head. "No. There won't be anything in there. The only food we packed was nonperishable."

Conrad insists, "Check it, just in case."

I shrug and take a look in the fridge. I'm surprised to see a giant pancake covered in fruit and cream sitting there all alone on the shelf with a plastic fork and knife. I turn to him and ask, "Where did that come from?"

Conrad gets up from the couch and stands next to me. "It's Christmas Eve breakfast, just like my mom used to make. Take a bite." I am amazed as I take it out of the fridge. It smells amazing. I'm about to ask where he got it from when Conrad puts a finger to my lips to quiet me. "I noticed how hungry you were when we got home from work last night, so I walked to the restaurant down the street this morning and ordered this to go. I would have bought more, but I gave the rest of my money to you yesterday."

I can't help myself. It is the best thing I could ask for at this moment. I throw my arms around my friend. "Thank you! Help me eat it!" Conrad protests at first, but he takes a few bites off my fork. My mom does too as she bustles about getting her hair done and shoes on. She stops midbite when she realizes there is nothing left for Everley.

Mom pulls $20 out of her pocket and writes a note to Marcella and Ed telling them to get some food for Everley and everyone else for today. It won't be much, but it's better than nothing. Before we leave, Conrad slips a chocolate bar into Everley's shoe to surprise her when she wakes up. He is so sweet. He thinks of little things for the people he cares about while I've been so busy thinking about the big things like having enough money for two apartments and not getting caught by Patrolman Darius.

The Christmas music that is usually quietly playing as Casswell's is booming loud today. I knew it would be a busy day, but this is ridiculous. Conrad and I don't get a lunch break because our line of customers needing gift wrap never ends. Mr. Bronson brings us some kind of fruity health beverage to give us the energy to work through lunch. It helps, but my stomach starts to growl again an hour later.

I feel guilty leaving Conrad alone for a bit so I can use the lavatory, but it's that or wet my pants. I insist that Conrad do the same thing when I get back. My hands positively whir around each gift without my brain keeping up with what I'm doing. Conrad calls it muscle memory. I wrap a chemistry set without looking up or saying more than, "Hello, how are you today?" before I realize that the customer is a peace officer—I'm sure he notices my jolt of surprise when I hand it to him. "Have a M-merry Christmas, and thank you for shopping at Casswell's," I stutter.

The peace officer looks at me suspiciously for a second, but then looks at his watch and says, "Merry Christmas to you, too." He stops to talk to Mr. Bronson at the cashier station before he leaves.

Conrad puts a hand on my back to stop my shaking. I whisper to him, "It wasn't Patrolman Darius, but what if that peace officer is on his way to report to him? I think he suspects me." Conrad frowns at me but says nothing as he wraps gifts as fast as he can.

I am numb as I finish our shift. I don't even notice that we've worked an hour later than we were supposed to. Shelly and Lupe are always late, and the lines are still so long. Luckily, no one is here to escort me away in handcuffs, so I think we're okay. Conrad offers to clock us out in the employee lounge, which I'm grateful for. My mom meets us at our table, looking at her watch anxiously. "I hope Everley is okay. We've been gone so long, and I don't know if they bought any food."

Conrad is back quickly and puts a hand on Mom's shoulder, "I'm sure she's fine."

I push the door open to lead us out when I hear Mr.

Bronson yell from the cashier station, "Stop! Stop right there, you three. Don't you dare leave."

I look at my mom in fear. Her eyes are filled with terror, too. Conrad is the most composed of us, so he calls back, "Our replacements are here, Mr. Bronson. Is there anything else we can do for you?"

Mr. Bronson calls out, "Get over here right now. I have something to show you."

I am positively shaking in my boots now. Conrad has to pull me along with him to our boss' round cashier station. I will follow for now, but if we are found out, I'm going to run. Mr. Bronson puts a "Lane Closed" sign on his desk-like area and gives us all a long, hard look. "That Peace Officer that was in here today asked me to look into your records to see your start date and hours worked. So, I did and guess what I have discovered?"

My mouth is too dry to speak, but Conrad manages to mumble, "I don't know, what did you discover?"

"I hired you two and a half weeks ago and all three of you have worked all 17 days in a row with no days off, often starting early and staying late. John, you've done more double shifts than single shifts." Conrad looks at me and then at our boss. None of us say anything because we're not sure if this is a good discovery or a bad one. Mr. Bronson goes on, "I feel like a terrible boss for working you so hard. I want to make it up to you." He pulls two big boxes out from under his desk. "I want to provide your Christmas dinner and stocking stuffers, so take this with you, enjoy your first day off in over two weeks, and have a very Merry Christmas!"

My mom puts a hand to her mouth to cover her surprise. Conrad laughs. I start to cry; well, a tear or two leaks out. I was sure we were on our way back to Layland. I could hug Mr. Bronson right now, but my mom does it for me. I can barely stammer, "Thank you, Mr. Bronson. You make this store an enjoyable place to work."

Conrad picks up the heavier food box. "Thank you and Merry Christmas to you, too, Mr. Bronson!"

Our boss smiles at us and says, "I hope to see you all back after Christmas to help us with returns and shelf stocking. Can I count on you?"

Conrad smiles. "Absolutely!"

Mom and I each take a handle on either side of the lighter, gift-filled box and leave with smiles on our faces.

The walk home is slow and kind of painful for our arms, but we have nothing but smiles on our faces the whole way. We thought we'd have to stop and buy groceries after work, but we have plenty of groceries and presents at no cost to us. I can't wait to get back to the apartment and dig through these boxes with Everley.

The smell of baked potatoes greets us as we walk in the door. Everley almost knocks the box out of my arms when she comes around the corner. "Look! Look at what Ed and I did today! We decorated for Christmas!" She is absolutely right. The kitchen and living room are covered in white paper snowflakes, green paper Christmas trees, yellow stars, and red and green paper chains.

Mom and I set the box down on the ground and knead our arms as we look around the apartment in shock. "Where did you get the paper and scissors, sis?" I ask.

"Ed found the paper in the trash at the low-level school around the block."

Ed bounces on the soles of his feet. "It's called a primary school here, apparently. I borrowed scissors and tape from a teacher there. I am a janitor who has already racked up a few favors." Ed seems incredibly proud of himself for pulling this off, and I'm incredibly glad that he found something to do with Everley all day.

Everley gasps when she sees all the wrapped packages in our box. "What did you buy, Mom? Do we get Christmas presents after all?" She picks up a package that has a big round part wrapped, but a black handle sticking out unwrapped.

Mom picks up the box and moves it up to the countertop in the kitchen. "That is a box of surprises for tomorrow, so I hope you are on your best behavior tonight!"

Everley bounces up and down for a second, and then

157

forces herself to calm down and nod politely. She eyes the box in Conrad's arms. "What do you have, Conrad?"

He shrugs and sets his box next to my mom's. "I don't know, just the best Christmas dinner ever!"

Everley grins and starts pulling things out of the box. "I love ham and stuffing and corn and potatoes and green beans and cider and—cherry pie!"

Conrad covers the top of the box with his arms to keep Everley from taking everything else out. "Leave a few surprises for tomorrow, silly!"

Marcella looks at the potatoes Everley put on the counter. "I hope you're okay with potatoes two days in a row. That's what I made for dinner. I have a few ugly cinnamon rolls, too."

Mom quickly unloads the rest of the food box into the fridge and the nearest cupboard. "I could eat potatoes every day, Marcella. Thank you."

Marcella uses a folded in half sock to pull three large potatoes out of the oven. "I didn't have enough money to get cheese, but we have butter and salt and pepper, and they're hot."

Mom pulls a package of thin plastic plates and plastic utensils out of the food box. "I know these are disposable, but if we're careful, we can wash them and reuse them." She pulls three plates out and starts dressing the potatoes for us. The potatoes are delicious despite their meager toppings. Conrad eats his whole potato, peel and all within minutes. Marcella brings two small, shriveled-looking cinnamon rolls over and cuts them in half. "You can each have a half. We need to leave some for B."

Baldwin shows up an hour after we do. He has a box of surprises too. Everley jumps up and down to get a look inside. He smiles at her enthusiasm and lowers the box so she can see what is inside. Everley's smile turns into a frown. "What is this stuff?"

Baldwin keeps smiling. "They are two-way radios! Josie gave them to me." The smile melts off my face too. "She said that the news station was about to throw them out, so she snagged them for me. We'll be able to contact Rocky when he's at home now."

I am not surprised that Baldwin wants to use the radios to contact Rocky, but I wish he wanted to contact me, too. I won't be staying in this apartment forever.

Mom is in a particularly good mood after dinner and challenges Baldwin to a game of cardboard box checkers. Baldwin seems honored that she asked. I hold Everley in my arms as I watch them play, giggling every time someone loses a piece. They both have brilliant strategies, but Mom wins somehow. I kind of think he let her win, but then Ed challenges her, and she wins again, and before we know it, we've made two more cardboard box checker boards and we're in a full-on checkers tournament. Everley is the first one out, then Marcella, then Conrad, then Gordon, then me, then Ed. We even get Adamar to play, and he beats everyone, even Mom and

Baldwin. Everley makes Adamar a yellow crown out of paper and writes "Christmas Eve Checkers Champion" on it. I swear I see the corner of Adamar's mouth turn up when Everley places it on his head. We're all so happy to see him not miserable that we stay up even later to do some checkers rematches. I am not the only one who goes to bed smiling and excited for Christmas day.

Chapter 17

CHRISTMAS MORNING IS A BEAUTIFUL thing. I get to sleep in for the first time in two weeks. My legs finally urge me to get up and give them a soak. Mom and Everley are up, but Marcella is still sleeping. After my morning vinegar bath and aloe vera application, a delicious aroma leads me into the kitchen. My jaw drops when I see Baldwin and Conrad working side by side cooking bacon in the frying pan that Everley discovered in the gift box last night. I can't believe how nice they are being to each other. It is truly a Christmas miracle. The smell of bacon eventually brings everyone to the kitchen.

Marcella adds to the delicious smell by pulling a dozen donuts out of the kitchen cabinet. We eat our breakfast leisurely, except for Everley, who is jumping up and down looking at the box of gifts on the counter.

Once we finish breakfast, Mom tells us all to sit in a circle on the living room floor. She brings the box over and sets it by her feet. I can see what she is thinking, but I see a problem. "Mom, how will we decide who gets each gift?"

My mom blushes slightly. "I actually peeked at each of them, and I've written the name of who I think should have each gift on the top of them."

Conrad smiles and nods at my mom. "I can't wait to see how you've divided the gifts up! We should go youngest to oldest." Everley claps her hands at that news.

My mom laughs at her excited daughter. "Great idea. Here you go, Everley. Merry Christmas."

My sister rips the red wrapping paper off the gift in seconds. She has a white hat with a pom pom on top and a pair of matching mittens in her hands. "I love these! They are so pretty! Thank you, Mom."

"Don't thank me. Thank Mr. Bronson."

Everley puts the hat and mittens on and looks up at the ceiling and says, "Thank you, Mr. Bronson!" Mom and I look at each other and laugh.

Marcella goes next. She unwraps a pretty pink sweater.

She holds it up to herself and smiles. "Thank you, Mrs. Metty, I mean Mr. Bronson!"

Ed goes after that. He unwraps a best-selling book that I have wrapped a million times at Casswell's. "This looks like an interesting read, thank you!"

I snag the book when Ed isn't looking and read the back cover. It does sound good. "Hey, Ed, can I read this when you're done? I haven't read a good book in ages!"

Ed shrugs. "Sure."

Baldwin snags it from me and asks, "Can I read it when she's done?"

Ed chuckles. "Sure, I'll have to make a sign out sheet for it!"

Adamar goes next. He unwraps a red stylish shirt. It is the second time I've seen the corners of his mouth curl up into a smile since we crossed the border. I am so happy to see him happy that I throw my arms around him and say, "Merry Christmas, Adamar! I'm so glad you're my friend!" Baldwin claps him on the shoulder once I release him from our embrace. Everyone looks at him kindly or reaches out with empathy. Our depressed friend looks like he is barely tolerating the attention, but he needs it on a day like today.

I go next. I unwrap a long flowy black skirt that hides my legs without scratching them. "This will be perfect for work, thank you, Mom and Mr. Bronson!"

Gordon goes next and unwraps some leather winter

gloves. He puts them on and grins. "These will keep me warm when I leave work in the middle of the night! Thanks!"

Conrad goes next and unwraps a soft, red blanket. He looks at my mom who looks at him with eyes that know what terrible sleeping conditions he lives with. "Thank you so much, Mrs. Metty." He looks up at the ceiling like Everley did and says, "And thank you, Mr. Bronson!" That makes Everley laugh.

Baldwin goes next and unwraps a new pair of black men's business shoes. My jaw drops when I see them. This is the most valuable gift so far, but it is well-deserved and much needed. Baldwin's scruffy green sneakers are holey and falling apart. He picks the new shoes up and scrutinizes every inch of them before he says, "Thank you. I've never had shoes this nice before."

My mom looks at my boyfriend and says, "You are welcome from Mr. Bronson." It's nice to see Mom do something nice for my boyfriend. She holds up two remaining gifts and says, "We have two extra gifts, so I think we should all share them."

Conrad shakes his head. "No. You didn't get a gift, Mrs. Metty, so I think you should unwrap them and choose the one you like best for yourself."

My mom shakes her head. "Oh no. I chose the frying pan that we used for breakfast as my gift. I figured it was best to use it when we needed it instead of keeping it wrapped."

Baldwin nods at my mom. "That was very kind of you to share your gift this morning."

Conrad shakes his head again and touches my mom's arm. "No. The frying pan should be a shared gift, and you should get something just for you, Mrs. Metty."

I feel my head nodding and realize that almost everyone else is nodding too. Mom finally gives in and opens up the remaining gifts to reveal a foot massager and a giant box of chocolates. She shrugs and says, "I like the frying pan though. It's important for everyday use."

Conrad's eyebrows come together as he thinks. "You, Dandra, and Marcella made it so we could afford this apartment. You can keep the frying pan, but you get to keep something else just for you."

Mom shakes her head and closes her eyes. "It is not in my nature to take something for myself when I'm surrounded by kids who need more than I do."

Conrad takes my mom's hand and says, "You need things too, Mrs. Metty. I'm sure Mr. Bronson picked out many of these gifts with you in mind."

My mom looks at Conrad and says, "Okay. If you say so." She looks down at her calloused feet and says, "I feel so selfish, but I would like to keep the foot massager."

Ed bounces with glee. "Excellent choice! Now we can share these!" he declares as he opens the box of chocolates. He takes one and then passes the box around. Everley giggles with delight when it gets to her and picks out the biggest piece before passing the box on.

Baldwin clears his throat. "Conrad brought up a good point. We owe a lot to the girls who are probably wondering if they'll ever get their money back. I for one feel like Christmas is the best day to let them know how much we appreciate them. I say that you girls get to sit on the couch the rest of the day, and we'll make the Christmas dinner." He leads my mom to the couch and gets her feet set up in the foot massager.

Conrad looks at Baldwin sideways and says, "I agree with Baldwin's sentiment, and I'll add to that all the money that I still owe Dandra for my part of the apartment." He hands me the $36 he still owes me. I smile at my friend and hope that the rest of my $390 will start surfacing. Unfortunately, it doesn't. The rest of the boys just start cooking and don't say anything about the money they owe us. Conrad stands next to me. "Sorry about them. I tried to get the ball rolling."

I decide not to let my disappointment affect me. "It's okay. I'm sure they'll get it to us when they have it."

Conrad looks at my boyfriend who is busily giving out orders in the kitchen and then looks at me sheepishly. "I have one more thing I want to give you."

I can't believe that Conrad bought me more than the things he has already given me. "No, Conrad. You already gave me the scarf and the pancake. I didn't get anything for you."

Conrad doesn't miss a beat. "I didn't have enough to get

your coat back, but I will do that as soon as I can. Do you want to take a peek into my Casswell's bag?"

Obviously, I am still curious, but I don't have anything to give him. "Conrad, you are so sweet, but you also make me feel like a bad friend."

He squeezes my hand. "You are my best friend in the world—that's why I did it! I'm going to go get it." Conrad comes back with a red fluffy hat to match my scarf.

I wish I could scold him, but this hat is perfect. It's a Christmassy-red color, it probably didn't cost him too much, and it does match the scarf he gave me perfectly. I now have two things to wear in public that look respectable. "Thank you!" I squeeze his hand in appreciation. "You did a good job saving money for this apartment and still being the kind-hearted person that you are."

Conrad's face turns red at my compliment. "I thought you were going to be mad for a minute there."

I smirk. "I want to be mad at you, but I can't be mad at you for being yourself. I just wish I could give you something back."

His smile drops for a second. "There is one thing you could give me that doesn't cost a thing."

I'm not sure I'm ready to hear his answer, but I have to ask, "What is that?"

He looks at my lips for an uncomfortably long time. He seems to forget that we are in a crowded apartment with my mom, sister, and boyfriend looking over their shoulders at us.

One glare from Baldwin seems to bring him back to our current situation. "You know, I'd love a—hug."

I feel my held breath release. I can give him a hug. I can't help feeling that he deserves more. When I hug him, he holds me like he's never wanted anything more than this. It feels so— nice. Well, until I hear my boyfriend yell from the kitchen, "Hey, where's my Christmas hug?"

I let go of Conrad in an apologetic way and call to Baldwin, "It's on its way to you now!" Conrad looks sad as he watches me go, but then he picks up his new blanket and heads to his room.

I have to hand it to the guys. They know how to make a nice Christmas dinner. The ham is tender, the mashed potatoes are smooth, and the stuffing is flavorful. Even the corn from a can is the best I've ever had. Mrs. Abbot brings us—or Conrad—a Christmas cake in a disposable pan which comes in handy, and then she lends Conrad a couple of pots when he winks at her the way he does. I love seeing all nine of us filling our plastic plates heaping full without worry.

Once my mom decides to take a midafternoon nap, Baldwin takes me into his room. "I can't wait to give you your present."

I feel my heart skip a beat even though he really shouldn't

have. "We agreed not to get Christmas presents this year, didn't we?"

My boyfriend rubs the snake on his neck and then looks at his belongings in the corner of the room. "Yeah, but this one was free."

I look at the two-way radios in the box in the corner and hope that he is going to give me one, but he doesn't. He gives me something squarish wrapped in plastic bags. I unwrap it excitedly to discover a first aid kit. Baldwin winks at me. "They had us draw numbers for Christmas gifts at work, and this is what I got. I thought it might help you with your burns."

I take the white box from him and look through it quickly. It doesn't have any aloe or vinegar in it—the two things I really need. At least there are two pain pills in a little pouch. "Yeah, this is helpful. Thank you."

He hugs me and leads me to his bed on the floor. "I want to spend the last hour I have with you. Rocky is picking me up for work soon."

I am a bit miffed. "You are working on Christmas day?"

"Well, yeah. The news has to go out every day, and I'm one of the newest employees, so I have to take the shifts no one else wants."

"So there won't be anyone there but you and Rocky and an anchorman?"

"Pretty much," he says quietly.

I don't appreciate his vague choice of words. So, I just blurt out the question that is on my mind. "Is Josie working tonight?"

"Um, I think she might be."

I just nod my head and fold my arms across my chest. When he pulls one of my hands free, I look away. "Did you get Josie something for Christmas?"

He looks down at the ground. "Oh, not much."

My head snaps around. "What did you give her?"

"I told you I wouldn't spend any money on Christmas this year, and I didn't."

"But you gave her something."

He starts fiddling with the plastic bags my present was wrapped in. "The first aid kit I won came in a two-handled bag, and she liked the bag, so I gave it to her."

I try not to be mad about the free bag he gave Josie, but a bag would have been more personalized than a first aid kit. "I hope she liked it," I say without emotion.

"She seemed to, but enough about her. How has your first Christmas on the run been?"

I sigh as I think about all the things that made me smile today. There were quite a few. It really has been a good day despite the unfavorable turn our conversation just took. I can't help but smile. "It has been a surprisingly good Christmas. I really can't complain. We are in a safe place where Patrolman Darius won't find us. We have jobs and good food and presents, and each other." When I say those last words, Baldwin pulls me in for a long kiss. It is the longest kiss we've ever had. He is the same Baldwin as he was in Layland, but he's a little bit different too. Being here with him reminds me of our first date stargazing back in Layland. We were so lost in each moment with each other back then, and I finally feel that way again with him now. I forget how much time has passed until Adamar knocks on the door.

He barks, "Rocky is here to pick you up, B, and Mrs. Metty wants to talk to Dandra."

Baldwin bumps into my legs as he gets to his feet. I cringe but don't say anything. My boyfriend helps me to my feet and hugs me before he goes. "I hope your mom doesn't rush you guys into your own apartment too soon. I like sharing a place with you and having moments like this."

I smile and hold him as long as I can, but I know that this is too good to last, especially if my mom has noticed how long we've been in here together.

Chapter 18

IT'S CHRISTMAS NIGHT, AND WE SHOULD be playing checkers again and singing songs, but instead my mom marches me into our room and gives me an hour-long talking to about why I can't be in Baldwin's room alone with him. I swear I can hear Everley and Marcella snickering from the other side of the bedroom door. It feels so unfair.

I assure her that nothing happened, but she doesn't care what I have to say. I have angered momma bear. "Mom, he was just giving me my Christmas present."

"Do I dare ask what his hour-long present was?"

"He gave me a firstaid kit that he won at his work party."

Mom raises her eyebrows in amusement, but then growls, "I assume that isn't the only thing he gave you."

I know why she's looking at me like that, so I just admit, "He kissed me too. But that is all. He shares a room for crying out loud. What more do you think we would do?"

Mom looks into my eyes for a long time as if trying to read my mind. "I don't know because I don't know Baldwin very well. I hope you are telling me the truth."

"I am."

"Fine. Just don't pair off in his room and shut the door again. This is going to be a nonnegotiable rule until we get our own apartment. Are we understood?"

I turn my head to the wall and say, "Yes, Mom. Can I go play checkers now?"

Mom scowls and shakes her head. "No, I think you should go to bed early tonight. You need to rest, heal, and be ready for work in the morning."

I roll my eyes. This is so ridiculous. "Fine. Goodnight and Merry Christmas."

At least I get to take one more vinegar bath while under room-arrest. Marcella tries not to laugh at my frown when she comes to bed hours later. I try to send a "Merry Christmas" thought through the wall to my friends from my uncomfortable floor bed.

My eyes pop open the morning after Christmas, and I wish I could have more than one day off from work, but we can't go back to Shasta's apartment yet, and my mom wants us to get into our own apartment as soon as possible. She even goes downstairs to talk to Mrs. Abbot before breakfast. I hope my mom is less grouchy when she gets back. Mrs. Abbot tells Mom that she will have a two-bedroom apartment available in 10 days. Mom turns into a hard-nosed business woman the minute she gets back. She tells the anti-gamers at breakfast that they have 10 days to repay our money back to us. Conrad raises his eyebrows at me after she gives Baldwin and his friends the ultimatum.

He follows me to the couch as I put on my shoes. "I'm surprised that your mom is so grumpy this morning. She was so sweet and giving yesterday."

I feel my cheeks turning red. "I don't want to talk about it."

He whispers so only I can hear, "I'm pretty sure I got the gist of what she is feeling through the walls last night. Something about you being in Baldwin's room alone with him."

I scowl at my friend and say under my breath, "We only kissed. She's all worked up about nothing."

I see Conrad's shoulders visibly relax. "Well, I bet she's going to keep a closer eye on the two of you from now on."

I laugh humorlessly. "Yeah, that's a bet you can put money on."

The walk to work is less frosty than the conversation at breakfast, to my relief. We are greeted by Mr. Bronson at the door of Casswell's and shown our temporary registers and how to do returns. I never thought I would say this, but I miss wrapping presents. Dealing with grouchy customers who want their money back is way less fun and doesn't include tips.

I love this new twist to our jobs even less when a peace officer comes in to talk to Mr. Bronson. I feel like I am holding my breath the whole time the officer is in the office with our boss. I finally breathe again when Mr. Bronson tells us to go on our lunch break. Conrad uses his special way of talking to people as we follow Mr. Bronson to the break room. "What did that cranky officer want? Let me guess. Pictures of your employees?"

Our boss growls, "Yes. I told him that it is not my job to give him pictures of my employees, so if he wants them, he'll have to come here and take them himself."

Conrad looks at me cautiously and asks, "What did he say to that?"

Mr. Bronson snorts, "He was not happy, but he said he would return tomorrow to take the pictures."

Conrad shoots a worried glance at me before he turns the charm back on for our boss. "If he wants to waste his time harassing good workers like us, then he deserves the disappointment he'll get when he finds nothing to report."

"That's basically what I said to him, but he insisted that he has to do his job."

We sit down next to Mom in the break room and tell her the bad news as we eat our lunches. Mom thinks we should stay home tomorrow, but I'm not sure that Mr. Bronson will let all of us do that.

When our shift is done, I feel my heart beat harder and faster as we go to clock out. Mr. Bronson is doing a crossword puzzle and having another cup of coffee in the break room next to the time clock. He looks up as we walk by. "How did you like returns?"

I grimace and say, "They aren't as fun as wrapping gifts, that's for sure."

He chuckles and winks at my mom. "I'm glad you pushed through it anyway. I probably won't need all of you tomorrow. I'll need one of you on the register and one restocking, but one of you can stay home if you'd like."

I look at my mom and try to think of how to respond to this, knowing that a peace officer is taking pictures of all employees tomorrow. My mom knows exactly what to say. "My younger daughter was hoping that we could take her sledding. Would it be possible for both Dani and me to get off work tomorrow?" My mom looks into Mr. Bronson's eyes and says,

"We just need one more day with family before school starts again. We will be back here and ready to go the next day."

Mr. Bronson rubs his temples with his fingers and takes a sip of coffee before he answers. "I suppose it won't hurt anything to wait a day to restock the returned items. "Go ahead and enjoy your day off!"

We leave happier than we were a few hours ago, but I'm still worried for Conrad. He is the main person that Patrolman Darius has been assigned to find and bring back to his father. I ask the question we're all thinking as we walk home. "What is Conrad going to do about the pictures?"

My mom looks at him and says, "We'll have to try everything we can think of tonight to make him look unrecognizable for his photo."

Chapter 19

WE SPEND THE WHOLE EVENING in our lavatory with Conrad trying different things to make him look different. His hat and glasses help quite a bit, but on closer inspection, Patrolman Darius might want a closer look at him. We decide to shave his head and put coal dust under his eyes to make him look like he has unhealthy addictions. It's not a perfect solution, but it's the best we can do. I feel a pang of sadness when I sweep his black locks of hair into the trash for some reason.

Marcella gets home late with a messed up walnut carrot cake from the bakery for us. When she offers Conrad a piece, he declines it. "I can't have walnuts. They make my tongue and cheeks swell up like a balloon."

I almost laugh at how great that news is. "Conrad, if you eat this right before your pictures, your cheeks and jaw will change shape! That is the perfect way to disguise you!"

"But what do I do afterward? You know, when I can't talk to customers with my swollen tongue?"

I suddenly remember something I saw in my first aid kit. There are allergy pills and an allergy gel in there. I'm sure of it. I pull out the kit and hand them to Conrad. "If these don't work, tell Mr. Bronson that you need to go to the doctor. I'm sure he'll let you leave."

Conrad takes them from me and pretends to smile. "I hope this works."

Baldwin puts his arm around me and says to my friend, "It will work if you make it work. Show us how determined you are to stay here."

Conrad glares at my boyfriend and says, "I'll be fine. I don't need your advice."

I worry about my friend as I watch him spin around and march to the boys' lavatory, slamming the door as he goes.

Baldwin growls, "He and I are never going to be friends."

I look at him curiously and ask, "Why?"

He pulls me closer and pushes a piece of hair behind my ear. "Because of you, obviously." He leans in and kisses me until my mom clears her throat behind us.

I try to be excited and playful for my sister's sake when we go sledding at a nearby hill. I thought my mom was just making up a story when she asked for the day off yesterday, but she tries to always tell the truth, so we go sledding, without sleds.

I forget how lucky I am to have parents who remember the days before the gaming district. They used to go sledding all the time in the winter back in Layland. I never saw anyone my age doing it, but we always did. I didn't think it was possible to sled without, you know, a sled, but my mom surprises me once again.

She makes sure we have double layers of clothes on and our hats and scarves and Everley's mittens snugly in place, and then she makes us sleds out of cardboard, tape, and plastic bags. They work surprisingly well once we have an established sledding track down the hill. We try to set records for going further each time. When Everley and I go together, we go the farthest. When Mom joins us, we usually start spinning in circles and don't go as far. Everley notices how quiet I am as we trudge through the snow back to our apartment. "What's wrong, Dandra?"

I smile at her and say, "Nothing. I just hope Conrad's picture goes okay today." I am literally waiting on pins and needles until the *creak* of the door announces his arrival.

His face is still slightly swollen. I immediately bombard

him with questions. "How did it go? Did they suspect you? Did you go to the doctor?"

Conrad looks at my worried face and declares, "I think we're okay. The peace officer looked at me funny while he was taking my picture, but he didn't ask me any questions."

I am dying of curiosity. "Did the allergy pill and gel work? How did it feel? How do you feel now?"

He goes into the lavatory and looks in the mirror at his face. He touches his jaw and looks at his tongue. "I took the pills and rubbed the gel on the inside and outside of my mouth as soon as the picture was taken. I couldn't talk for a full 30 minutes after my picture, so I asked if I could go on my lunch break early." Conrad rubs a bit more allergy gel on his jaw. "I could feel the pills and gel loosening my tight face as I started back to work. I purposely chose the farthest register from the line, so I'd have the least customers to talk to."

I surprise myself by hugging him. I was truly worried that he would get found out. I suppose he might still get found out if Patrolman Darius recognizes him in his photograph. Looking at him now, I feel pretty confident that his picture will be unrecognizable.

Mom makes fried potatoes and ham for dinner tonight, and the anti-gamers really like it. Some money even gets turned in to us. After dinner Mom counts what we are given and what more we will need once it is all paid back.

She says excitedly, "We will need $2000 for the first and

last month's rent for our apartment. We were owed $450 for me plus $300 for Marcella plus $390 for you, Dandra. Out of the $1140 we are owed, $540 was paid back today. So once we have the last $600 paid back to us, we will only need $860 more."

I think of the black sock in my backpack that has $120 in it from Conrad paying me back and my tips from my last days as a gift wrapper. Mom and I will get paid again before the 10 days are up. We should have the money we need in time. It's nice to see Mom in a good mood again.

I find out that I like restocking shelves better than talking to grouchy customers with returns. Whenever I'm given the choice of what to do, I choose shelves. Mom doesn't mind either job, but Conrad likes interacting with the customers. He has a gift with people that I don't think I could even pretend to have.

The money we are owed keeps trickling in over the next week. Ernestine is released from the detainment center, but her house is still being watched sporadically throughout the day and so is Shasta's. Mom gathers all of us girls together to discuss how safe we feel about going back to Shasta's. Mom lists the pros and cons for us. "Shasta has more furniture and food, but her house gets checked on every hour or two throughout the day. If we don't memorize their patrolling schedule, we'll get caught. If we stay here until we get our own apartment, we will keep sleeping on the floor and cooking our meager food out of our meager pans, but we won't be watched."

Marcella mumbles, "I don't see what's so bad about staying here until our apartment is ready."

Everley agrees with her. "I miss my friends at Shasta's house, but Conrad and Ed and everyone are our friends too."

Mom insists that we put it to a vote, and it's no surprise that my mom votes that we go back to Shasta's. It's also no surprise that Marcella votes that we stay with the anti-gamers. Everley looks at me and says, "How are you going to vote, Dandra? I want to vote with you."

I know that my mom won't be thrilled, but I feel safe here. I explain my reasoning as I vote. "This apartment complex was already searched. It is not on an hourly surveillance like Shasta's house is, and I like being in the same place as Baldwin. I vote to stay here." Everley votes the same way I do.

Mom isn't happy, but she isn't angry either. She is the adult here, and she could override my vote, but I think she's resigned to the fact that we are better off here. The good news is that life in the apartment is getting a bit more comfortable. The anti-gamers are used to finding things for free or in the trash, so we soon have a couple of single wide beds, several lumpy mattresses, a scarred up, but functional table, and some chipped, but working dishes.

I am in shock when the boys vote unanimously to put the two twin beds in our room for Marcella and me to sleep on. Our bedroom is by far the biggest in the apartment, but with a queen size bed against one wall and two twin-sized beds against the other wall, there isn't much room to walk around.

I complain to Baldwin about it. "It isn't fair that we have all the beds. You should put one bed in each bedroom."

He gives me a knowing look and shakes his head. "But then how do we decide who gets the bed and who gets the floor? It will save us a lot of headache to give them all to you girls. Besides, I couldn't live with myself if I was sleeping on a bed, and you were sleeping on the floor in the room next door. I know Gordon feels the same way about Marcella."

I frown. "I can see what you mean, but I still don't like it." Something Baldwin said suddenly jolts me awake. "Are Gordon and Marcella together?"

Baldwin looks at me like I'm slow in the head. "They haven't made it official, but they definitely like each other."

I feel like an idiot. I've been sharing a room with Marcella for weeks, but I've been so preoccupied with my own problems that I haven't noticed what is going on with her. I should be a better roommate.

Our jobs are changing yet again with the new year, so Mr. Bronson asks Mom to take several boxes of clothes and curtains that haven't sold all year to a local charity to make room for next year's inventory. He even asks her to use his fancy car to do it. She agrees to do it but takes the clothes and curtains to our apartment instead. There are enough curtains to cover all of the windows of this apartment and most of the ones in the future girl apartment too.

Mom sighs with satisfaction when all of the windows have new curtains hanging over them. "Privacy is a good thing for us," she says as she drinks some hot apple cider that Marcella made after work. "I just wish we were in our own apartment with privacy from the world and—the boys." She gives Baldwin the stink eye when he squeezes my arm as he walks by.

Chapter 20

MY MOM GETS HER WISH sooner than later. I really just want to put up my feet and rest after work, but Shasta stops by to tell us that Mrs. Abbot called her to let us know that apartment 113 will be available tomorrow. This news puts my mom into a preparedness frenzy. She pesters the anti-gamers until she gets every last dollar we're owed from them and starts making a list of what we can bring with us from this apartment, and what we still need to buy or scrounge for free. Mrs. Abbot said that the previous tenants left a table with four chairs and an oversized armchair that she was hoping the boys could haul off.

We of course, want to keep them, and the boys agree to let us have all of the beds from this apartment.

Mom leaves for the frugality store down the street after she makes her list. It's a store that sells used items for cheap. Everley goes with her. I wish it wasn't dark so early or so slick. My legs are killing me after standing all day at work, so I don't go with them. I'm glad she is excited and has a purpose, but I'm worried about how we're going to show Mrs. Abbot IDs for the apartment tomorrow.

Mom comes back from the frugality store with five pots and three pans, a set of dishes, three blankets, and two pillows. I'm not sure how the two of them carried it all. Mom looks at me excitedly. "I bought a couch as well! They put a sold sign on it for me and said we could pick it up tomorrow. It was the cheapest one there, and not much prettier than that green monster over there," she says as she points to the green couch that came with this apartment, "but it is a whole lot better than sitting on the ground."

Everley pulls a blanket out of the bag she brought in and says, "The couch is striped red and green like Christmas, and Mom says we are going to share the pots and pans with the boys."

Ed looks at the pots and pans my mom is unloading from her bags and frowns. "I could get you guys stuff like this for free."

My mom looks at him skeptically. "It was dollar day at the

frugality store. You can't get household things much cheaper than this. Besides, I doubt that the primary school throws out couches, pans, and bedding on a regular basis."

Ed shrugs. "Maybe not these things, but they throw out useful things all the time, and my janitor friend cleans for a hotel on the weekends, so he gets thrown out bedding and furniture quite often."

I am glad that the boys have a way to replace all the things that we are taking with us. I encourage Ed to keep his eyes and ears peeled. "This friend of yours is a good connection to have. Let him know that you guys could use practically anything he can give you for free, especially beds." I feel terrible that not one guy has a bed in this apartment. They gave Adamar the extra mattress they found for free, but that's it.

My Everley-style alarm clock goes off way too early for my liking. "Get up, Dandra! We're moving today!" Mom is so happy that I'm afraid that the boys will be insulted by her unnaturally peppy ear-to-ear grin. She made sure we packed as much as we could last night and placed the $2000 we need for our first and last month's rent in an envelope. The boys promise to help us move the furniture once we get our keys. We won't be able to move much this morning ourselves because we still have to go to work.

As I shove all of the toiletries I just used in my scruffy backpack, I ask Mom, "Who is going to watch Everley while we're at work?"

Mom looks sullen for a minute. "Well, Marcella can."

"Yeah, but not all the time. What about when Marcella is working?"

"She is ten, Dandra. She can take care of herself when she's not at school."

I scoff, "But we haven't signed her up for school. Who is going to watch her tomorrow?"

Mom's peppiness goes down a notch. "I—I guess we may still need the boys' help after all."

I'm glad Mom is acknowledging this; I put my hand on her arm. "We will have to help each other if we want to survive in this country, Mom."

She nods. "I know, but it's time I took a day off and signed Everley up for school. I should also start tutoring if I can find any students."

I start to feel anxious with this to-do list. "Yes, but let's not get ahead of ourselves. What are we going to do about showing ID for the apartment?"

Mom purses her lips together and says quietly, "I have a plan. I don't feel good about it, but it's the only way I know how to make this work."

I have never seen my mom look so devious before. "Do we need Conrad to come with us to sweet talk her?"

Mom shakes her head slowly and pulls out her worn wallet. "I asked Mrs. Abbot how many IDs she needed to see since you, Marcella, and Everley are still school age, and she said that only I needed to show ID."

I look at her wallet knowing full well that the only ID in there is from Layland and will get us locked up for being wanted refugees. "What ID are you going to show her?"

Mom pulls a United Cities ID out of her wallet and hands it to me. It is of a lady about the same age as my mom and has bright blonde hair like my mom. That is where the similarities end. This woman wears more makeup and looks like someone just ran over her favorite cat. I look at my mom questioningly. She lowers her eyes to the ground and says, "This customer brought back returns yesterday, and I couldn't help noticing that she kind of looked like me. I asked to see her ID even though she had a receipt and her payment method. I kept her talking and distracted, and I didn't give this back to her."

I am shocked that my sweet, honest mother did this, but I am grateful all the same. "I'm sure she'll notice that it is missing and come to Casswell's for it today."

"I know. I just need it long enough for Mrs. Abbot to make a copy. It's time to do that right now. Will you come with me?"

I laugh humorlessly. "Yes. Everley can bring her support, too. You're a good mom. You did what you had to do. The lady will never know what we used this for. Just be sure to sign the rent agreement with this name."

Mom looks down at the ID and says, "I guess I'm Linda Greenway at the apartment and Laura Moore at work. Make sure I remember that. In fact, I better write that down." She pulls a piece of paper and a pencil out of her bag and does so.

Conrad knocks on our partially open door as he peeks in and says, "I overheard your plan. Maybe I should do the same thing, so I can show Mrs. Abbot ID."

Mom closes her eyes and sighs. "Wait till we see how my attempt goes first."

Conrad shrugs and says, "Why don't I come with you?" I nod, glad he offered. Any distraction we can get will only help us. He continues, "I'll come in as soon as you start signing papers." I think it is better to not show up at the same time. We don't want Mrs. Abbot to know that we've been living with the guys all this time.

Mom, Everley, and I hold hands and make the cold walk down to the apartment office area together. We let go of hands when we see our faces on a "Wanted Persons" poster on the office door. Mom gasps and freezes.

She finally unfreezes and looks at me. When I shrug, she turns to Everley, "Go back to the boys' apartment and wait there for us." Everley nods and runs back the way we came. Mom turns to me and says, "Don't look her in the eye if you can help it. We—we can't turn back now. We have to do this." I nod bravely and follow her lead. The bell jingles when we shut the door. "Hello, Mrs. Abbot, how are you this morning?" Mom asks our landlady as we approach her desk.

Mrs. Abbot looks up at us and pops a piece of candy from the bowl on her desk into her mouth before saying, "Well enough, how about yourself?"

Mom's smile is happy but nervous. "We've been looking forward to this day for weeks, do you have the papers and keys ready for us?"

Mrs. Abbot walks to a filing cabinet behind her desk and says, "Yes I do." She plops a file folder on the desk in front of us that is labeled, "Shasta's Complex Friends." She glances at our feet. Did Shasta drop you off? Where are your things?"

Mom gulps and says, "Oh, yes. She dropped us and one load of belongings off at apartment 113 and is going back for another load. Marcy is outside watching our things."

Mrs. Abbot's eyebrows come together suspiciously, but she opens the folder and pulls out a couple of keys that have 113 engraved on them. "John and his friends agreed to haul off the extra furniture that was left behind, so don't worry about that."

Mom smiles nervously. "Con...John is so helpful, and he promised to help us move in today." Mom takes the piece of paper that Mrs. Abbot hands to her. She pauses before signing the fake name found on the borrowed ID. I worry for a second that she has already forgotten the name she's supposed to use. "There you go, Mrs. Abbot. Here is our first and last month's rent." Mom's hands shake slightly as she extends the thick envelope filled with cash to our landlady. "Can I send my daughter out with a key to start moving our things in?" Mom moves her hand toward the keys.

Mrs. Abbot stops her from touching the keys with her own hand. "Not so fast. I have learned from my mistake with John and his friends that I need to get copies of the IDs before I hand out keys. They still haven't come back to take care of that for their own apartment."

As if on cue, Conrad walks in the door like he owns the place. "Hello, Mrs. Abbot, my favorite landlady! How would you like to taste the best hot apple cider in the world? My roommate just made this, and it is to die for!"

Mrs. Abbot smiles as Conrad hands her a chipped mug full of Marcella's cider. "I'm making copies of IDs right now, John. Where is your's?"

Mom pulls out the stolen ID, and Conrad takes it and hands it to Mrs. Abbot. "I don't have it on me at the moment, but I will bring it by after work. It's looking like a busy day for me what with all the furniture you need me to haul out of apartment 113, and the furniture I'm moving in for my friends here, and shoveling the sidewalk once this snow stops so you don't slip…"

Mrs. Abbot listens to Conrad as she makes a copy of the fake id for her file. She looks at the card and pauses for a second longer than is comfortable before she hands the ID back. "I appreciate your help, young man, but I still need a copy of your

ID. Stop keeping me waiting." She hands the keys to Mom and says, "That's all I need. Be careful moving everything in on these slick sidewalks." She then turns to Conrad and says, "I'll see you after work."

Conrad gives her one more dashing smile and says, "Wouldn't miss it for the world! Come on ladies, let's get you moved in!"

We leave the office quietly, but as soon as we are outside, I ask, "What are you going to do about the ID you promised her after work?"

Conrad waves me off. "I will be such a good little helper today that she won't remember that I didn't give her my ID yet."

"You won't be able to distract her forever, you know."

"I know, but I have to keep trying." We all shudder as we pass the wanted poster. If those are posted all over the city, our lives are about to get harder than they already are.

Our apartment is on the first floor of the building, so we don't have to go up any stairs to find our new front door. Mom is positively trembling with excitement as she turns the key in the lock. Everley bursts in as soon as the door is open. She twirls around and around the living room/kitchen area. The apartment looks similar to the boys' apartment except the master bedroom is slightly smaller on one side of the living room and there is only one bedroom and a lavatory on the other side of the living room/kitchen area which is a bit smaller as well. Everley sets her box of belongings and backpack on the left-behind table and collapses into one of the kitchen chairs. "I like this place already!"

Everley's enthusiasm makes my mom laugh. Her thrill at being away from the boys is obvious. We all run upstairs and grab boxes to take down. Marcella straps on her backpack and grabs a box. It doesn't take very long to move our few boxes and bags of belongings into our new apartment. I plop down into the oversized brown armchair that was left behind. It is a bit worn, but it is pretty comfortable. We should definitely keep it. We can hear Gordon and Baldwin's grunts and groans as they carry one of the twin bed frames down the stairs. They are careful not to scratch the walls and the doorframe as they bring it into apartment 113. I give Baldwin a kiss when he sets it down in my new room.

Gordon clears his throat. "We should get this set up before Ed and Adamar show up with the other bed frame." I step out of the way and watch them work.

It only takes the two guys a minute to get the bed frame put together and positioned correctly. We squeeze into the corner of the room as Ed and Adamar come through with the next bed frame. My mom helps Conrad bring down the mattress for my bed. She keeps looking at her watch. She probably wishes she had asked for the day off, but she didn't, so we have to get to work.

Conrad sees the longing in Mom's eyes as she flutters

around the apartment and says, "Should I tell Mr. Bronson that you aren't feeling well today?"

Mom sighs as she looks around at everything that needs to be done, but she shakes her head. "No, I don't want to lie to him. I may see if he will let me leave early though. I would like to be home by the time Marcella leaves for work."

Conrad nods. "Okay, if that's the case, we better get going."

Mom looks around the apartment frantically for a second, and then pockets her key and says, "Thank you for bringing these beds in for us. Are you willing to bring down the queen bed and maybe the couch from the frugality store down the street?"

Gordon and Marcella squeeze by with the second twin mattress as Mom looks at Baldwin with a pleading gaze. Baldwin nods at her and says, "Gordon and I can get one thing and Ed and Adamar can get the other. Which one do you prefer, Adamar?"

"The bed of course. It's a much shorter distance."

Baldwin rolls his eyes. "Okay, Gordon and I will go get the couch. Meet you guys back here in half an hour." He gives me a quick hug and says, "Have a good day at work; we'll get the big things moved in for you and I'll check in on you after dinner tonight."

I hug him tighter than he hugs me and give him a quick peck on the lips. "Thank you!" I pull away and look at everyone else in their shabby coats and gloves. "Thank you, everyone.

Especially you, Marcella." She is putting our dishes and pans away in the cupboards while the rest of us are talking. "Leave a few things for me to put away after work!"

Marcella agrees and shows Everley where to put the plates Mom bought at the frugality store. She waves me off and says, "There will be plenty to do when you get back. See you later!"

Mom, Conrad, and I say a quick goodbye and head to Casswell's. I hope the drivers are careful on the ice today, I'm so distracted, I might get hit. Conrad keeps looking at me while we walk to work. "Are you okay?"

I nod distractedly. "Yeah. I'm sure this will be good thing."

He reaches out and squeezes my hand. "I'll help you get everything the way you want it after work."

I squeeze his hand back and then use that same hand to adjust my hat and scarf. "Thanks, we'll be fine. I'm more worried about you and Baldwin. You won't have any females to keep you two in line."

Conrad chuckles. "I get my own room today. Things should get better for me too."

Chapter 21

WHEN WE GET TO CASSWELL'S, WE FREEZE
as our own faces greet us at the front door, on a wanted poster.
Conrad tells us to act normal as we walk in. The store is
unusually empty. I look at my mom and know that she wishes
she had stayed home. After we clock in, Mr. Bronson gives
us our orders. "John, I want you on the return registers with
Lupe, and I want one of you to restock everything that came in
last night, and one of you to start organizing and planning the
clothing displays for the New Year with Shelly."

Mom decides now is a good time to remind Mr. Bronson

that she isn't going to work here anymore since school is starting again. "Mr. Bronson, I would like to do the restocking today since my time here is about done. I have another job when school is in session."

Mr. Bronson looks saddened by this news. "I forgot about that. I'm so used to having you here, Laura. Unfortunately, the restocking is drying up fast. I may not need you for the whole day today." He gestures around the mostly-empty store with one hand.

Mom nods understandingly. "That is actually good news for me. I have so much to do at home right now. We're reorganizing and redecorating, so I would appreciate some extra time at home today."

Mr. Bronson looks at Mom miserably and says, "Will you come back tomorrow? Or will this be your last day?"

Mom looks at the empty store briefly and says, "I don't think you need me anymore this season, so today should be my last day." Mr. Bronson's face droops. She continues, "I'd like to come back on my next break from school if you have an opening, though."

Mr. Bronson takes Mom's hand and says, "Of course you are welcome back any time. I'll make sure I save something for you to do every summer and every Christmas. You can count on that."

Mom sighs with relief. "I will look forward to it. Thank you."

Mr. Bronson sighs too, but not with relief, more like sadness. "It won't be the same around here without you. I'm already counting down the days until summer break!" That makes Mom laugh. Mr. Bronson looks at the two of us listening in and says, "Don't worry about these two. I'll keep an eye on them when you're not here. I'll even chaperone them on the way home today if you want me to."

Mom waves his comment off. "They are just friends. They don't need a chaperone, but thank you."

Mr. Bronson and Conrad exchange a look that I can't decipher. Mr. Bronson looks at his watch. "Time is ticking by quickly; let's get to work, shall we?" Mom slips the borrowed ID to Conrad when our boss' back is turned and heads to the restock area.

I haven't had to work with Shelly very much, but for a middle-aged woman who wears too much makeup and takes too many smoke breaks, she has some very creative ideas about the new clothing displays for the new year. She puts me to work setting up racks of clothing by the combinations she thinks look best together. I'm supposed to put six of each size of each item on each rack. A shirt style with a coordinating pants style goes on one side of the rack, and a different shirt with a different coordinating pants style goes on the other side of the rack. I have to locate a lot of boxes in the warehouse with varying amounts of dust on them and then hang the contents on the racks without getting them dusty. It's a brainless job, and

I appreciate that. It reminds me of wiping down dusty shelves at the Tifton Library to be honest. I smile at that thought.

The mindlessness of my movements comes to a complete stop when I see a familiar black jacket covered in Layland insignia entering the warehouse. My heart starts pounding. What is Patrolman Darius doing here? I hide behind the rack of clothes I'm working on and listen to him talk to Shelly once she gets back from her smoke break. His voice is just as forceful and creepy as ever. "Hello, there. What is your name?"

Shelly sounds almost as nervous as I feel. "M-my name is Sh-Shelly Cray."

"There's no need to be nervous, Shelly. I just have a few questions for you."

"Okay."

"I am looking for some people who snuck into this country illegally."

"I-I was born in this country. Illegal is a word I try to stay away from, sir," Shelly says while shoving something deep into her coat pocket.

He looks at the hand in her pocket suspiciously but doesn't let that distract him from his mission. "When did you start working here?"

She eyes the GameCom on his arm as she says, "Three weeks before Christmas."

Darius scribbles something down on his notepad. "That

is about the time that the wanted individuals snuck across the border."

Shelly's hand shakes as she pushes her brittle, overly-dyed red hair behind her ears. "I told you. I was born in this country, in the hospital on 32nd Street as a matter of fact."

Darius looks up from his notepad. "I believe you, but did anyone else start working here near the same time you did? Someone suspicious maybe?" Oh, no. Shelly is about to give us away.

Shelly looks confused as she says, "Well, Lupe started working here the day before I did, and then John, Dani, and Laura started working here the day after me."

Darius keeps scribbling in his notebook. "Do any of them seem suspicious to you? Like they don't belong in this country?"

Shelly looks like she would say or do anything to make Darius go away. "Well, now that you mention it, Laura is always looking at me in a shifty way when I go outside for a smoke. I think she might be a suspicious person."

"What is so suspicious about her?"

Shelly twirls a piece of hair around her finger and says, "There is something in her eyes that just bothers me. I don't know how else to describe it."

Darius finishes writing in his notebook and slips it into his pocket. "Thank you for the tip. I will look into your suspicions."

I choke back a sob as my frustration at Shelly burns inside. She was starting to grow on me, and now she has put my least-favorite person in the world on our trail. I watch through the clothing rack as Patrolman Darius goes into the office from the warehouse side. The door is open a crack, so I sneak over there to listen. I hear Darius say to the office secretary, "Let me see all the paperwork on your employee named Laura."

"I need a last name, sir. Laura who?"

Darius isn't very patient with her. "I don't know her last name, but she started working here less than a month ago and her name is Laura."

The secretary fumbles around in a filing cabinet for a while and says, "This is all I have on her." She reads through the two papers in the file and says, "She was hired for temporary Christmas work. She asked to be paid weekly in cash. She did not give us a phone number, but this is her address."

"Is she working today?"

"I believe so, but if I am not mistaken, I was just told this morning that today would be her last day. I'm not sure if they had a full schedule for her today or not, but since sales are at a record-low, probably not."

Patrolman Darius growls, "Write this address down for me. I'll be back to get it. I need to talk to Mr. Bronson."

I quickly sprint back to my clothing racks and start opening boxes. Shelly startles me when she comes around the rack to talk to me. "Where have you been, Dani?"

I have to think fast. "I was—taking a smoke break."

Shelly narrows her eyes at me. "I didn't know you smoke."

I look down at my feet. "I just started. It—calms my nerves."

Shelly pulls a pack of cigarettes out of her pocket and takes one out of the box. She runs it along her nose and breathes it in. "I remember being there myself, kid." She puts it back in the box and shakes her head. "It's a hard habit to break. I think you should think twice about this. You don't want to be broke and have lungs as black as coal, do you?"

"No, I guess not."

"Then find another way to calm your nerves. I don't want to hear you talk about this again. Do you hear me?"

I nod obediently. "Yeah, I understand." Shelly starts walking away. I call out to her, "Where are you going?"

She doesn't turn around as she says, "To take a smoke break."

"What? But you said..."

Shelly shakes a manicured finger at me. "Do as I say, not as I do, kid."

I wait for the outside door to close behind Shelly. I have eight minutes before she notices that I'm missing. I run silently to Mr. Bronson's office and listen through the wooden door. I can hear both men raising their voices at each other. Patrolman Darius says, "You never got a picture of her like you were told to, and right when I'm here to question her, you let her quit?"

Mr. Bronson retaliates, "She was hired for temporary Christmas work. Christmas is over. There was nothing more for her to do today or tomorrow or the next day. What do you expect me to do? I am a business man. I can't pay people to sit around here waiting for you to interrogate them."

"It seems like you are protecting her."

My boss bristles. "I try to protect all Casswell's employees from unneeded harassment. She was a fine employee who wouldn't hurt a fly. If you want to spend your day hunting her down, you will have to do that without my help."

"Mr. Bronson, I have not had this kind of resistance from any other businesses in town. It makes you and your employees seem awfully suspicious."

"I run the largest and most respectable department store in all of Herrington, Mr. Darius. Senator Brock Hamble himself bought two trucks full of Christmas presents here a few weeks ago. Do you see this list?" Mr. Bronson holds up a two-page list and goes on to say, "I have to do all of these things every day to make the four levels of this department store run as they should. Interrogating my employees about where they come from and where they are going next is not on my list." My boss shakes the list at Patrolman Darius. "Please allow me to do my job, and I will allow you to do yours. Feel free to interrogate any employee here today, or chase down Laura Moore as she walks home, but leave me out of it."

Darius bristles. "Maybe I will chase her down. One of the few pathetic things you have on your records is her address. I'll just collect that from your secretary and be on my way." I hear heavy footsteps coming toward the door. I think my eight minutes are up.

I feel my heart beating in my throat as I sprint to my clothing racks. Darius goes into the office for just a few minutes before marching out the side door. I rip boxes open with a vengeance and hang the contents up with the same forceful energy. Shelly comes back from her smoke break and stops me from putting too many things on the same rack. I've lost count for some reason. Mr. Bronson walks towards me with a newspaper pinned between his arm and his body. "Dani, can I have a word with you in my office?"

Chapter 22

I TRY TO LOOK CALM. "Uh, sure, sir." I walk with
him to his office and sit down in the proffered seat. "What is
this about, sir?"

Mr. Bronson frowns at me for a second and says, "Sorry.
I just had an irritating conversation, but it has nothing to do
with what I need to talk to you about." He looks at the paper list
I saw him waving at Darius and says, "I, uh, just wanted to find
out what kind of schedule you want to work since school starts
tomorrow."

I feel my tense body relaxing. "I was hoping to work less—maybe every other evening after school?"

Mr. Bronson nods and looks at his computer screen. "That will work. John wants to do something similar. Do you want to work the same days as him, or on opposite days?"

I don't really care, but I know Conrad likes working at the same time as me, so I say, "The same days if possible."

Mr. Bronson looks at me for a second and then back to his computer screen. "Oh, okay. He asked for the same days as you, but I just wanted to make sure that is okay with you. Your mom made it sound like you two weren't as interested in each other as I thought you were."

I stammer to say anything. "I-I like Con-John very much, but we are just friends. I actually have a different boyfriend."

Mr. Bronson nods. "I know. I've had many late-night chats with John about you."

I feel my eyebrows coming together. "You have?"

"Yes. Does that surprise you?"

I frown slightly. "Well, yes. He knows that I have always just wanted to be friends."

Mr. Bronson's eyes keep moving from my face to his computer screen. "You're right. He knows that. I may have just misunderstood your feelings. You seem to enjoy his company quite a bit."

I shrug. "I do. He has always been my closest friend, or

almost always. Anyway, I do want to work with him, and that's all I have to say about that."

Mr. Bronson clicks something on his computer and then turns to face me. "Okay. I will make that happen." He waits a second and says, "Before you go, please look out for your mom for me. I'm afraid she may have some trouble headed her way."

I try to play dumb. "Oh, what kind of trouble?"

Mr. Bronson throws up his hands in frustration. "They are still looking for the Layland refugees, and the officer who was in here today got a tip that your mom is a suspicious person. He must have absolutely no leads on this case because he wants to investigate her." Mr. Bronson shakes his head and takes a sip of coffee. "She left once she had all the returns restocked, so he wasn't happy about that, and I told him that today was her last day. He wasn't happy about that either. I've done all I can to keep him away from her, but he has your address from her file, so he is probably on his way there now."

I am glad that our address on file is Shasta's house, and not the apartment building, but I feel terrible that Shasta is about to be interrogated. At least she is used to having her house watched by now. I try to keep my face calm and say, "What a silly inconvenience. Hopefully he doesn't take up too much of her day."

My boss looks exhausted. "I hope not. Would you like to go on break now? The lunch rush is over, and the store is pretty dead right now."

"Sure, thank you, Mr. Bronson, and thank you for standing up for my mom."

"No problem, kid. Have a good break."

When I get to the break room, I see Conrad reading a discarded newspaper at our usual table. His face looks swollen, like he ate a walnut. He points to our pictures on the front page and frowns. "Did you see Patrolman Darius when he was here?"

I roll my eyes in frustration. "Yep."

Conrad lowers his voice. "Did you talk to him?"

I lean closer to him and say quietly, "No, but Shelly did, and she stuck him on my mom's trail."

He sighs with relief. "We're lucky he went after your mom instead of us. She left over an hour ago."

"What happened to your face?"

Conrad scowls and runs his fingers over his bulging jaw. "I took a couple of walnuts off the cake Marcella gave me and put them in my coat pocket just in case. When Darius came in the door, I thought he was here for me, so I popped a lint-covered walnut in my mouth."

I raise my eyebrows and unwrap my sandwich. "Good thinking! Did you talk to him?"

Conrad glares at his food. "Yep. He made the rounds of the store, looking through a stack of pictures as he walked and then got in my returns line. He said that my picture looked suspicious, so he came to look at me in person."

Fear grips me around the throat. "Were you swollen by

then? He may have recognized your voice even if he didn't recognize your face."

"I was definitely swollen. I spoke with a high-pitched accent, kind of like Lupe's, except slurry from my swollen tongue. Anyway, he asked me when I started here and if I thought any other employees were acting suspiciously. I didn't give anything away, but he didn't look impressed with me."

"Do you still have the allergy pills and gel?"

"I took all of the pills last time, but I still have some gel. It is slowly working. I can talk at least."

I swallow a bite of sandwich and say, "Mr. Bronson said Patrolman Darius probably went to Shasta's house. What if he comes back here when he doesn't find her?"

"Does he know you are her daughter?"

I shake my head. "No."

Conrad looks around the almost empty break room. "The store is dead today. I've only had five customers at my returns register. Maybe we should ask to go home early?"

I have had a bad feeling in my gut ever since I laid eyes on Patrolman Darius today. I was lucky enough to hide from him once, but I worry about him coming back. "Yeah, I think that's a good idea, just in case he comes back."

When we enter Mr. Bronson's office, I see our pictures staring up at me from the front page of his newspaper again. Conrad sees it too. He looks at me in a way that says, do something about that. He keeps our boss talking while I figure out what to do. He clears his throat. "Mr. Bronson, I can't believe how empty the store is today. Can you?"

I see a bottle of Casswell's Christmas Cream on Mr. Bronson's desk. I've wrapped many bottles of this stuff since I started working here. I interrupt Conrad's conversation with our boss for just a second. "Can I try some of this cream on my dry hands, Mr. Bronson?"

Our boss says, "Sure, keep the whole bottle if you'd like. It's a good product, and I have plenty more."

"Thanks." I move the bottle on top of his newspaper and push the lotion plunger down with more force than is necessary. It squirts all over our pictures on his newspaper. "Oops." I take a tissue from the box on his desk and wipe the paper until it's blurry.

Conrad ends his conversation with our boss by saying, "I don't want to waste the company's money with so little to do today. Is it okay if we go home early?

Mr. Bronson looks at his smeared newspaper and frowns slightly. He probably wishes I would quit doing that. Or maybe he saw the picture before I tampered with it. He clears his throat and says, "I think you're right, John. You and Dani don't have enough to do today, and with school starting again tomorrow, you should have some time to get yourselves ready. I will see you after school the day after tomorrow. Be safe now."

Conrad wipes a chocolate bar wrapper on the wanted poster as we leave through the front door. As we walk home, I ask Conrad a question that has been on my mind since I heard Mr. Bronson defending my mom to Patrolman Darius. "Do you think Mr. Bronson suspects that we are the wanted refugees?"

Conrad thinks for a minute and says, "I don't know. He acts like he doesn't suspect us, but there are posters out now, and the news has sure been posting our pictures all over the place. It seems like he either doesn't know or he knows and doesn't care."

I think about what Mr. Bronson said about school and ask, "Does school really start tomorrow?"

Conrad nods. "According to Lupe, there are many different kinds of schools here with different areas of focus, and some started a couple of days ago, but most started today or will start tomorrow."

I look around the big, clean city we now live in. "Which one should we go to?"

Conrad shrugs. "Probably the one that is closest and free."

I sigh. "We need Shasta's help."

He nods. "Or Rocky's."

I scowl when I realize how hard it is to talk to our friends now. "I hope Shasta doesn't get in trouble for housing a suspicious person."

"Shelly has no proof of anything. It will blow over."

"I hope so. I also wish Shasta and Ernestine's houses weren't being watched, so we could talk to them right now."

Conrad sighs. "I know."

As we're walking by a small, fancy shoe store, not far from our apartment building, Conrad suddenly grabs my arm and pulls me inside. I look at him questioningly, but he shoves me toward the corner of the store, away from the other customers. "Look at these shoes, aren't they nice?"

I look at the red high-heeled shoes with a price tag way out of my price range and look at him questioningly. "If I saved for six months, I might be able to afford these shoes. Why are you interested in them?"

Conrad's eyes aren't on the shoes, they are looking out the giant wall of windows that look out on the street. Patrolman Darius suddenly walks by with five peace officers behind him. I feel my breath catch in my throat. Conrad's grip on my arm slides down to my hand, but his eyes are still looking out the window. "Just keep walking, just keep walking," he says as Darius comes to a stop.

I can see Darius' face mouth the words, "Check the store."

Conrad pulls me as fast as he can to the back of the store. "I need to use the lavatory. Come with me."

I don't argue and shuffle run as fast as I can to the single toilet lavatory with him. I hear the bell on the store door jingle right as we get to the lavatory door. Conrad grabs the doorknob, but it's locked. He cusses under his breath. We can hear heavy footsteps coming down the tall aisles of shoes. We hear a toilet flush, but that means we still have to wait. A peace officer I've never seen before approaches us at a march. Conrad pulls me closer until we are practically hugging, and then he kisses me. Not just a little kiss, a kiss that means we are not interested in talking to anyone else, for a while. I close my eyes and just play along. My heart is beating out of my chest, and I bet Conrad can feel it because we are smashed so close together. His hands move up and down my back. I hear the heavy footsteps stop, and the lavatory door suddenly opens. I open my eyes long enough to see a businesswoman with long black hair walk out. Our lips never part, but Conrad pulls us sideways into the lavatory and slams the door shut.

I feel my tense body suddenly relax. I sort of melt into Conrad's arms. Our lips finally part, and my head finds his shoulder, and I just lean against him, letting him hold me as we listen to what is going on outside the door. Heavy footsteps march around the store for several minutes. One set of heavy feet even wait outside the lavatory door for a while. Eventually the officer knocks. Conrad says in a low voice, "Occupied," and suddenly starts kissing me again noisily this time and slamming us against the lavatory door. I play along until the heavy footsteps leave and we hear the bell on the front door jingle multiple times and then go silent.

Conrad's lips leave mine, and I crumple to the floor. I put my head on my knees and hold myself there. He follows me down to the ground and puts his arms around me. I close my eyes and just let him hold me until my heart slows down. I open my eyes and look at him. He looks so—worried. He touches my cheek softly and says, "Are you okay?"

I look into his worried eyes and wonder which thing he's talking about. It takes me a minute to find my voice. "That was—close."

He leans closer to me. "I'm sorry if I scared you, but I saw them coming, and then I saw one coming for us again, and then I think he was waiting for us."

I replay the whole situation in my head as he talks. "I know. Your quick thinking saved us for sure." I pause and look blankly at the wall for a second. We could have pretended to do what we actually did once we were behind the locked door, but we didn't..."We should—you know, leave."

He looks even more worried than he did before. "Don't you want to talk about it?"

I wish I could, but I'm in shock. I don't know what to say to him. Kissing him was different than the last time. He stole that kiss at his house in Layland, and I hated it. I hated him in that moment. He was helping his father lie about my dad's murder. But this time, he was trying to save me. He did save me, and judging from how this kissing session went, he still has feelings for me. The big question is, do I have feelings for him, too? I didn't push him away. I didn't hate it. I was scared out of my mind, but I kind of liked it, but I have a boyfriend...

The worry in his eyes breaks my heart, but I need some time before we talk about this. "Uh, yes, we should talk, but not right now. I'm sure the owner of this store wants his lavatory back, and we need to make sure my mom is okay. Those officers were right by our apartment, and Darius is hunting her down."

His eyes look sad as he says, "I want to talk now, but you have a point. I guess we better go."

The employees look at us funny as we leave, but we just hold hands and don't make eye contact with anyone. I take my hand back to scratch my nose as soon as we walk past the store. The walk home is quiet, and cold. I don't like it. I like it when Conrad is warm and happy. He drops me off at the door of apartment 113 and says he'll come back to check on me after dinner. I nod blankly at him. I just hope my mom is okay inside.

I have to knock on the door because Mom and Marcella have the two keys to our apartment. Maybe I should ask Mrs. Abbot to make one for me. The door opens, and Everley lets me in. "You're home early! Do you want to see how we've fixed up our new place?"

I force a smile on my face and say, "Yes! Show me everything!" She shows me the master bedroom that she and mom will be sharing first. She shows me that the boys set up the queen bed and that she made it with the bedding from Shasta's house. The lavatory connected to this room is a bit smaller than the one in the boys' apartment, but it has a full tub that my legs already want to try out. Then she shows me the new-to-us red and green striped couch in the living room with the brown overstuffed armchair across from it. If we need more seating, we can always pull a chair or two out from the table that was left here. She shows me each cupboard and drawer in the kitchen that she put dishes, pots, silverware, and food in. She smiles extra big when she takes me to my new room. "Close your eyes, Dandra."

I close my eyes and let my sister lead me into my new bedroom. When she says, "Open your eyes!" I see both twin beds made with new-to-us matching pastel green blankets from the frugality store. New green and white curtains are hanging in the window from the Casswell's donation box, and a new-to-us dresser is sitting against the wall between the two beds. I pull open the drawers to find my clothes in the first and third drawer and Marcella's clothes in the second and fourth drawers. My sister sits on what I assume is my bed because my backpack is sitting on the floor underneath it and says, "What do you think, Dandra? Do you like it?"

My head is still on overload, but I curl up the corners of my mouth. "I love it. Where did you get the dresser?"

"Oh, Baldwin bought it for you when he went to pick up the couch at the frugality store this morning."

Baldwin bought it. Baldwin is my boyfriend. I look at my sister and say, "Oh, that is so sweet." I feel more than a little bit guilty for kissing Conrad thirty minutes ago while my boyfriend was buying and moving furniture for me, but it was a protect-myself kiss, right?

The last room Everley shows me is the lavatory that

Marcella and I will share. My handy gallon of vinegar is sitting in the corner of the tub. I immediately turn on the water to start my vinegar bath. "I love the whole place, sis. Did Marcella help you do all of this?"

"Yeah, she helped me put things away until Mom got home. When Mom got here, we hung up all the curtains."

"Where is Mom now?"

"Oh, she said that she wanted to sign us up for school, so she left to do that right before you got here."

"She knew which schools to go to?"

"No, she said she was going to talk to Shasta first."

My head starts pounding. I run the timeline of Darius' movements throughout the day in my head and pray that Mom wasn't seen coming in or out of Shasta's or walking down this street. She could easily have been caught. "Well, I hope she gets home soon." I absent-mindedly start taking off my clothes for my bath. I think it embarrasses Everley.

"Sheesh, I guess I'll leave," Everley says as my exposed skin makes her blush.

"Sorry, my legs really need a soak. Go pick out what you want for dinner, and I'll help you make it when I'm done with my bath, okay?"

"Okay."

Chapter 23

I SAID IT WAS MY LEGS that needed this soak, but really, it's my brain that needs this still, quiet moment. I relive everything I heard and saw while Darius was at Casswell's today. Mr. Bronson tried to cover for us, and Conrad ate a walnut for us. Then I relive the walk home. Conrad. Conrad hid us right before Patrolman Darius saw us. I touch my lips with my fingertips. Conrad hid us again by—kissing me. Not just fake kissing me, he kissed me with passion. Twice. I close my eyes and dip my head under the water. The gurgly water sounds so peaceful. Why can't my life always be this peaceful?

When I emerge from the water, a question burns through my mind. Do I like Conrad as more than a friend? A second question follows the first. Is what I have with Baldwin better than what I could have with Conrad? A third question makes me wonder why it wasn't the first. Is Mom okay? Patrolman Darius almost found me just now; he could have found her.

I wish I felt better, but I don't really as I get dressed. Everley wants to make cheese sandwiches and tomato soup for dinner. We have exactly the pots and pans needed, so I get lost in the process. I really start to worry when we finish dinner and Mom is not home yet. She was taken by Patrolman Darius. I just know it.

"Are you okay, Dandra?" my sister asks.

"I'm fine, sis," I say blankly.

"Then why are you crying?"

I reach up and wipe the tears that I didn't notice rolling down my cheeks. "I'm just worried about Mom. Patrolman Darius was looking for her at work today. I'm afraid he might have—you know—found her."

Everley looks upset. "What will we do if she doesn't come back?"

Seeing my sister's worry makes me find some courage. "If she doesn't come back, I will take care of you, and I will not stop until we find her."

Everley's eyes become a fountain of tears. "I thought today would be a good day, but now I'm worried about Mom."

224

I stand up and walk my sister to the couch. We sit down and hold each other for a few minutes. We cry, but don't say anything for a while. Everley turns to me and asks, "When you are sad, who do you wish was there to comfort you?" She wipes her tears and says, "I wish Mom was here to comfort me, but since it's her that I'm worried about, I'm glad I have you here."

I think about that question for a minute. Who do I wish was here right now to comfort me? I feel like a little girl, like Everley, in a lot of ways. I wish my dad was still here, and I definitely wish my mom was here to comfort me, but if they aren't an option for me anymore, who do I want to get me through this? Baldwin? Or Conrad? Who do I wish was here right now? Baldwin will have plenty of practical solutions to my problems, which is helpful. Conrad probably won't have any practical solutions for me, but he will hold me and comfort me. He's done it before.

Everley holds my hand and says, "I know Mom wanted us to be in our own apartment, but I kind of wish we had other people to talk to right now. I miss our friends. Can I go get somebody to sit with us tonight until Mom gets home?"

"I know what you mean, sis, but I'm not sure which friend I want to talk to right now."

"Really?" She looks at me like I'm an idiot. "Are you having boy problems?"

I close my eyes and sigh, "Well, maybe, sort of."

Everley's eyebrows come together. "You have a boyfriend. Do you want me to go and get him for you or not?"

"I think so…"

Everley smirks at me. "Let me guess. You aren't sure if you want Baldwin to come over because he will probably make a plan that involves everyone helping you pay the rent on this place because he thinks Mom is gone for good, when really, you just want a shoulder to cry on."

I am shocked at how much my sister picks up. "Well, yeah. That is part of it."

"What is the other part?"

"Well, Conrad and I almost got caught by Patrolman Darius ourselves today, and we ended up hiding from him, alone for a while."

Everley smiles. "What's wrong with a little alone time with Conrad?"

I roll my eyes at her Conrad crush. "He kind of made me think that he likes me."

"He does."

My sister's bluntness takes me by surprise. "Well, we don't know that for sure, but if he does, what should I do? I have a boyfriend."

Everley looks me in the eyes. "Did Conrad kiss you?"

My cheeks turn to fire because this is not where I wanted this conversation to go. I was purposely steering away from anything to do with—kissing. "Uh, well…"

BAM, BAM, BAM. Everley and I both turn to the front door. A million possibilities run through my head of who could be on the other side. Should I answer it? What if it's Patrolman Darius? What if it's Mom? I take Everley's hand and tiptoe to the front door. I can hear heavy footsteps shuffling around on the other side. I place my ear against the door hoping to hear a voice.

It sounds just like the peace officer outside the lavatory in the shoe store. I am not going to open that door. I put my finger to my lips to shush Everley and show her how to tip toe away from it when she lets go of my hand, grabs the doorknob, and throws the door open. I scream, "No!" but it's too late.

Chapter 24

THE WIDE-OPEN DOOR allows big feet to walk into our apartment. They belong to Conrad. He isn't wearing a coat and his hands are shoved deep into his pockets as he shivers in the January cold. "Hi, is this a good time? I told you I would check on you after dinner."

Everley throws her arms around Conrad and starts crying. "Mom isn't back yet, and we think Patrolman Darius took her. Dandra thought you might be Patrolman Darius and didn't want me to open the door, but I knew it was you. You always check on us."

Conrad looks at me, and when he gets a blank look back, shuts the door and leads a crying Everley to the couch. We all sit down, and she cries into his shoulder for several minutes. I am thrilled that I'm not getting arrested and hauled back to Layland, so I sit there and watch my sister cry. Conrad reaches over and takes my hand. I decide I need more than that, so I claim his other shoulder and feel the tears start to stream down my cheeks as well. Conrad finally says, "Your mom could be just fine, you know."

I look up at him, wipe my tears and say, "She went to sign us up for school. It's now 7:00 pm. How many schools are open this late? Something must have happened to her."

Conrad lifts Everley's head up and dries her tears. "Ed works at the school Everley will go to. He says there are office workers and teachers there until 5:00 pm."

"Yeah, but it doesn't take two hours to walk home!"

Conrad wraps his arm around me and holds me like he'll never let me go.

We are startled when the doorknob suddenly jostles around, and the door opens. My mom walks in looking haggard with multiple bags on her arms. Everley and I jump up and run to hug her. She looks confused and overwhelmed. "Why are you crying, girls? What's wrong?"

Everley says through her sobs, "Patrolman Darius was looking for you today at Casswell's, and we thought he found you!"

Mom drops her bags to the ground and hugs Everley tighter. "Oh, dear. I'm sorry I worried you. I did visit Shasta today, and she told me that he came looking for me, but she told him that I found a job in another city and moved out. He has no idea I live here now."

I feel some stress leave my body. "Oh, good. I've been so worried about you. Darius almost caught Conrad and me on our walk home from work."

Mom grabs my face and kisses my forehead. "I'm glad he didn't catch you." When Everley and I continue to cry, Mom finally realizes how close we were to trouble today. She holds us for a long time, and then says, "You girls are so strong. You did so well today. No more tears. Let's talk about the good things that happened today." She takes a step back to look at our faces and almost trips on her shopping bags. "Help me put these groceries and towels away, will you? Then I can tell you about the schools I signed you up for and the two tutoring students I met today."

Conrad and Everley help Mom put the groceries and supplies away while I dish up her dinner and put it at the table for her. She listens to us talk about our crazy day as she eats. When she's done, she gives Everley a piece of paper with her teacher's name and the primary school schedule. She pats my sister's hand and says, "I think you will like your teacher. I met her, and she was very nice. The school itself is extremely clean

231

with brand new books and models and items so high tech that I'm not even sure what they do."

Everley squeals with delight. "Brand new books! I can only imagine what they look like!" The poor kid grew up with dusty books from the Tifton Library and my dad's personal library. The low-level school's books were falling apart when I went to school there.

Mom passes a piece of paper to me as well. It has a schedule with seven classes and seven different teachers. I remember the poor remaining teachers at my mid-level school who had to teach things they didn't know and only had a few of us in each class. I feel so spoiled now. "Do they have more than one teacher for every subject?"

"They have many teachers for each subject. I hope I picked some good ones for you." Conrad takes the paper from me and looks at my schedule intently, almost like he's trying to memorize it. Mom looks at him curiously and asks, "Are you signed up for school yet, Conrad?"

My friend is just smiling at the relief on all of our faces. "No, I'm not, but if Ernestine and Rocky think it's safe with wanted posters everywhere, everyone in our apartment is going to sign up tomorrow morning. Do you think it's safe, Mrs. Metty?"

Mom shrugs. "I had a very different day from you guys. I felt very safe at the schools. No one mentioned the posters at all."

Conrad nods. "Perfect. Maybe I'll get to sign up tomorrow after all. Is there anything special that I need to bring?"

Mom shrugs. "Well, they asked for a few documents that I didn't have, but they said that because the laws changed a couple of years ago, anyone can start school without all the paperwork completed and that I could bring citizenship documents by later."

Conrad looks at my mom with concern, "Do I have to have a parent or guardian sign anything?"

Mom's eyebrows come together as she walks her dishes to the sink. "I did sign a few things today, but like I said, they told me that the law won't stop anyone from starting school even if the paperwork is incomplete. We may need to get Shasta or Ernestine to sign as guardians for the rest of you."

Conrad nods as he stares at my schedule. "Did you sign Marcella up?"

Mom answers slowly, "Yes, should I have signed you up, too?"

He shakes his head. "No, it's okay. I mean, yeah, it would have been nice, but I can do it."

Mom's eyes fill with regret. "I should have signed you up, too, Conrad. If you have any problems tomorrow, let me know, and I'll figure out a way to help you."

"Thanks, Mrs. Metty." Conrad smiles at Mom like she's his flesh and blood. "So tell us about the tutoring students you found today."

Mom lights up. "I was just waiting in a line to sign Dandra up for classes when I heard the boy ahead of me complaining to his mother that he didn't pass his math class last term and he didn't think he could pass the class this term either, so I told them that I was a math and science tutor and would love to give him some one-on-one help so he could pass his class. The mom was so excited that we exchanged information, and she wants me to work with him twice a week and maybe more. She also said her niece needs some help in math, so she gave me her information as well."

I smile at my mom's good news. "That's great, Mom. Are these students the same ones who posted for a tutor at city hall?"

Mom shakes her head. "Nope, I plan to contact those students tomorrow. I may have five students my very first week!"

I nod as I look around our sparse apartment. "Are you going to tutor them here?"

"No. I don't want anyone knowing where we live. The schools are open until 5:00, so I can meet students in the school library for an hour or so when they get done with classes, or I can meet them at their own homes, or the city library. That's my plan for now."

The sound of our front door jangling around makes us all turn to see where the noise is coming from. Marcella bursts through the door, throws a box of messed up pastries on the counter in the kitchen, and says, "I'm going to the boys' apartment to play chess once I've had a bite to eat, if that's okay."

I can tell from the look in Mom's eye that she doesn't love this plan, but she isn't Marcella's mom either. She says, "That's fine, but don't stay out too late. You start school in the morning. I have your schedule in my bag."

Marcella grabs a sandwich and a messed-up donut and says, "Sounds good. See you in a couple hours." She's gone as fast as she arrived.

Mom stands up slowly and says, "I think I will use my foot massager once I'm done with the dishes. I feel like I walked half the city streets today."

Conrad jumps to his feet and says, "No, I'll do the dishes. Everley, will you help your mom set up the foot massager?"

Everley grins. "Sure." She grabs my mom's Christmas present out of their room and puts it on the floor in front of our brown armchair. Mom sits down and lets Everley place her feet in the mysterious box and push the start button. Mom closes her eyes and sighs with pleasure.

Conrad washes while I dry and put away the dishes. It takes about 10 minutes. Everley decides to take a bath so she's ready for school in the morning.

I realize as Conrad and I sit down on the red and green couch that my mom is snoring. Conrad nudges me with his elbow and says, "Do you feel better now?"

I smile. "Yes, a hundred percent better."

Conrad starts to pick at the edge of the couch and whispers, "Are you ready to talk about what happened in the shoe store?"

I see the worry creeping back into his eyes. I look at my mom's sleeping figure and shrug. "Uh, yeah. I guess—I guess we should."

He sighs and says, "I can tell you don't want to talk about this, but I haven't been able to think about anything else since I grabbed you and kissed you at the shoe store."

His vulnerable eyes are hard to look away from. I force myself to look at my hands. "What part are you still thinking about? Getting away from Patrolman Darius or—kissing me?"

Conrad's voice gets softer as my mom snores nearby, "Oh, 100% kissing you."

I feel butterflies in my stomach, and I suddenly remember how it felt to kiss him. His arms around me were so warm. He made me feel safe. He's right here, and we aren't hiding for our lives this time. I kind of wonder how that same kiss would change if we repeated it right now... I lean in a little bit, and then he leans in. I close my eyes and prepare myself for his lips when...*BAM, BAM, BAM.* Someone else is at our door.

Mom startles awake and looks at me. "Will you get the door, Dandra?"

"Yeah, Mom." I notice how disappointed Conrad looks as I stand up and walk past him. The door creaks just a bit as I open it.

Baldwin bursts in and gives me a big hug and a kiss. "Did you see your dresser? Do you like it?"

I smile. "Yeah, I saw it. It's perfect."

Baldwin takes my hand and walks me to my room to look at the dresser while he explains how he got it. "When Gordon and I picked up your couch at the frugality store, I noticed three dressers standing in a row by the door. I looked at the price tags and knew that I didn't have enough for all of them, but I figured it wouldn't hurt to talk to the manager about them. I asked if he would give me a deal if I bought all three of them. He said that if I paid full price for two of them, he'd give me the third one for free! So now you have a dresser!"

I try to be as excited about his deal as he is, but my smile doesn't quite match his. I love the dresser, I really do. Pulling clothes out of a bag or a box every day is not very fun. I think my hesitation is because it seems like he only gets joy out of giving me things that are free instead of getting joy out of making my life better.

I force a smile on my face. "Thank you so much for the dresser. This room will be so comfortable and convenient for Marcella and me."

Baldwin stands a little taller. "Right? I think if I wait a week, I may be able to talk the manager into a deal on desks, so be waiting for that!"

I smirk as I see his excitement. "Oh, I will." I lead him back to the living room.

The grin on Baldwin's face falls off the minute he sees Conrad sitting on our couch. "What are you doing here?"

Conrad glares at my boyfriend. "I told Dandra I would check in on her after dinner. We had two encounters with Patrolman Darius today, and I think she's been feeling unsettled all day long."

My boyfriend's head snaps around. "Is this true?"

I nod. "Yeah."

He looks at me like I'm some sort of miracle. "How did you get away from him?"

Conrad smiles for the first time since seeing Baldwin come in the door. "We hid together."

My boyfriend asks, "Where?"

My friend gives me the same eyes he gave me before Baldwin knocked on the door. "In a shoe store lavatory." A secret smile plays at his lips.

Baldwin glares at Conrad. "You act like I should be jealous of that, but that sounds disgusting."

Conrad shrugs. "Disgusting is not the word I would use to describe it." He stands up and gives me a hug. "I think I better get going. I have to get signed up for school bright and early, after all. See you in the morning, Dandra." His eyes linger on mine as he walks to the door.

"Bye, Conrad," I say quietly as he leaves.

Baldwin looks at me curiously as he sits down on the couch and pats the seat beside him. "I can't stand that guy."

Everley comes out of her room wearing hand-me-down pajamas and wet hair. "Did Conrad leave already? I didn't get to say goodbye," she says with a frown.

Mom stands up and yawns. "Yes, he said he needed a good night's rest before his first day of school in this new country. You all need that, so why don't I braid your hair, Everley, and read you a chapter in your book, and tuck you in, which will take about 15 minutes, and then we'll all go to bed!" Mom gives Baldwin a pointed look as she steers Everley to the bedroom.

Baldwin chimes in, "I agree, Mrs. Metty. I planned to leave in 15 minutes anyway." When the bedroom door closes with a click, he puts his arm around me. "So what do you think about these new sleeping arrangements?"

I shrug. "I haven't had a chance to sleep yet, but I think this apartment will work out all right. Mom seems happier."

"Marcella isn't happier."

"She's used to living with you guys. She only has to sleep here. It will be all right."

"Yeah, I'm sure it will. Did I tell you about the broken side tables and bedding Ed brought home from a hotel tonight?"

I pick at a spot on my arm. "Nope."

Baldwin sighs with contentment, "Yeah, things are getting cozier all the time."

I like the fact that Baldwin is easy to please. "Is it just like the old days in the basement of the library?"

Baldwin chuckles. "Yes, and no. We definitely didn't have

spoiled brat Conrad at the library, and we couldn't bring big things in through the basement window without causing a scene, so it's nice to bring in bigger furniture without a worry."

"Do you miss all the secret passageways and secret note drops?"

Baldwin laughs, "Yeah. That was fun. Adamar misses that part more than I do, though. Charlisa dropped him a note almost every day."

I lay my head on his shoulder and remember all the good times we had in that dusty old library. "What do you miss the most about Layland?"

Baldwin traces the fingers of my right hand with his pointer finger and says, "I miss feeling like I was making a difference."

I frown and look at him sideways. "You don't think you're making a difference here?"

He picks up my hand and kisses it and then sets it back down and starts tracing it again. "I'm doing my best to make life better for my little adopted family here, and they definitely have more freedoms now than they've ever had, but Ernestine, Shasta, and your mom have made most of that happen. Starting the anti-gamers gang and learning things that weren't being taught to us at school and spitting in the face of Zane Chesterton felt so—fulfilling. I made those things happen. I found the basement of the library. I saved all my friends from rotting in the streets. I made them want to learn and contact people from other countries with radios. I accomplished so many things there. Here I'm just trying to put a roof over our heads and feed us."

I can see and even feel what he's saying. I take his hand and say, "I know what you mean. I felt like I was making more of a difference in Layland than I am here too, but we won't always be in survival mode. We have our own roofs over our heads now. Patrolman Darius will eventually give up and leave us alone. We'll be able to learn and build things at school and join clubs and change the world for the better here, too."

Baldwin looks into my eyes and smiles. "There's the girl I love so much. Will you help me make this world a better place, just like you did in Layland?" He pulls me in and kisses me.

"Absolutely," I say as I go in for another kiss.

The sound of my mom's bedroom door opening makes us stop and pull away from each other. She clears her throat. "School starts bright and early in the morning, you two. See you after breakfast, Baldwin?"

"Yes, ma'am," he says as he gives me one final kiss and walks me to the door. "See you in the morning, Dandra."

"See you," I say as I close the door behind him.

I flop on my bed and pull the blankets over my head until

Marcella comes in an hour later. I squint as she turns on the light. "Where have you been?" I ask.

"You know where I've been. The real question is where have you been today?"

I don't have patience for this. I'm tired. "Why do you care where I've been?"

Marcella turns out the light and climbs into her bed. "I don't care, but Baldwin and Conrad do."

"Why do you say that?"

"From what I gathered from their yelling match, you spent too much alone time with both of them today."

I cringe as I imagine a yelling match between the two guys I care more about than anything. I turn my head toward Marcella in the dark and say, "I spent the day trying to not get caught by Patrolman Darius, Marcella. Did I have to hide with Conrad? Yes. Did Conrad check on me when I thought Darius had my mom? Yes. Did Baldwin come to check on me as well? Yes."

Marcella is quiet for a minute. "Like I said, I don't care what you do, but I don't like seeing B hurt. I'm just going to ask you one last question. Did you kiss both of those boys tonight?"

I sit quietly as the tears stream down my face. I finally answer her softly, "Yes."

Chapter 25

MARCELLA AND I DON'T SAY ANYTHING to each other as we get ready for school. Everley is as excited and energetic as she used to be in Layland. "Is Conrad going to walk to school with us like old times, Dandra?"

Marcella glares at me as I answer, "Yes, I think we're all walking together, except you have to go to the primary school, so you and I will have to take a turn that way one block before everyone else."

"Perfect! What are we waiting for? Let's go!" She pulls me by the hand to the door.

"Don't forget your lunches!" Mom says as she hands all three of us a sandwich and an orange. We stuff them in our backpacks and wave goodbye to her. The last thing we hear as we shut the door behind us is, "Make it a great day, girls!"

I appreciate her sentiment, but it goes in one ear and out the other once I see Conrad and Baldwin scowling at each other as they walk down the stairs from apartment 218. Everley is oblivious to the tension in the air, so she calls out, "Good morning, everyone! Let's go to school!"

Conrad gives me one cold look and then latches on to Everley and says back, "Good morning to you, too. How many steps do you think it is from here to school? Let's count them and find out." They lead the group out and I am more than happy to just follow them.

I start walking alone, but Baldwin eventually ends up walking beside me. He has a pained look on his face. "Good morning, Dandra. Would you mind having a private lunch and conversation with me at school today?" he asks in a tone more formal than usual.

"I-I would love to, thank you," I say as warmly as I can.

He nods at me and continues to walk beside me in silence. When we get to the turn off for Everley's school, Ed tells us exactly where to turn and what door to go through before we set off by ourselves. Everley turns to me and says, "Why is everyone so quiet and grouchy today?"

I try to smile and say, "They had a fight at their apartment last night, so they aren't as excited about school as they should be. Hopefully they are in a better mood when we walk home."

I walk Everley to the door right as Shasta drops off Nelle, Peggy, Deedee, and Mina.

Everley jumps up and down. "Hi, Nelle!" She turns to me and says, "You can go now. I have friends who can help me."

I feel a little bit displaced. "All right." I give my sister a hug and leave her with our former roommates. "Mom said she would pick you up after school. Have a good first day!"

My sister waves at me and walks into the building. Shasta waves me over to her van. She looks like she's aged since the last time I saw her. She gives me a curious look and says, "Everley seems excited about school, but you don't."

I force a smile on my face. "I am. I really am. It was a rough morning, but things will just get better."

"I think it will. You'll probably make some new friends. Just don't use your real name and don't spend much time with your Layland friends. You will blend in better if you aren't seen as a group."

My heart sinks. "You're right. I'll tell everyone. See you later." I wave at her and start walking to Herrington South Tertiary School. The one-minute walk is a good time for me to clear my head and focus on what I'm about to do. Shasta's words keep ringing in my ears. I worry that having all the anti-gamers register for classes at the same time will look suspicious. Maybe Baldwin's snake tattoo will do the trick. I almost run into

Adamar and Gordon as I walk in the front door. The door has an all-too-familiar "Wanted Persons" poster on it. Adamar looks green around the edges. He bursts through the door and races to a giant garbage can. "I'm gonna be sick!"

I cringe as he loses his breakfast. "I think you guys better go home and try again tomorrow."

Gordon pats Adamar on the back. "I think you're right." He waves goodbye and starts walking our sick friend home. I feel bad for Adamar, but this is probably for the best. Those two can register over the next day or two without looking suspicious. I see Conrad and Baldwin standing in a line in the main office area. They look like they want to kill each other still. Remembering Shasta's advice, I keep a safe distance from them, take out the schedule my mom gave me, and start walking to my first classroom, 121, Chemistry.

I see Marcella walk into the nearest lavatory looking sad. She needs a lot of support that Gordon usually gives her. I would give it to her, but I'm worried about being recognized together—I just keep walking, even though it makes me feel like a jerk. When I get to room 121, I have to push through a group of girls to get through the door. The room is full of two-person lab stations. I see a seating chart projected on the front wall, so I find my seat and sit down. We rarely had seating charts in Layland, but we were lucky to have enough students to have a class at all once the education law changed. According to the seating chart, there are 30 students in this class. I jump when someone calls my name from behind me.

"Dani. Dani!" a male voice says. I look behind me and see Ed across the aisle and a row back from me.

I frown at him. "Are you registered already?"

He smiles and hands me a stack of loose, bent papers and a pencil. "A friend from work helped me register a couple of days ago."

I hold up the papers and pencil. "Did your friend give you these, too?"

"Yes, but I pick up forgotten papers and pencils at the primary school all the time."

We stop talking as soon as his lab partner sits down by him. I wait for my lab partner, Bonnie Smith, according to the seating chart, to sit down by me. I hope she isn't nosy. The bell rings and still no lab partner. The teacher takes the seating chart down and puts up a pop quiz in its place. "Please take out a piece of paper and number it from one to ten. This pop quiz shouldn't be too hard. They are all review questions from last term."

I feel myself start to sweat. I don't know the answer to the first two questions. Did my Layland school teach me anything? Am I really the least-smart student in this room? I am not used to this feeling, but I don't let it overwhelm me. Thanks to my dad, who always taught me things as we dug the tunnel, I do know the answer to the next two questions, and by the time the teacher says, "Time is up, please pass your papers forward," I am pretty sure I got seven out of ten questions correct.

The teacher gathers the papers and changes the projection on the wall to a list of instructions. "We are going to start a lab on metals today. You will be working with your lab partner, but turning in your own lab report, so please pull out another sheet of paper and send someone to collect the items listed on instruction number one."

I wish my lab partner was here today. I wait to see where everyone else is going to collect their supplies before I leave my seat. I just do what I see the other students do until I get back to my lab station. I can hear everyone around me dividing the tasks that need to be done and getting to work. I look at the door and silently plead for my lab partner to walk through it. It doesn't work, so I just start going through the steps by myself.

I have to ask the teacher how to start my heat source, but other than that, I feel like I am keeping up with the rest of the class more or less. I am still scratching down notes of what happened when I applied heat to metal number two when the bell rings. I have to hurry and put my supplies in a box, label it, and put it on the shelf in the back for tomorrow. My teacher says I did well by myself as I run out the door. I am going to be late for my next class. I quickly look at my schedule to see which way to speed walk. English, 207. That sounds like it is on the second floor of this building. I skip every other step up the stairs and make it to room 207 right as the bell rings. I slip in and sigh with relief that everyone is still deciphering the seating chart on the wall, so I haven't missed anything.

I am the last seat in the far corner of the room. It's a good thing I like reading and writing because this would be an easy seat to fall asleep in. No one is sitting in the seat in front of me, and a husky guy with a big smile is sitting in the seat to my right. He winks at me. The teacher, Mrs. Haynes, takes down the seating chart and puts up a thought-provoking question in its place. She says, "Open your notebooks and write a paragraph about how you would answer this question and why."

I don't have a notebook for this class yet, so I pull out one of the papers Ed gave me and write the question at the top. *If you could do anything to change the world, what would you do and why?* I lean over to the guy with the big smile and ask, "Have you taken a class from this teacher before?"

He responds, "Yes. She's a good teacher."

I follow up with, "Who will read our responses?"

He gives me one of his big smiles and says, "Just the teacher, and she doesn't collect our notebooks until the end of the term, so I doubt she reads them thoroughly, if you know what I mean."

That is exactly what I needed to know. I have so many things I want to change about this world, but I don't want to be found out if I write about Layland. I put my head down and start writing. I am so intent on my response that I don't even notice the boy who comes in late and sits in front of me.

When the teacher asks if anyone wants to share their response, a familiar voice in front of me says, "If I could change anything in this world, I would open the border between Layland and the United Cities, so people could move or visit between countries without harassment from peace officers in their homes, businesses, and schools all the time." Half the class starts cheering and clapping, including Mr. Big Smile sitting next to me.

The teacher nods and says, "That would be a big change for the world. Can you think of anything we could do to make that happen, Mr.—what is your name again?"

The blonde head in front of me turns toward the teacher revealing a snake tattoo on his neck. "Blake, Winston Blake, but you can call me Win." I was so intent on writing my paragraph that I didn't notice he was the one who sat in front of me.

Baldwin goes on a tirade about how every other border around the United Cities is open, and how it would only take a forward-thinking politician with good international relations to change the law. I kick his chair in irritation. Does he want us to get found out? It's our first day at school for crying out loud. He ignores my kick and says, "I bet Brock Hamble would be willing to change the law. He changed the Complex Law two years ago. Maybe I'll write a letter to him today about changing the law about the Layland border wall. I bet he's as sick of the searches and interrogations for the refugees as we are." Half the class starts cheering again.

I shake my head when Baldwin turns around to stretch his back and winks at me. I can't help but grin. As much as I worry about getting found out, this is Baldwin. He makes things happen.

It's nice to have a familiar face in my first two classes of the day. I don't know anyone in my United Cities History class third hour, but it's fascinating to learn about the Complex Law that was repealed only two years ago. It affected the lives of every family in this country for over a hundred years.

Fourth hour I have a cooking class with Marcella. We make breadsticks that don't take very long at all, and I'm already planning on making them for dinner this week. After the bell rings for lunch, Marcella and I walk toward the cafeteria, but not too close together. I see Ed talking to a girl from my history class at one table and Conrad sitting alone a couple of tables away. I wish I could sit by him, but I am supposed to meet Baldwin for lunch and—a chat. Marcella sits down by a girl from our cooking class and starts eating the sandwich Mom packed for her. I stand in the doorway of the cafeteria awkwardly until Baldwin taps me on the shoulder and starts walking to a bench by the gym door. He sits down, and I sit next to him, but not too close. Both of our lunches have their own seats between us. He sighs and takes a bite of apple. I pull out my sandwich, but I wait to hear what he has to say before I start eating.

My boyfriend swallows and asks, "Did you kiss him yesterday?"

I consider asking him who "he" is, but I don't think it will do me any favors to play stupid, so I just bite the bullet and answer honestly. "Yes, but there was a peace officer walking right toward us. We were trying to hide in plain sight."

My boyfriend nods like he expected my response. "Was it your idea?"

"No."

Baldwin looks relieved by that. "Do you like him as more than a friend?"

His questions are to the point and hard for me to answer, even to myself. "I-I don't know. He saved me twice yesterday, and I feel more connected to him now."

Baldwin sighs. "Conrad is under the impression that you are in love with him. He wants me to step aside and let you two be together. Is that what you want?"

I don't care who sees us, I turn to face him and take his hand. "No. I never said anything like that to him."

"But do you want to be with him?"

I am at a loss. "I-I don't know. I need to think about it."

Baldwin stands up and says to the wall above my head, "Let me know when you have made up your mind." He leaves without another word.

He is so cut and dry Baldwin-like that I am left feeling like a disgusting pile of garbage.

I sit there alone and rethink my life until the bell rings. A quick look at my schedule tells me that I have an exercise class, then math, then speech. I am sitting as close to the gym door as humanly possible, so it takes one second to get to class. I am so lost in my thoughts that I don't realize that Conrad is standing right next to me until he's asked to add his name to the roll. He writes his fake name down and then stands a foot or two to the right of me.

The teacher finally gets his roll updated and says, "Those of you who have exercise clothes to change into, go change now. The rest of you, bring yours tomorrow. You will need to find a partner, grab a worksheet, and pick a stopwatch to record how many of each of these exercises you can do in one minute. We will do this again in a month to see how much you have improved. Grab what you need and get to work everyone.

Conrad looks at me cautiously and says, "Will you be my partner?"

I sigh and say under my breath, "We really shouldn't, so we aren't recognized together." He nods in disappointment. I look around the gym for an open partner to claim, but I don't see one. We are the odd ones out. I feel bad for being snippy. We have to be partners now. I say, "Trouble is unavoidable these days. I'll be your partner."

The corners of Conrad's mouth curl up as he grabs two

worksheets and a stopwatch for us and then walks with me to a corner of the gym where no one will hear us talking. He looks at me cautiously. "How did your chat go at lunch?"

My face drops. "What did you tell him last night? Your big mouth is the reason everyone is walking around on pins and needles today," I say irritably.

My friend's eyes flare with fire. "I just couldn't handle him bragging about the goodnight kiss you sent him off with last night."

I lean toward him and whisper-yell, "Conrad, what do you expect from me? He is my boyfriend, and we had a very good, thoughtful conversation last night. I would say that the conversation outranked the goodnight kiss."

Conrad smiles at that remark. "You almost kissed me last night. Not to save our skins, just because you wanted to. You had the look." He looks at me like he wishes I had "the look" now. I scowl as he goes on to say, "I wish Baldwin had waited ten seconds longer to show up last night. I think everything would be different today if he had."

I have no words. I just sit there and fume until our teacher says, "Listen up! One partner needs to set the stopwatch for one minute and count how many pushups their partner can do. Then switch. Go through each exercise on the list. Get to work!"

I pick up the stopwatch and throw it at Conrad. "Time me." My anger pushes me to do more pushups than I thought possible for my weak arms to handle. Conrad counts quietly until the watch beeps.

He leans close to me and asks, "Dandra, am I wrong though? Did you want to kiss me last night?"

I don't know how to respond, so I click the watch and say, "Your time has started, go." I count his pushups quietly until the watch beeps. It gives me time to think. As he catches his breath, I say quietly, "I did want to kiss you. I wanted to know if it would be different if we kissed because we wanted to instead of because we had to."

Conrad grabs the watch and says, "I wanted to."

I can see pain in his eyes. He deserves so much better than what I have given him. He deserves to be happy, genuinely happy. Can I make him happy? Will making him happy make me happy? I stammer as I say, "Wh-what's next on the list?"

"Sit ups." I get in position, and he says, "Go."

I don't have near the energy that I had a minute ago as I do my sit ups. I collapse when the watch beeps. "Conrad, I like you, but I like Baldwin too."

He tosses me the watch and gets into position. "We should have had that kiss last night. Promise me you won't make up your mind until we've had that kiss."

I am taken aback. "Go." As I count his sit ups, I say quietly, "Okay."

When the watch beeps, he sits up and looks me in the eye. "What did you say?"

"I said, okay."

Conrad looks relieved. He doesn't pressure me to promise anything else as we finish our exercises. Once we have our papers turned in, we just wait for the prepared people to change back into their regular clothes. His eyes never leave me. He reaches out and takes my hand for a brief second before the bell rings.

We walk side-by-side until we get into the hall, then we have to act like strangers to blend in. I watch him walk away from me and feel a sense of loss. In Layland, the anti-gamers acted like strangers to keep their gang a secret, but Conrad and I never kept our friendship a secret.

Chapter 26

MATH IS EASY AND UNEVENTFUL. I don't know anyone in the class, and the review is challenging, but not intimidating. I'm pretty tired by the time I walk into speech class. I have to keep my shock in check when I see Baldwin, Ed, and Conrad in the same class with me.

The seating chart has us sitting near each other in a diamond shape. The person sitting in the middle of our diamond introduces himself to me almost immediately. "Hello, my name is Thomas Barlowe. I am the president of the Herrington South debate team. Are you in this class by choice or by necessity?" He pauses while I try to think of a response. He continues, "I am always looking for new debaters to join my team."

I cringe as I burst his bubble. "I hope to learn a lot in this class, but I am definitely taking it out of necessity. Sorry."

Thomas frowns as the teacher gets the class started. "Hello, class. I am Mr. Whitlock. I hope you have enjoyed your first day of the new term because I'm about to drop a big assignment on you." The students around me, except for Thomas, groan quietly. "Your grade in this class will be comprised of four speeches. This should not surprise you since this is a speech class." Everyone around me, except Thomas, groans again. "You will give your first speech exactly one week from today at an academic assembly for the city council."

Thomas does a happy dance in his seat and mutters under his breath, "I knew he would pick this class! I can't wait!"

Our teacher smiles at Thomas and goes on. "The city council meets to decide how to distribute money to the tertiary schools in the city the week after our academic assembly. I cannot express to you how important this first speech is to you personally for your grade and collectively for our school. I wish I could give you more time to prepare, but Headmaster Barlowe has asked that this class represent our school at the academic assembly. Thomas, did you talk your dad into choosing this class?"

Thomas puffs out his chest and says, "Maybe."

While I'm fighting the urge to leave now and drop this class, Baldwin raises his hand, "Can we give our speech about any academic topic?"

Mr. Whitlock shakes his head. "No. As soon as I take the seating chart down, I will project the topics you may choose from, two people per topic."

Thomas raises his hand. "Won't it be weird if two of us talk about the same thing side-by-side?"

"Great question. Yes, that would be weird, so we will have a dress rehearsal in class on Friday. The person who does the best job presenting their topic will get full marks and present their speech at the academic assembly. The other person will get half credit and not present at the assembly, so choose your opponent wisely."

My jaw hits the floor. Which is better, getting full marks and exposing myself to political leaders or getting an F on an assignment that is one fourth of my grade and keeping my identity secret? I look at Conrad and see him battling the same question in his mind. Baldwin seems unfazed. Ed gets my boyfriend's attention and mouth's the words, "You're going down, B!"

As soon as the topics appear on the wall, everyone jumps out of their seats to sign up. Well, not everyone. I hang back with Conrad to see which topics disappear and which opponents need a contender, Baldwin jumps up at first, but then hangs back once the sign up frenzy happens. I am not surprised when I see Thomas approach the interactive projector confidently and write his name on the wall with his finger next to "Herrington South's Educational Advancements." If I don't want to speak in front of the city council, I should put my name right there next to his. A quiet girl with a stutter takes one of the spots for "Math is the Path to the Future," but the other spot is open and looking like an easy winner. Ed signs up for "Communication is Key." I'm definitely not signing up for that one. That would mean that one of us is guaranteed an F. Baldwin takes a step forward and signs up for "Needed Improvements for the Future." His opponent jumps up to the wall quickly, so I'm guessing he has a lot to say about it. I keep looking at "Literacy is Lucrative," and finally sign up for it. Conrad mutters under his breath to me, "What should I do?"

I mutter back, "It's up to you. Guaranteed no speech or guaranteed speech?"

Conrad looks at me and then looks at Baldwin's confident face before he grabs a spot. He signs up for "Math is the Path to the Future." I'm a little bit surprised but impressed that Conrad is willing to speak in front of the city council. He sits down and lets out a long-held breath.

Mr. Whitman walks to the wall and says, "Christopher is the only one not here today, so I guess he will be your opponent, Thomas."

Thomas mutters, "Yes!" under his breath. I'm guessing Christopher is not a very impressive speaker.

Mr. Whitman goes on to say, "You will have the rest of class to get acquainted with your topic, so gather your things and follow me to the school library where there are books and computers that can help you find the information you need."

I slip my backpack on and sidle up to Baldwin as we walk with our class to the library. "Wouldn't the responsible thing be to walk to the office and drop this class? We will be putting our faces right in front of government officials if we do this."

Baldwin looks at me like he's never disagreed with something more. "Absolutely not. This is the first time I've felt like I'm making a difference since we got here. You do what you want, but I'm giving my speech." I slow my steps down and watch him go into the library ahead of me. This feels incredibly risky to me, but as I see Baldwin's determination, I hate feeling left behind. If he is determined to give his speech, I may as well do mine, too.

Chapter 27

THE WALK HOME IS ALMOST AS QUIET as the walk to school was. Marcella is always quiet when Gordon is missing. Baldwin smiles at me but doesn't talk to me. He just listens to Ed explain how he is going to approach his speech. I am glad that Baldwin is in a better mood. I'm still extremely worried about these speeches. We've done so well to keep under the radar. I feel reckless planning to speak to city council members face to face. Conrad doesn't look very comfortable either. Baldwin interrupts Ed after he looks at his watch. He starts walking quickly because he needs to be at the National

News Station as soon as possible for his evening news shift. We all pick up our pace and get home quickly. I ask, "Is Rocky giving you a ride to work?"

He shakes his head and says, "No. Josie."

Of course.

Once we're at the apartments, Marcella says she's going to check on Gordon and Adamar. Conrad and Baldwin follow her up the stairs. I walk to my apartment alone and knock on the door. Everley opens the door and gives me a big hug. "I loved my first day of school, Dandra! Nelle ate lunch with me. Guess what? If I get all of my assignments in on time this week, my teacher is going to take my class to your school for an assembly!"

"That's great, sis! Where is Mom?"

"She is tutoring some kid at the library. She said we would have to make dinner."

I look through the fridge and cupboards until I find some chicken, vegetables, and rice. I have enough seasonings to make a chicken and rice bake that takes an hour in the oven to cook. I hope Mom doesn't get mad at me for cooking the only meat we have. I throw everything together in one of our baking pans and pop it in the oven while Everley finishes telling me about her first day at school. When I finally get a chance to speak, I say, "I need to soak my legs for a bit, doctor's orders, so knock on the door in an hour so I can take the food out, okay, sis?"

Everley nods. "Okay. I'm going to get my homework done at the table so I can go to the assembly."

"Great idea, sis. See you in an hour." I shut the door to the lavatory and start filling the tub. I try to think about my own homework. What should I say about reading and how it helps people make money? Literacy definitely wasn't lucrative in Layland, but my study today in the library opened my eyes to jobs in the United Cities that I didn't even know existed. I love to read. I worked in a library for crying out loud. I should be able to kill this speech. I lay back into the water and think about all the good things I witnessed at school today. It was amazing to have full classes of students who wanted to be there. My mind turns to the negatives though. The speech to politicians is a negative. Baldwin's disappointment and ultimatum is a negative. Conrad's disappointment is a negative too. I promised him that he would get the kiss that was stolen from us. When will he want to collect on that kiss? I suddenly have goosebumps even though I am totally submerged in warm water. Knock, knock. "What do you want, Everley?"

"The food is ready. Come take it out."

"Okay. I'll be there in a minute."

The chicken rice bake is a perfect golden brown on top. Everley wants to dig right in, but I send her to get Marcella and see if Mom is walking down the street yet. I open my speech notes on the table and jot down a few thoughts I had while in the bath while I wait for my sister to come back. Everley is holding Marcella and Gordon's hands when she comes through the door. "I brought an extra dinner guest, Dandra. I hope you made enough food."

I smile and clear my homework from the table. "I think I did."

I pull out a chair and invite Gordon to sit down. I hand Everley some cups and forks to set at the table while Marcella starts dishing up plates for everyone. We definitely have enough for one extra. I will probably be taking leftovers to school tomorrow for lunch. Mom walks in as I'm putting the last plate on the table. She smiles when she sees us. "It smells delicious in here. How was school?"

Everley gives Mom a big hug and repeats everything she's already told me. Mom looks at Marcella and me and asks, "What about you guys?"

Marcella shrugs and says, "It was okay. I guess."

I try not to let my speech ruin everyone else's day too. "It was great, Mom. I learned a lot in just one day."

Gordon starts nibbling at the chicken on his plate. "What about your speech? Aren't you in the same class as Ed and Baldwin?"

I frown slightly when he brings it up. "Yeah, that is the only bad part."

Mom looks at me confused. "Why is that the bad part? You've never shied away from a speech in past classes."

I push the food around my plate. "It's not the speech itself that has me worried. It's that I have to compete for the chance to give the speech, and if I win the spot, I have to give the speech to the city council at an academic assembly next week."

Mom pats my hand. "You'll win the spot. I'm sure of it."

"Thanks, Mom, but what if the city council recognizes me?"

Mom frowns for a second. "I'm sure we can disguise you well enough. No one has recognized you yet, right? I want you to give that speech. I will be so proud. I will even come watch you give it."

Everley says through a mouthful of chicken, "I will too. That's why I have to get all of my homework in on time, so I can go!"

I don't love the turn this has taken. "I still think this is risky. How is Adamar doing, Gordon?"

Mom looks at our guest. "What is wrong with Adamar?"

Gordon shrugs. "He got sick and barfed the minute we got to school. I think it's nerves more than anything. He seems fine now."

I look at him and insist, "When you two sign up for classes tomorrow, don't sign up for last hour speech."

Gordon snorts. "I wouldn't touch that class with a ten-foot pole, but I'll be sure to be in the audience watching you next week."

I roll my eyes. "Thanks a lot."

Mom starts clearing the table before I have even touched

my food. "Finish your dinner and get working on that speech, Dandra. You have work after school tomorrow, so I suggest you use your time wisely.

"Yes, Mom."

Chapter 28

I DREAM OF GIVING MY SPEECH that night. I have a big ridiculous hat and wig on. While I'm giving the speech, Thomas from my speech class rips off my disguise and then drags me away to Patrolman Darius at the big gray building behind Shasta's house. I wake up in a cold sweat. It was just a dream. I am in bed, safe.

Everley keeps everyone in a good mood as we walk to school. She is excited to see Nelle at lunch and wants to invite her to hang out at our apartment soon.

All of my classes seem easy now that the last class of the

day has such a big assignment. My lab partner shows up today, so chemistry is much easier than yesterday. Baldwin passes me a note in English class that says, "You look nice today, but you seem worried. Are you okay? Have you made your decision?" Mrs. Haynes hovers close to our desks after he gives it to me, so I don't dare send a note back. As we're leaving class, I say, "I can't make that decision right now. I need to focus on my speech. Will you give me that long?"

Baldwin shrugs and says, "Sure," before he turns the opposite direction.

Adamar joins my History of the United Cities class, but he doesn't talk to me or even look at me. Gordon joins the cooking class that Marcella and I are in. She is in a much better mood today than yesterday. Our soup turns out perfect.

At lunch I am so full of soup that I just go to the library to research the topic for my speech more. Conrad follows me there, but I shake my head when he tries to sit by me. I may get a chance to talk to him in one of our classes or at work, but I don't want anyone to think that we are linked in any way. It turns out Conrad and I can't talk in exercise class because we have to run a mile and then lift weights in gender arranged groups.

By the time we get to speech class, I have a rough outline for my speech. Mr. Whitlock has us walk to the library again so we can find facts and figures to back up our arguments. He says we should just meet in the library for the next two days.

Baldwin glares at me when I consider sitting across a table from Conrad, so I sit in a corner by myself instead. Every time I turn around to look at everyone, they are anxiously engaged in their research, even Conrad. I get so overwhelmed that I lay my head down on my table and try not to cry.

"What's wrong?" a deep voice asks me.

I look up to see Ed looking at me like I have two heads. I wipe my eyes and say, "I hate that they both hate me."

Ed scrunches his nose and says, "So do I. Maybe you should just choose one of them and put us all out of our misery."

"I wish I could, but I like them both for very different reasons."

Ed shrugs and says, "Maybe you need to find someone who has all of the things you like about the two of them in one body."

I laugh. "If only it were that easy."

When the bell rings, I see Mom walk in the library with a math book and a stack of papers. She looks at me and says, "Have you been crying?"

I do not want to talk about boys with her, so I say, "I just want to get this speech right. It's stressing me out." It's not a complete lie.

Mom squeezes my shoulder and says, "You can do it. Just take it a paragraph at a time."

"I will. Thanks, Mom."

I don't have to worry about walking between two guys

who hate each other after school because Baldwin takes off at a speed walk to get to work on time. I'm pretty sure Josie is driving him again, but I don't know for sure because it is impossible to talk to him.

Conrad and I set off for Casswell's alone. The walk is quiet for a while. I ask him, "How is your speech coming along?"

He shrugs. "I'm giving it all I have. I hope it's enough to impress my judge."

"You mean Mr. Whitlock?"

"Mmmhmm," he responds.

Mr. Bronson greets us at the door like old times. "I'm so glad to see you two! How is school going?"

Conrad grins as we walk with him to the employee break room to clock in. "Great. How is business going?"

Mr. Bronson frowns. "Not so great. January is always a slow month. That is why we don't usually keep our Christmas workers after the new year."

Conrad puts a hand on Mr. Bronson's shoulder. "Do you want us to leave? Is there not enough to do?"

Mr. Bronson shakes his head and waves his comment off. "No. I told you to come today, but I was thinking that we may need to reduce your hours to two nights a week during the month of January. Will that still work for you?"

I wish I could pull out a piece of paper and do the math quickly. I need to make $350 a month in order for us to make our rent. More if I want to help with food and supplies. Conrad does some quick math in his head. "That will be fine for a couple of weeks, but I need to work three or four shifts a week after that to pay my rent."

Mr. Bronson looks concerned. "I could give you an extra shift a week of deep cleaning if that helps."

I feel like I'm back at the Tifton Library for a minute. Conrad nods. "Yes. I will take that. Dani, if you don't have any savings, you may want to take it too."

I trust Conrad and his mental math. "Yes, I'll take a cleaning shift too."

Mr. Bronson smiles. "Perfect. For tonight, I need you two to restock the new clothing lines Shelly brought out this week, the entire toy department, and the home furnishings. I want the shelves overflowing."

Mr. Bronson yawns and says, "I'll be leaving at 5:00, but my assistant manager Mrs. James can answer any questions you have. The store closes at 8:00 during the month of January, so be sure to clock out no later than 8:30."

Conrad smiles and says, "No problem, enjoy your evening off, Mr. Bronson."

The smile falls right off Conrad's face when we get to the warehouse. "I'm barely going to make my rent this month. I don't know what I'm going to eat."

I assume that if he's worried about his rent, I should be worried about mine too. "I have a cooking class right before lunch at school. I can wrap up whatever we make for our lunches. Will that help?"

Conrad smiles. "Yeah. That will help. Thanks."

I am curious. "Are you out of savings? I still have some."

Conrad doesn't look me in the eye. "No, but I was hoping to get—it doesn't matter. I'll make it work."

"How much is your rent with your own room?"

"$500 a month."

That is quite a bit for how little we will be working. I ask, "How much is everyone else's rent sharing a room?"

"$375 a month."

I frown. "Maybe you should let the guys know that rent is going to be tight this month. Maybe they will pitch in some money or some food to help out."

Conrad shakes his head. "No. I'll figure it out."

I look at all of the boxes of clothes, toys, and home furnishings we need to restock by 8:30. "I'll take the clothes, you take the toys, and then we can work together on the home furnishings."

"Okay. When do you want to take a break? Do you have any food on you?"

"I have a sandwich I didn't eat for lunch today. It's probably warm and soggy by now."

Conrad holds out his hand, "Give it to me and I'll put it in the breakroom fridge. If you share it with me, I'll share a bag of chips with you."

I am absolutely shocked with Conrad. He has never tried to save money like this in my memory. I hand the warm sandwich over and say, "I'll meet you at 6:30 for a 15 minute sandwich break here in the break room."

He nods and says, "See you then."

I take an inventory notepad with me into the clothing department on the second floor and start counting how many sizes of each item are missing. The new year displays Shelly and I set up are selling faster than everything else in the department except coats, hats and gloves. I feel a small sense of pride in that. I find an empty rolling cart to fill with restocks. I need entire boxes of hats and gloves, but I have to restock one medium and two larges of the black velvety coats, and one medium and one extra-large of the white velvety coats. It's going to be a long night.

I finish restocking the entire clothing department a few minutes before 6:30. I grab an inventory notebook and head to the home furnishings on the third floor when I realize that I'm already down a medium velvety white coat. I'll have to remember to grab one when I load up the home furnishing restocks. Conrad takes the elevator down to the home furnishings right at 6:30. I can hear his stomach growling. I'm not sure I saw him eat lunch in the library today now that I think about it. He puts a hand on his loud stomach and says, "Are you ready to eat yet? I sure am."

I stop scribbling on my inventory notebook and say, "Yeah.

275

Let's eat." Our trip down to the first floor in the elevator is quiet, but quick.

We have the entire break room to ourselves. It's probably dinner rush for the cashiers, and the office workers have probably left. Conrad buys the biggest bag of chips that the food machine has, pulls the less-than-appetizing sandwich out of the fridge, and puts them on the nearest table. He offers me a chair and then goes back to the fridge and pulls out a stale bottle of soda that has been in there for a week. He grabs a plastic knife and two plastic cups out of the cupboard. He cuts the sandwich in half, exactly in half, but he still tells me to choose which half I want.

I can't believe what I'm seeing. This is not the Conrad I know. He is finding free things to embellish what we have and smiling at me while doing it. He looks as attractive as I've ever seen him. My rich, cocky friend is finally on my level and smiling about it. I can't help myself. I reach over and pull his face toward me. His eyes look like they can't believe what is happening as I pull him in for a kiss. I did promise he would get this kiss after all, and I actually want to give it to him. I'm glad this kiss isn't as aggressive as the ones at the shoe store. I just close my eyes and enjoy it. Enjoy him. His stomach growling makes us stop. Conrad laughs. "I-uh, sorry. Can I have another kiss for dessert?"

I try to hold back a grin, but I can't. "I'll think about it."

Conrad is so sweet and courteous, and he doesn't complain

about my mom's mediocre sandwich. I feel happier than I have in a long time. Conrad gets the dessert he wants after all…

We are all grins as we restock the home furnishings. Conrad throws me into the wheeled cart on top of the curtains and pillows and speeds me down the warehouse aisles like we own the place. He steals another kiss when we go up the elevator to restock the throw pillows on the model living room sets. Who knew Casswell's could be so fun?

I dread looking at the clock because I know it's about 8:30, and that means the fun ends and a long walk in the cold begins.

I clock us out in the break room and pull on my scraggly coat. Conrad immediately takes it back off. I know he's in a playful mood, but we were told to be out by now. I turn around to tell him that when a white velvety coat gets placed on my shoulders. Conrad smiles when he sees my surprise. I shake my head. "No, Conrad. I can't take this. You need enough money to eat this month. Return it."

Conrad won't budge. "Nope. I promised I would get it for you as soon as I could, and I can today."

I sigh. "But you don't want to eat free, stale food and cheap junk all month."

Conrad shrugs. "Yes, I do, and you can't change my mind."

"Oh yes I can."

"No, you can't. Not this time. Just let me buy my favorite girl something she likes and needs."

I can see that fighting with him about this will get me nowhere. I stand there speechless as he puts the coat on me properly and puts my red hat and scarf around my neck to get me ready for the cold January streets.

I can see Mrs. James turning off all the lights in the store, but I don't care. I grab Conrad and give him a kiss, an aggressive one this time. We have to peel ourselves off each other when the lights go off in the break room and we have to feel our way out of the store. Conrad laughs and takes my hand to guide me to the front door.

I feel so warm as we make our cold walk home. The coat helps, but Conrad's hand in mine and the smile lighting up his whole face could melt a snowman on New Year's Day. I am on cloud nine until we get to my doorstep. He holds me like he never wants to let me go but then says, "What about Baldwin?"

I sigh and say, "I'll tell him tomorrow at school. Please don't tell him tonight. I don't want to make everything weird and uncomfortable for everyone else again."

Conrad nods and says, "Does this mean you choose me? Can I finally call you my girlfriend?" His eyes are so sweet and earnest.

I feel so bad for everything I've put him through. "Yes. I choose you." He smiles like it's Christmas day again. I put a finger on his lips and say, "But don't tell anyone until after school. I need to tell Baldwin first. He isn't going to like this."

Conrad nods and gives me one last kiss. "I'll be thinking about you until I see you walk through this door again!" It is torture letting go of his hand and watching him walk up the stairs. His eyes are so glued on me that he slips and falls on his raw legs.

I laugh even though I know he must be in tons of pain. "Are you okay? I'm so sorry!"

He jumps up and says, "I can't feel a thing! This is the best night of my life. Goodnight, Dandra."

It's 9:30 and Everley and Mom are already in bed when I get inside. I eat the leftovers my mom wrapped up for me and run myself a quick vinegar bath. I hum my favorite song as I start my nightly routine in the bedroom. Marcella glares at me as I climb into bed. "Why are you so happy?"

I play dumb. "I don't know. I just had a good day."

She keeps glaring at me. "It didn't seem like it earlier."

I try to remember what I was like at school today, but all I can remember is dinner with Conrad, and kissing Conrad, and restocking housewares with Conrad… I try to keep my secret a little longer. "The day got better. Goodnight, Marcella."

She turns out the light and says, "You give me whiplash, Dandra. Goodnight."

Chapter 29

I WAKE UP WITH A SMILE on my face. Marcella continues to glare at me as we get ready and eat breakfast. Everley is thrilled to have me smiling in the morning for once. "Dandra, I have all my homework done on time, I am going to be at your academic assembly for sure!"

"Yay! I'll make sure to wave at you when I see you!"

Everley looks taken aback. "You will?"

"Yep! Let's get going to school! Are you ready?"

Everley grabs her backpack and hands Marcella's backpack to her. "We're ready! Have a great day tutoring, Mom!"

Mom kisses my forehead. "I want an update when you get home from school today."

"An update about what?"

Mom looks at me like she knows more than she claims she does. "Oh, you know. Your life."

I just smile and shrug. "Okay. See you, Mom!"

"See you."

Marcella glares at the white velvet coat as I zip it up. "I thought Conrad took that back."

"He did, but he bought it back yesterday."

Marcella glares at me harder. "Hmm."

It is all I can do not to run to Conrad and throw my arms around him, but I need to show Baldwin the same respect he has shown me. Baldwin looks at me in my new coat and big smile and then at Conrad before frowning and saying, "Good morning, girls."

I smile like I have all morning and say, "Good morning, Baldwin. It's the perfect day to walk to school, isn't it?"

He looks up at the overcast sky and says, "If you say so."

I purposely walk behind everyone else with Everley by my side. She grabs my hand and then grabs Conrad's hand and starts swinging our arms back and forth. We steal glances at each other every chance we get. When it's time for me to turn early and take Everley to her school, Conrad keeps holding our hands and walks with us. I see Baldwin glare at us before walking on with the rest of our friends to school.

282

After we drop her off, we walk a foot apart with our hands aching to touch the other person's. I try to look ahead, but my head keeps turning to the side and looking at Conrad. It feels so awkward that I just start giggling. Conrad laughs too, and by the time we get to school, we have to massage our sore cheeks from laughing so hard. It's going to be a struggle to stay away from him today. I point to the door. "You go in first. I'll follow 20 seconds later."

He nods and says, "See you soon." I count to 20 in my head and follow him into the school.

Baldwin is immediately by my side and says, "Dandra, can I have a word with you privately?"

The smile on my face droops a bit. At least he doesn't want to drag this out. "Sure. Where would you like to go?"

Baldwin's face is a statue. "To the library."

I think of how fitting that is considering the first relationship talk we ever had was in the Tifton library. "Okay." I follow him and sit at a table with him far away from everyone else.

He looks at me and says, "What is going on? It looks like you have made your decision."

I hate seeing the pain in his eyes, but I am not going to put him through any more pain. "I have made my decision."

"And?"

I look at his worried face and whisper, "I choose him."

Baldwin's shoulders droop, but he doesn't look shocked.

After a few moments of silence he asks, "Can I ask if the coat bought you?"

I bristle immediately. "No. I chose him last night before I knew he bought the coat. I am not someone who can be bought, Baldwin." I stand up and turn to leave when he grabs my hand.

His face is regretful. "I'm sorry. I know you can't be bought, but can you at least tell me why you chose him?"

I look at him and feel bad, but not bad enough to change my mind. "I like you, Baldwin. I like you a lot. You do so much good for so many people, but sometimes, I just want to be higher on your list. I want you to spend time with me and do things for me because you like seeing me happy."

Baldwin recoils. "I thought I did that. I made you cookies."

"You did make me cookies, but Josie knew everything you were doing before I did. I felt like an afterthought. Make sure you make cookies for Josie."

I get up and walk out without a second glance.

Chapter 30

I GET MY CHEMISTRY LAB DONE easily with the help of Bonnie Smith. Baldwin sends me a note during English class that says, "I'm not with Josie."

I send one back that says, "Will you be with her by the end of the month?"

He sighs when he reads it but doesn't send another note back.

Adamar's frown becomes my goal to turn into a smile during history class, but it doesn't work. The gourmet hot sandwiches we make in cooking class smell delicious, but I save mine to split with Conrad during lunch. At lunch I see Conrad walking toward me in the hall, and I wish I could run to him, but we still need to blend in if we don't want to go back to Layland. I jerk my head toward the library, and he follows me there. We share the sandwich and a few kisses between bookshelves before the bell rings. Ed sees us while he's working on his speech with Thomas from our class. That means Baldwin will know what we were doing soon enough.

We play a sport in exercise class with a ball and a hoop, and I can't stop laughing when Conrad tries to get the ball in the hoop but misses every time. I even enjoy writing my speech for the first time because Conrad is sitting next to me and winking at me whenever I steal a glance at him.

Baldwin doesn't walk home as fast as he has the last two days. I'm pretty sure he has work again and doesn't want to miss his ride with Josie, but he walks slowly, like a defeated soldier. Conrad and I walk near each other, but we don't hold hands or show any public affection.

Josie is waiting for Baldwin in the parking lot at our apartment, and I finally get to meet her. Conrad takes my hand and leads me to the old, clunky car she's driving. He beams at me and says, "Hi, Josie. I'd like to introduce you to Dandra." I drop his hand as soon as we get to the open window of her car.

Josie is a short girl with green expressive eyes and thick blonde hair that lands just below her ears. She turns those eyes on me and doesn't look away for a long time. "Hello,

Dandra. I've heard so much about you, from Win." Her eyes immediately look at Conrad and then back at me.

I say, "I've heard so much about you, too."

She looks unsettled as she says, "I'm just giving Baldwin a ride to work. I'm not trying to steal him or anything."

I smile and say, "Thanks for giving him rides to work. I appreciate that. We actually broke up today."

She raises her eyebrows at me. "Really?"

I nod. "Yes, and he's feeling down. He needs a friend right now. I'm glad he has you."

Josie's eyes dart around furtively. "Uh, yeah. I'm always here to help."

I sigh and say, "I have a speech to get ready for the educational assembly, but I'll see you around, Josie."

She says, "Yeah, see you," as her car window closes.

Conrad walks me to the staircase, gives me a quick hug, and whispers, "I'll see you after dinner."

I whisper back, "I'll be missing you until then. Remember, we need to get our speeches done tonight."

He nods. "I know," and starts walking up the stairs. Baldwin has changed into his work clothes and rushes down the stairs, passing Conrad on his way. He doesn't acknowledge either of us. I just see pain on his face, and I feel responsible for it. How can my heart be so happy and sad at the same time?

I watch out the window of my apartment as Baldwin climbs into Josie's car. She immediately wraps her arms around his neck. It's obvious that she likes him. His blank face doesn't reciprocate her feelings back though. I think he'll get over me quicker than he thinks he will.

My bath helps to calm my mind. I did the right thing, right? Yes. Yes, I did. If I could have the wish of my heart, I would spend the whole evening with Conrad, but I have to get my speech done tonight. I have work tomorrow after school, and the next day I have to present it to the class to see if I get 50% on the assignment or if I get to present it to the city council on Monday. Well, as busy as I know I am, one thing makes me happy. Conrad and I can always work on our speeches together as we cuddle on the couch...

Chapter 31

MY SPEECH IS PRETTY MUCH READY. I have one fact I need to check while I'm in class today, but other than that, I think it's a good speech. Conrad says it's good. I wish he would let me read his speech, but he says that he wants it to be a surprise tomorrow when we present to the class. We openly hold hands as we walk to school for the first time. Marcella is still being cold to me and says as we're walking, "If you act like a couple at school, you'll be easier to recognize. We were on the Herrington news again last night." I want to say that she and

Gordon aren't hiding their connection very well either, but I don't.

I try to ignore the cold looks I get from Ed in Chemistry class and Baldwin in English class, and Adamar in History class. They told me to make a choice, and I did. I don't want to lose their friendship over this. We need each other still. I finally feel warm and happy when Conrad takes me to a private bench in the English hall during lunch. We share the tempura vegetables I made during cooking class and talk about who we expect to see at the educational assembly. Conrad thinks we should invite Mr. Bronson. I am not so sure.

I say, "He is a big part of our lives, but we still have Patrolman Darius snooping around work, and seeing us sitting on that stage for so long might trigger a thought that he's seen us in one of his newspapers."

Conrad shakes his head. "You've destroyed our faces on all of his newspapers."

My eyebrows come together. "What if I haven't? What if he has another copy at home? It's too risky."

Conrad frowns. "He's like the father I wish my father would be to me. I still want to invite him."

I am surprised to hear this. I ask, "How is he like a father to you?"

Conrad's face turns red. "You know, he gave us Christmas presents and Christmas dinner."

"Is that all?"

Conrad looks at me like I'm the most captivating thing he's ever seen. "He told me I had a chance with you. He told me not to give up even though you had a boyfriend."

I shake my head as I take another bite. "Why would he say that?"

"He cares about us, I think." Conrad eats the last bite of my culinary creation and says, "I am proud of my speech, and I want Mr. Bronson to hear it."

The bell rings. I clean up our lunch mess and say, "We'll talk about this later."

We don't get another chance to talk about it in either of our classes. We lift weights in gender groups again in exercise class, and we are assigned partners in speech to fact check each other's speeches. I'm partnered with Thomas, and he makes me fact check all of my figures, not just the one I was worried about.

We finally get a chance to talk after school as we're walking to work. I nudge him in the side. "If you had your way and could ask anyone in the world to come to the educational assembly, no matter what country they live in, who would you want to be there?"

Conrad thinks for a minute and says, "My mom, my brother, your mom, Everley, Mr. Bronson, and maybe Mrs. Abbot."

I am not surprised by most of these people, but I am surprised by Mrs. Abbot.

"Why Mrs. Abbot?"

He shrugs and says, "She likes me!"

I squeeze his hand. "You're easy to like."

He leans in and whispers, "Not as easy as you are to like." He steals a kiss that makes me want to stop walking and just hold him. But, we can't be late for work, so we keep walking. I look at him deep in thought and ask, "Are you sure you wouldn't want your dad there?"

Conrad's mouth hardens, and he says, "I—I don't—know. He used to be a good dad. I used to want him at everything that I did, but I don't know if he has anything worth admiring left in him."

I sigh and ask, "Do you think you'll ever see him again?"

His eyes grow thoughtful, and he says, "Studying the topics in speech class has made me believe that the border wall law could change in my lifetime. I think I will see him again one day. I hope having me gone is changing him. I hope he stops drinking and being married to his despicable job. My mom and brother need him."

"Do you need him?"

He looks at me and says, "You are my family now. I'll be okay with or without him."

My heart goes out to him. When we get to Casswell's, I say, "I think we should invite Mr. Bronson. He is the only father figure either of us has now." Conrad's smile makes my day.

Chapter 32

THE YAWN THAT ESCAPES MY MOUTH is loud enough to wake the dead. I didn't sleep well last night. It is Friday morning before the academic assembly that will happen on Monday. I have to give my speech to my classmates, my teacher, and our headmaster. If I outspeak my opponent, I will get full marks and give this speech to the city council. If I don't present my topic better than my opponent, I will get a 50% on this speech that is worth a quarter of my final grade, and I will sit in the audience and watch everyone else give their speeches instead.

I originally thought it would be better to get the failing grade and keep my identity safe from the city council members, but my mom and Baldwin changed my mind. They made it seem like an honor to put myself out there and make a positive change for my school and myself. I'm not quite to the "this is an honor" mindset, but I've loved watching every member of my speech class work so hard and learn so much. I'm finally living in a learning community like my father wanted me to have.

I even think Conrad has changed during the course of our speech preparation. He doesn't usually do things for the greater good, but he has worked like a dog to write the best speech he can. I haven't read it, but I have full confidence that he will earn full marks and share his speech at the assembly. He is very convincing with his words—just ask our landlady, Mrs. Abbot.

I almost start my shirt on fire during chemistry class. Bonnie Smith pushes my arm away from the heat source in the nick of time. I am just so nervous about my speech; I can't focus on what I'm doing.

During English class, Baldwin passes me a note. It says, "Good luck on your speech today. I hope you get full marks."

I send a note back that says, "Thank you. You don't need good luck. I know you'll amaze us all. P.S. Did you invite Josie to come watch on Monday?"

His note back says, "Thanks, I miss you. Yes, I did invite Josie."

I feel so bad that I have broken his heart. He did force me

to make a choice though. I write a note that says, "Don't hate me, Baldwin. Josie seems nice. I can see why she's your friend."

He doesn't write back.

In History class, we go over current events. Apparently, there is a big trial going on across the border in Layland. I zone out during most of the class discussion until I hear who is on trial for murder and invasion of privacy. The man's name is none other than Zane Chesterton. During lunch, Conrad takes me for a walk outside because I keep sweating. I don't tell him that the sweat is from my nervousness instead of the exercise. He seems nervous too. During exercise class, he and I jump rope next to each other. I look at the wall blankly as I jump and mumble, "Are you ready, Conrad?"

He jumps faster. "As ready as I'm going to be. I'll just be glad to know if I pass or fail and move on from this."

I jump slower. "I don't want to fail, but I don't want the city council to watch me speak either."

My boyfriend says, "You'll know which it will be in a couple of hours."

I don't want to add to his jitters, but I have to ask, "Have you been to History class yet?"

Conrad looks at his feet. "Yes."

"So you know about your dad?"

"Yes."

I take his hand. "Are you okay?

He squeezes my hand, but he doesn't look at me. "I'm okay."

I try not to worry about Conrad while I fill out my math worksheet. I have no memory of what I did. I hope I don't fail that too. I'm so sure I'm going to fail, and I can't handle that. I would rather speak to the city council than fail. I know that now.

I feel sweat dripping down the back of my neck as I sit in speech waiting for class to start. Our teacher has placed a table and two chairs in the back of the classroom for himself and our headmaster. As soon as the bell rings, he says, "Welcome, class. Today is the day you present your speeches. Mr. Barlowe and I will each grade you as you present, and then we will add our scores together. Whichever person scores higher for their subject will receive full marks and present again on Monday, and the other person will receive half marks and watch from the audience. I have the subjects written on little papers in this hat. I will pull one out at a time, and have both students present." He lifts up the hat, puts his hand inside, pulls out a slip of paper, and says, "We will start with Educational Advancements. Christopher, you will go first, followed by Thomas."

Christopher is very nervous, and I can't hear half of what he says about the educational advancements our school is pursuing. Thomas on the other hand is very confident and persuasive. Even if one of the judges hadn't been his dad, he definitely won his spot today. Ed and his partner go next. They take different approaches to the need for communication in the United Cities. I understand why Ed promotes more communication between countries, but I'm not sure if our teacher will think his take on the subject is better than his partner's. They both do a good job. Two students I don't know go next. Baldwin's partner acts quiet and reserved during class, but when he stands up to speak, he is very forceful. Baldwin just smiles and nods through his opponent's speech.

When it's his turn, he takes a different approach. He talks about how everyone wants to be comfortable and safe as they learn and grow. He makes me want to be a better person as I listen to his own drive to become more than his drunk dad was.

He really gets me when he says, "This country is doing well in so many areas, but it needs to improve in one important area: it's bigotry toward those who are not perfect. You may think that I am only speaking of the Complex Law that until two years ago shut all people who were imperfect in any mental or physical way out of the public eye, but that is not the only bigotry this country struggles with. Three of the four borders of this country are open to travelers between the countries, but the border to Layland is closed. No one is allowed in or out between these two countries. Why is that? On the surface, it appears that Layland, the country of low education and filthiness is trying to keep their citizens from leaving, but the truth is, the Layland Border Wall Law came into effect the same time as the Complex Law. It came into effect for the same reason as the Complex Law. Layland is not perfect and is being hidden from the United Cities' public eye. Since one law has been repealed to outlaw bigotry, the Layland Border Wall Law should also be repealed. This is the most needed improvement for the future of both countries." Baldwin pauses, looks down at his new shoes in a half bow, and sits down.

The silence in the room is deafening. I have to pick my jaw up off the floor. I think everyone in the room is in shock. Did everyone know that the two laws happened at the same time for the same reason? I certainly didn't learn that yet in United Cities History Class. I look around at the shocked faces in the room and hope we don't get sent back to Layland right now. Then I hear clapping coming from the back of the room.

Our headmaster is on his feet clapping. "Well done, young man. I haven't heard someone speak this forcefully for change since Brock Hamble's final campaign speech two years ago. I am very impressed, and I think the city council needs to hear this." The rest of us in the room slowly start clapping until the room is filled with thunderous applause. I steal a glance at Baldwin who is looking very pleased with our response.

The shock has not worn off when I get called up to speak. I rearrange my papers to give me a few seconds to calm down. I give Baldwin a confused look and then start my speech. My voice is a little shaky. "Literacy. Literacy or the ability to read and understand what others are trying to say helps everyone in every job..." I feel the shakiness leave my voice as I get going. "There are those who think that a minimal education is enough to live a fulfilling life, but the more we read, the more we know, and the more we know, the more we can change our communities for the better."

I feel like I finish strong, and the judges clap for me, but when I listen to my opponent, I'm not so sure my speech is the best one. Conrad's subject is the last piece of paper pulled from the hat. The girl with the stutter goes first. She is hard to understand, and she runs to the garbage can and throws up after she is done. The sound and the smell throws the whole class into a frenzy. I offer to take her and the garbage can to the bathroom. When I get back, Conrad is already done with his speech, and Mr. Whitlock is about to post who will be presenting on Monday on the wall. My feet shuffle to a stop. I didn't get to hear it? Why didn't I think about that before I left?

I send an apologetic look to Conrad, but he doesn't look sad. He actually looks pleased with himself. Our judges don't take long to add numbers and discuss things between themselves. They post a piece of paper on the wall with their results.

The class starts whispering and moving toward the speech results. I feel sweat dripping down my sides. Conrad walks up to me and says, "Let's go look."

I approach the wall slowly. I didn't do as well as I wanted to. I scan the scoresheet from the top down. Thomas gets full marks, Ed gets full marks, Baldwin gets full marks, Conrad gets full marks! And—I get full marks! All four of us will be presenting at the academic assembly on Monday.

The boys are so excited and brag the whole way home from school about how well they did. I don't join in because I don't think I did very well, and I am as nervous as ever about the four of us standing in front of the city council, especially considering the content in Baldwin's speech. I have a terrible feeling that he will be found out if he says those things to the city council. I am going to ask him to change it.

When we get back to the apartments, Mrs. Abbot is standing in the doorway of the apartment office. She calls us over. "I bet you're happy to be done with school for the weekend. Would you boys be willing to move a bed out of an apartment for me?"

Conrad pulls out his best smile and says, "Yes, of course we will! We would do anything for our favorite landlady!" He brags to Mrs. Abbot about giving the speech at the assembly and invites her to come watch.

Mrs. Abbot smiles at my boyfriend and pats his cheek. "You should be proud, John. Of course, I'll come and hear your speech."

Conrad looks at me adoringly. "Actually, four of us will be giving speeches. You'll want to hear all of them. Especially Dani's."

Mrs. Abbot raises her eyebrows as she looks at me and

the others behind me. She scratches her chin and pauses for a second before saying, "All four of you are speaking? It was a special honor in my day. I bet it will be a show worth watching."

Conrad is all smiles, but I feel awkward and unworthy of being grouped with them. I just hope Monday goes well.

Chapter 33

CONRAD AND I HAVE OUR FIRST cleaning shift today. I get a feeling of DeJa'Vu when Mr. Bronson hands me a bucket of hot water and Conrad a bucket of cleaning supplies. "I want you to dust and sweep the warehouse and mop it. When you are done with that, I want you to wash all of the windows that you can reach."

"No problem, Mr. Bronson," Conrad says. We start to walk away, but Conrad turns around and asks, "Mr. Bronson, will you come to our speeches at the academic assembly Monday?

We both worked so hard on them, and not many students get this kind of honor."

Our boss looks at us and then at the papers in his hand. His eyes stay on his papers when he says, "Yes. I would love to. I participated in one of those once when I was your age. I wouldn't miss it for the world…" Mr. Bronson seems distracted and wanders back to his office. I am about to ask Conrad if he finds Mr. Bronson's behavior odd, but my boyfriend is so happy that he agreed to come that I don't want to change the subject.

I have to teach Conrad how to clean. He has lived a very pampered life. I decide to dust since I'm so good at it from my days at the Tifton Library while he sweeps. As we work, I ask him, "Who ended up getting the bed you guys moved yesterday?"

Conrad wipes his face and says, "Gordon did. Adamar, Ed, and Gordon all have a bed now. Once Baldwin gets one, I'll be next."

"Why are you last if you pay the most for the rent?"

Conrad rolls his eyes. "I'm last because they still don't like me—actually they especially don't like me now that we are together."

My curiosity is sparked at his comment. "Are things getting any better between you and Baldwin?"

Conrad shrugs. "Uh, not really. He really let me have it after you broke up with him. He seems happier in general today, but he still glared at me as I left for work."

My eyebrows come together. "Why do you think he is a bit happier today? I made him pretty mad last night when I told him to change his speech so it wouldn't talk about Layland."

Conrad dumps the dust pan into the garbage can and says, "He invited Rocky and Josie to come to the assembly. They both said they would go, so I think that made him happy."

I decide to get a new dust rag since mine is black. I ask, "Are he and Josie a thing?"

Conrad shrugs. "I don't know. Why do you care?"

I clear my throat. "Well, it just seems like they've been friendly for a while now, so I assumed it was only a matter of time."

Conrad looks at me and asks, "If they are, will you be jealous?"

I feel my cheeks redden. "No, of course not. I just want him to be happy."

Chapter 34

I WAKE UP GROGGY AND HUNGRY. My stomach growls, but I want to have my vinegar bath before I have breakfast. Hopefully Mom or somebody will make something by the time I get out of my bath. My legs are looking and feeling much better than they did a month and a half ago, but it will take months for them to fully heal. I probably won't be wearing shorts in public this summer.

When I'm done with my bath, the smell of bacon and eggs leads me out of the lavatory. My jaw drops when I walk into the kitchen to find Conrad making breakfast. My mom and Everley are already at the table eating. I run up to my boyfriend and ask, "What are you doing here?"

He hugs me and says, "You know, I just wanted to have breakfast with my favorite girls."

I lean close to his ear and say, "I thought you didn't have money for food."

He hugs me and says, "Mrs. Abbot gave me a tip when we moved the bed. I bought bacon and eggs with it."

I whisper back, "You shouldn't have, but I'll make some toast to go with it."

Mom and Everley finish quickly, and Marcella grabs a couple of slices of bacon and leaves to go see Gordon. Conrad and I get the table to ourselves while we eat. "Thank you for this; it's so good to eat some meat."

"Some day, I'll feed you meat at every meal."

I look at him sideways. "What do you mean by that?"

He looks pleased with himself. "I want to take care of you, and I want you to be happy."

I squeeze his hand and say, "You do make me happy."

He takes my hand in both of his. "Do you want to go for a walk?"

"Sure."

Mom clears her throat and points to my backpack full of homework. "If you go for a walk, you better be quick. You've been neglecting your other homework and chores since you started your speech."

Conrad nods at my mom. "You're right, Mrs. Metty." He starts stacking the dirty dishes on the table and looks at me. "Get your warm things while I wash the dishes."

"Okay, but let's put aloe on together first."

He looks at me sheepishly, "Uh, ok."

I grab my bottle of aloe and pull up my pant legs. My legs look red around my knees, but pink everywhere else. Conrad doesn't volunteer to pull his pant legs up, so I pull them up for him.

I gasp when I see how much worse they are than mine. There aren't any white infected spots, but there is still some black tissue around his knees. His legs are red; nothing is looking pink like the majority of my legs. "Are you taking vinegar baths and putting on aloe morning and night?"

"Most of the time."

I scowl at him. "Conrad, I don't want you to lose your legs! I need you whole!"

He leans into me and says, "I will do better. The infection is gone at least."

I roll my eyes. "Yes, thank goodness for that." I put aloe on for him, so he'll know how thoroughly I do it. He pulls his pant legs down and seems unusually enthusiastic about washing the dishes.

I put the aloe away and get dressed in my warmest clothes. My new coat, hat, and gloves will keep the winter chill off as we walk. Conrad finishes at the kitchen sink just in time.

The way Conrad looks at me makes me feel like a million coins. He gives me a quick peck on the lips and says, "Let's go."

Conrad leads me to a park with freshly shoveled sidewalks, pretty trees frosted with snow, and children making dozens of snowmen around the swing set. He points to one of the snowmen that a girl has put a red hat and scarf on. "That one looks like you," he says as he jostles the pompom on my red hat.

I laugh. "It does look like me!" We walk to a nearby bench and sit down to watch the children play. Their joy and energy are contagious. "Did you ever make snowmen when you were that age?"

Conrad shakes his head. "I don't think so. Actually, yes. I did once with you and your dad, but that was the only time."

That makes me frown. "Why not?"

Conrad shrugs. "My dad was too busy getting the gaming district up and going to take my brother and me outside to play in the snow." He sighs and says, "They wouldn't have been white and pretty like these snowmen anyway. They would have been full of dirt and litter."

Images of Layland's litter-strewn streets fill my head. "Do you ever think about Layland?"

Conrad sighs. "Yes. Every day."

I look around the bustling park and say, "Do you think it could ever be clean and active like it is here?"

Conrad pauses before he answers. "Yeah. I think it could.

It would take years and years to change things, but if someone wanted it badly enough, they could start cleaning the cities up."

"But—my parents and I tried to do that. Things would stay clean for a few hours, but there were always more people making it dirty than cleaning it up. We never made progress."

Conrad takes my hand. "You just needed more people to join you."

I sigh. "You helped me sometimes, but other than the anti-gamers, no one else ever joined us."

My boyfriend nods. "They were too busy at the gaming district."

I roll my eyes. "Even if they weren't at the gaming district, no one stands up for things there. Remember when I asked the parents waiting to vote about the educational reform bill to vote to keep us in school until age 18, and they just laughed at me."

Conrad squeezes my hand. "My dad was right there speaking against you that time. They were too scared to stand up to my dad."

Thoughts whir around in my head about what I could have done differently as we stand up and start walking around the park again. I look at my boyfriend, who is deep in thought, and ask, "Do you think everyone is scared of your dad?"

He doesn't answer quickly, and his eyes look far away. "No, not everyone. He is on trial after all."

I sigh. "The only people I know of who would stand up to him don't live in Layland anymore."

His eyes are still far away. "So true."

My hands are getting cold. I grab his hand and squeeze it. "We should head back soon. I don't want my mom to worry. I also want to pick out an outfit and practice my speech a few times."

"Yeah, we should head back." Conrad is strangely quiet as we walk back home. I hope I haven't brought all of his bad memories with his father back to haunt him.

As we approach my door I ask, "Are you feeling okay? Did our Layland talk upset you?"

He gives me a small smile. "No. It's good to think about what was, what is, and what could be." He takes off his fake glasses and kisses me. "Good luck on your speech tomorrow."

I like seeing his face without a disguise. I hug him a little tighter than normal and wish I didn't have to let him go. "Thanks. I can't wait to hear yours. I was so sad that I missed it in class."

He kisses me again and says, "It won't get a standing ovation from the judges like Baldwin's did, but I hope you like it."

Chapter 35

THE DAY OF THE ACADEMIC ASSEMBLY is here. I put on my best lavender dress and spike my hair to the best of my ability. I put on more makeup than I have ever worn in my life. Mom believes that the makeup will disguise me more than anything else. Mom insists that the boys wear makeup, too, and it makes me giggle as she puts it on their scowling faces. All of my friends and family from Layland have decided to skip class or work to be at our speeches. I'm glad I get to skip all of my classes before lunch today. I don't know if I could focus on Chemistry and English with all the pressure I feel to give this speech. I hope the sweat stains in my armpits aren't visible to the audience.

When we arrive in the auditorium, the ten of us who are giving speeches are given chairs behind the podium on the stage. I can't see very well with the bright lights in my eyes, but I'm pretty sure I see my mom and Everley on the third row behind the city council members that we are presenting to. I wave, hoping that Everley sees me. I am pretty sure I see Dr. Hamble, his daughter Elira, and another gentleman who looks related to them walk into the auditorium. I bet it's Greggory Hamble, Baldwin's boss. I guess I shouldn't be surprised to see them. They are the biggest humanitarian donors in the city, according to Shasta. Speaking of Shasta, I think I see her tall form sticking up from the middle of the crowd.

The five council members look very stern and serious. To say I am intimidated by them would be an understatement, especially the two women. They look like they had a bowl full of nails for breakfast. Everyone else in the audience blends into the seats. I hope the people we invited were able to make it, for Conrad's sake. Calm yourself, Dandra. You can do this.

My heart is beating so hard, I can feel it in my throat as Mr. Whitlock approaches the podium. "Welcome, everyone to the Herrington South Tertiary School Educational Assembly." Everyone claps enthusiastically. It's so nice to hear people supporting education like this. It makes me genuinely smile for the first time since stepping onto the stage. Mr. Whitlock introduces the 10 topics that we will be presenting on, and then introduces Ed as the first speaker by saying "Our first speaker will be Ernie Stevens speaking on the topic 'Education is Key.'"

Ed, also known as Ernie, looks confident like he always does, and he does a great job on his speech, when he says, "I have had a lot of things taken away from me in my life. The one thing that I know will never be taken away from me is my education, my knowledge," I feel more inspired than I did the first time I heard him say it because it's true. No one can take my knowledge from me either.

Then two other students go. Once they are done, Baldwin walks to the podium. I expect to hear different words than he gave on Friday in class, but his speech is exactly the same. When he mentions Layland, I see my mom gasp. My heart starts beating even harder in my chest. I hope there aren't any peace officers in the crowd.

When he lists the political acts of bigotry that the United Cities has had in place for over 100 years, everyone in the crowd is waiting with bated breath to hear him end with, "Since the Complex Law has been repealed to outlaw bigotry, repealing the Layland Border Wall Law should now follow. This is the most needed improvement for the future of both countries. Thank you for your time and consideration, Herrington City Council." I am shocked when the crowd applauds louder than they did for Ed. A few rows even give him a standing ovation. I realize as I watch him return to his seat that he could be the next Brock Hamble if he had enough money to run a campaign. I am proud of him for sticking to his convictions even though mentioning Layland is a risky move. I know I can't top his speech and applause, but I have to go right after him.

I start out just as shaky as I did in class and my armpits are just as sweaty. "Literacy. Literacy or the ability to read and understand what others are trying to say helps everyone in every job..." When I see Everley smiling at me and my mom listening to me with pride in her eyes, I feel more confident, and my voice stops shaking. "Literacy can help a person with nothing, no hope build a bridge to hope and possibilities, and success." I end much stronger than I began, and the audience actually claps for me, but not as loudly as they did for Baldwin, but I'll take it.

My mom smiles at me and gives me a thumbs up sign. If she is happy, I am happy. My body relaxes as I sit back down in my seat. I have done what I came here to do. I won't have to give that speech ever again. The only worry left in my mind is for Conrad. I have to wait for four more speeches before I can hear him speak. His opponent was so nervous and visibly sick in class that Conrad won the competition without even needing to try. I hope he did try though. I hope he gives a speech he can be proud of.

He looks scared as he approaches the podium. He gives me a nervous smile before he sets his speech on the stand. "Hello, everyone. I know what you're all thinking. 'Math is the Path to the Future' sounds like a boring topic." The audience laughs. Conrad smiles that dazzling smile of his and goes on, "I thought the same thing at first, but as I have researched this topic and thought about my own experiences with math, I am convinced that math is not boring. Math and numbers give us the data we need to move forward in a positive direction."

I am so nervous for him. I hope he can deliver what he is promising. He goes on to say, "Someone very close to me has a business that has made him very wealthy. He crunched numbers for years to come up with the perfect formula of what to charge his target audience to get them to pay for his services on a monthly basis..." Very few people in the audience know who he is talking about, but I do. Conrad says, "He crunched numbers for years to come up with the perfect variety of services that customers would keep coming back for."

Conrad looks down at his papers. "He used numbers to keep track of what people in opposition to him were doing and where they would be at any given moment. He used these numbers to eliminate his competition." He pauses and sniffs before going on. "He used math to make his business dreams come true. He made the numbers work in his favor. I wish I could say that this story has a happy ending, but unfortunately, this man spent so much time crunching numbers that he lost— his family."

Conrad's face shows the pain that this statement entails.

I wish his dad was the dad he needs. My boyfriend goes on to say, "Another person I am close to has had to start over with nothing. They have used math to know how much money they need to put a roof over their head and how many hours they need to work and how long it will take before they can provide needs and wants for themself and the people they love. They use math in their work to sell and give the right amount back with returns. This person was encouraged to drop out of math and to drop out of school for that matter. Luckily, they did not do that. Without math, this person would still be at the absolute bottom without a plan to get to where they want to be.

Math is the path to the future, whether the future we create benefits only ourselves or benefits many is up to each one of us. Use numbers to make a plan for yourself, to better yourself, like both men I have spoken about, but don't let the multiplication of money distract you from what matters most like the first man did. Make math work for you and those you care about. Make it benefit the world."

He is a grand finale worth waiting for. I feel myself jump to my feet and applaud him with everyone else. The whole auditorium gets to their feet after that. I'm not sure if it's just for Conrad, or for all of us, but I think we have done a good job until our headmaster, Mr. Barlowe comes to the stage, puts a hand on Conrad's shoulder, and says, "Please sit down everyone. I, for one, have been absolutely inspired by the speeches we have heard today. I'm even contemplating the changes I want to make in my life starting now. I wish I could send these impressive students out to the audience to shake hands as you leave, but I'm afraid I can't let anyone leave the auditorium yet."

He pats Conrad on the shoulder again, and then sighs. I sit back down and shudder as a familiar figure in uniform approaches the stand.

Mr. Barlowe wipes his ample forehead with a handkerchief and says, "This man to my left, who says his name is Patrolman Darius has accused this young man of being a wanted Layland refugee. I will turn the microphone over to him to explain how this meeting will proceed." The crowd breaks out into muffled cries of disbelief, and I feel my heart drop into my feet.

Chapter 36

PATROLMAN DARIUS STRUTS to the microphone and takes control from Headmaster Barlowe. He also puts a firm hand on Conrad's shoulder and says, "Evening, everyone. I'm sorry to disrupt this fine meeting today, but I have—reason to believe that this young man is a wanted refugee, but is not the only wanted refugee in this room." The auditorium erupts into whispers as he catches his breath. "We have been searching for these wanted persons night and day for over a month, so please be patient while we collect those who broke into this country illegally, and then we will let you all get on with your day."

Conrad leans toward the microphone and says, "I am the only wanted refugee here, Patrolman Darius. Please let the audience go, and I will come quietly with you back to Layland." The crowd breaks out into another round of gasps.

Patrolman Darius is as blinded by the light as I am, so he shields his eyes and squints into the audience several rows back. "Is he telling the truth? Are any of the other wanted refugees here right now?"

A voice I know I've heard before cries out, "He is not telling the truth. There are three more refugees on the stand right now."

I try to place the voice, but my heart is beating its way into my skull, and the pounding is all I can hear. Patrolman Darius pulls out some handcuffs and puts them on Conrad. My boyfriend doesn't even fight him. He is willing to sacrifice himself to save the rest of us. I fight against my tears. I can't give myself away. Patrolman Darius then turns around and looks at the rest of us sitting in our chairs as still as church mice. He walks in a straight line along the front of us looking into our faces. We must have disguised ourselves pretty well because he walks to the microphone and says, "No one is leaving this auditorium until three of you step forward and give yourselves up to my custody."

I feel like I'm about to faint. My mom and sister are beside themselves crying in the audience. I try to think of a way to save them, but mom looks like she is about to give herself away. I'm torn, what do I do to save the most people? Should I turn myself in to save them? I don't have the chance to decide before Baldwin steps forward and says, "I can understand why my dear landlady, Mrs. Abbot, believes that there are more of us from Layland on the stage today, but just because we live together, it doesn't make us all refugees. Conrad Chesterton and I, Baldwin Kole, are the only refugees on the stage. We separated ourselves from the rest of our original group, and we thought we were clever enough to go to school here and blend in with the other students. We were obviously mistaken and wish we had taken the safer path the other refugees took over a month ago. Please take us back to Layland and let everyone else in this auditorium go."

The crowd gasps. I can see the city council members turning to each other and asking, "How can these impressive speakers be the wanted criminals everyone has been looking for?"

Patrolman Darius is speechless for a moment and then squints out into the audience again. Mrs. Abbot shakes her head and says, "He's lying, too. There are at least two more refugees in this room, maybe more."

I see my mom bawling, and I can't let her give herself away. I love them too much, and Dad worked too hard on the escape tunnel to have them go back. I step forward

323

and say, "I am Dandra Metty. I am the last refugee in this room. Please let everyone else go."

"Ah hah!" Patrolman Darius marches up to me and grabs my face. He looks into my eyes and says quietly, "This is the last time you trick me, missy." I can hear outrage in the crowd as he roughly lets go of my face.

He marches back to the microphone and says, "Headmaster Barlowe, thank you for your cooperation. We have apprehended the three Layland refugees that were the masterminds of this escape. We are satisfied with these arrests and encourage everyone else to leave the auditorium at this time."

Headmaster Barlowe takes the microphone again and says, "Open the doors please, and thank you all for your attendance today and your cooperation. Please exit through the three doors in the back in an organized manner."

Some people jump up and run to the exits as quickly as they can, but not everyone. People I don't know stay in their seats and look at the three of us with something I can't identify in their eyes—sadness, pity, maybe? The three Hambles stay in their seats. They appear to be in a deep conversation. Dr. Hamble is probably realizing why Conrad and I have cement burns. Mrs. Abbot stays in her seat and glares at us all. Adamar stands up from his seat halfway down the auditorium and struts to the stage. "I am a Layland refugee, and I turn myself in." He looks happier than I've seen him since we snuck under the border way.

I shake my head in dismay as I hear Ed shuffle forward from the seats behind me and turn himself in as well. I can see my mom and sister walking toward me instead of away from me, and I shake my head harder. I mouth the words, "No, please don't! We worked so hard for this, don't give this up! No!" Tears start to fall down my cheeks.

My muttering doesn't stop them. My mom and Everley walk to the stage and turn themselves in. Mom turns to me as they handcuff her and whispers, "I'd rather be in the detainment center with you, than free without you." Her tears make mine fall faster.

My tear-filled eyes look for Marcella and Gordon and hope that they are walking out with the crowd. They have each other. They could be all right. But I see them look at each other for a long moment and then stand up and start walking toward the stage, holding hands and crying as they take each step. When they join us, they say the same thing to Baldwin that my mom said to me. We're all a big family now, and it's too hard to separate yourself from your family.

The auditorium is emptying out now. I see someone I recognize on the sixth row staying firmly in his seat. Mr. Bronson finally stands, looks at us, and puts his hand over his heart. He kisses his hand and waves farewell to us and walks slowly out of the auditorium. Shasta, Ernestine, Rocky, and

Josie give similar nonverbal farewell signs to us as peace officers force them out. They are particularly rough with Ernestine and Shasta. It makes me cry harder. I hope they don't get in trouble for helping us. Mrs. Abbot, on the other hand, stays in her seat and glares at my mom and me.

When peace officers have us all handcuffed, they shove us toward the auditorium doors. Patrolman Darius hands Mrs. Abbot a thick envelope. Our former landlady smiles sinisterly as we pass her. She finally hefts her body out of her seat and says to Mom, "I knew something was fishy when you signed your rental agreement. Linda Greenway works at my doctor's office. I had an appointment this morning, and as soon as I saw Linda, I knew that you had lied to me." She lifts the envelope and waves it in front of us. "I have big plans for your rent money and the reward money. Enjoy your trip back to Layland."

Conrad looks particularly betrayed. He pleads with our landlady, "Why would you do this? We didn't cause any harm. We tried to help you make your business better! I thought we were friends."

Mrs. Abbot smiles villainously and pats his cheek. "Oh, we were friends, honey, but you never showed me your ID, and this stack of cash is a better friend." She kisses the thick envelope and waves goodbye. Conrad looks absolutely crushed.

Patrolman Darius pushes me roughly toward the door, but the three Hambles block the way. Elira is in tears. Dr. Hamble has one arm around her, consoling her, but the man I thought was Baldwin's boss says, "Patrolman Darius, I am Senator Brock Hamble, and I would like to have a word with these young people before you take them away."

Patrolman Darius shakes his head and says, "Senator, you have no jurisdiction over me, and I have strict orders to get these refugees back to their country as soon as possible."

Brock Hamble looks at Patrolman Darius and then at the five peace officers that were assigned to him by the United Cities. "I may not have jurisdiction over you, but I have jurisdiction over them." He points to the men in peace officer uniforms. As if on cue, the five peace officers stand at attention and salute Senator Hamble.

Patrolman Darius sneers as he looks at his not-so-loyal helpers. "Fine. You have five minutes before I drag them back to where they came from."

Brock Hamble raises his eyebrows at Patrolman Darius curiously and then looks at the nine of us. "I don't think it will be necessary to drag these people anywhere. I have seen nothing but civility and refinement from them since the moment I laid eyes on them. I'm sure they'll return with you quietly." He turns and looks me in the eyes. I feel like he can see right through me. He walks from me to each member of our group and looks them in the eyes just as deeply. He ends with Baldwin and holds his gaze the longest.

"I must say, when we agreed to let Layland send Patrolman Darius across the border wall to find you, I thought it would be a quick and easy job. I assumed that nine uneducated ruffians were loose in my home city wreaking havoc on all the things I love. I wanted you to go back to where you came from, and I wanted it done quickly. But now that you have been found and are going back, I find myself extremely reluctant to see you go."

I look at Conrad and see the same surprised look in his eyes. Brock looks at Baldwin and says, "You are not uneducated; you are not ruffians; in fact, I have not felt more inspired by a group of teenagers since my own sister escaped from the Complex of Undesirables years ago. I did not realize that the border wall law was enacted out of bigotry by the United Cities until now. I realize what the next step needs to be to rid the United Cities of the senseless bigotry I tried to stop two years ago. It's time to repeal another senseless law."

Baldwin smiles and leans toward Senator Hamble, "Yes! I completely agree! I knew you would be the one to stop it!"

"Silence!" Patrolman Darius slaps Baldwin across the face to shut him up. Baldwin recoils but does not stop looking at Senator Hamble.

Doctor Hamble reaches out to Baldwin and looks at the red mark on his cheek. The senator pulls his dad back as he approaches Patrolman Darius. "That is not necessary. He isn't hurting a thing. In fact, I suspect he and I will be amicable allies in the future when the wall comes down."

Patrolman Darius growls at Brock Hamble, "Your five

minutes are up." He then turns to the peace officers. "Let's get these people out of here, boys."

Senator Hamble steps aside to let Patrolman Darius through the auditorium door. As we leave, the senator calls out to our group, "I'm so glad I was here today and able to meet you. I know we will see each other again one day. Do what you can from your side of the wall, and I'll do what I can from mine."

Patrolman Darius erupts, "Enough! March to the van!"

We mutter our thanks to Senator Hamble and his dad and sister as we pass them on our way through the auditorium doors. We fall silent as Patrolman Darius and his additional peace officers lead us to a big van with tinted windows. I feel tears soaking into my dress as we leave the school parking lot. A small crowd of people silently watch us go.

Time and space seem distorted and unreal until we pass our apartment building. I'm suddenly awake again. We worked so hard to get those apartments. Mom wipes a tear off my cheek with her own cheek and leans on me to give me her version of a handcuffed hug. She gives one to Everley as well. I hold on to the feeling of her lean-hug like it's my last day on earth. We are not taken to the two-story, gray peace keeper building behind Shasta's house. They take us straight to the airfield.

Everything we brought with us and everything we've accumulated here will stay here. We are unloaded from the van into three separate peace officer helicopters. If my hands were free, I would reach for Conrad, who looks like a lost puppy, but I can't do anything but send him my thoughts through my eyes. His eyes are pained, but there is a spark in them that wasn't there when we entered this country. Our eyes keep us connected until I climb into a helicopter with Mom and Everley and watch helplessly as Conrad gets shoved into the next helicopter with Marcella and Gordon.

Patrolman Darius climbs into the cockpit of our helicopter and gives me an evil grin. "Zane Chesterton will be thrilled to see you."

I'm so tired of hiding and being submissive that I sneer, "It took you long enough. I'm surprised he didn't fire you."

Patrolman Darius growls, "I always find what I'm looking for."

I look my adversary in the eye and say, "I think Mrs. Abbot did the hard work for you. I hope you get less money than she did."

Darius spits on the floor. "Zane doesn't need to know how I found you. It just matters that I found you. My reward will be ten times what I gave her."

I don't engage with him. I just give my mom a lean-hug and turn around and look out the window as we lift off and fly above the beautiful city I've learned to love. It's so clean, and it has so many kind people who helped us start over here. Not everyone is kind, of course, but no country is perfect. I'm pretty sure I can see Dr. Hamble's dazzling mansion from here, and Casswell's.

The more I think about my situation, the more I realize that this is not my last day on earth. Yes, we got caught. We have to go back to our own country, but we know what we are capable of now. We know what a beautiful place any country can be. I like to think that Mom, Conrad and I helped make Casswell's the dazzling shopping experience that it was. We could do that again. Out of the 10 students who represented Herrington South's Tertiary School to their city council, four of them were from Layland. We could do that again.

My tears dry to my face as I think about everything we've done the past couple of months. We sure tried to make it in this clean, advanced country, and we could have made it. I'm sure of that, but as I think about the speeches we just gave and all the sacrifices our friends made to help us, I can't help but think that this is meant to be. We have learned so much by being here, but the place we really need to be is in our own country. We are going back to Layland, the country of laziness and litter, but once we're out of the detainment center, I think Layland will be surprised with what they get.

About the Author

Heather Hayes loves a good story. She believes a good story will entertain you and leave you feeling like a better person for having read it. She loves living in Idaho with her husband and five daughters. If she isn't writing, she is probably teaching English, watching a volleyball game, cooking, skiing, reading, enjoying the mountains, or planning a trip to somewhere new.

A Message from Heather Hayes

If you liked immersing yourself in Dandra's world, please tell your friends about it and leave a review on Amazon or Goodreads. It helps me out so much, and I love hearing from my readers.

Find more dystopian books by Heather Hayes on Amazon and HeatherHayesAuthor.com.

THE COMPLEX TRILOGY

The Complex Life

The Complex Law

The Complex Leader

THE DUST TRILOGY

Dust and Deceit

Dust and Dazzle

If you like a good story for younger readers, check out my other books:

Unexpected Magic

A Tale of Regrets

Rissy's Summer Son

The Fantastic Backyard of Imagination

Before the Store